DATE DUE

MAR 0 9 2010		
MAY 1 4 2010		
DEC 0 9 2010		
MAY 1 6 2013		
FEB 0 3 2015		
FEB 2 3 2017		

HACKING HARVARD

a novel by
Robin Wasserman

SIMON PULSE
New York | London | Toronto | Sydney

SIMON PULSE

An imprint of Simon & Schuster Children's Publishing Division
1230 Avenue of the Americas, New York, NY 10020
Copyright © 2007 by Robin Wasserman
All rights reserved, including the right of reproduction
in whole or in part in any form.
SIMON PULSE and colophon are registered trademarks
of Simon & Schuster, Inc.
Designed by Mike Rosamilia
The text of this book was set in Adobe Garamond.
Manufactured in the United States of America
First Simon Pulse edition September 2007
6 8 10 9 7 5
Library of Congress Control Number 2007928033
ISBN-13: 978-1-4169-3633-6
ISBN-10: 1-4169-3633-5

FOR MY FATHER,
who will always be number one

Power—including the capacity to shape the very categories used to classify candidates for admission and to designate specific groups as warranting special consideration . . . is at the center of this process. From this perspective, an admissions policy is a kind of negotiated settlement among contending groups, each wishing to shape admissions criteria and the actual selection process to produce the outcome they prefer.

—Jerome Karabel, *The Chosen: The Hidden History of Admission and Exclusion at Harvard, Yale, and Princeton*

Trust the system: admissions are generally fair.

—"Ten Tips You Need to Know," *Time* magazine,
August 21, 2006

IN THE BEGINNING . . .

THERE WAS THE PLAN.
AND THE PLAN WAS GOOD.

There are two kinds of geniuses, the "ordinary" and the magicians. An ordinary genius is a fellow that you and I would be just as good as, if we were only many times better. . . . It is different with the magicians. They are, to use mathematical jargon, in the orthogonal complement of where we are and the working of their minds is for all intents and purposes incomprehensible. Even after we understand what they have done, the process by which they have done it is completely dark.

—mathematician Mark Kac,
Enigmas of Chance: An Autobiography

*T*his story is not mine to tell.
It is, however, true—and I'm the only one willing to tell it.
It begins, like all good stories, once upon a time.

"I'm in."

The shadowy figure slipped down the hall, infrared goggles giving the familiar surroundings an eerie green haze. Dressed in head-to-toe black, a mask shielding his face, he would have been invisible to the security cameras if his partner hadn't already disabled them. Five minutes, blueprints from the firewalled Atlantis Security site, a pair of wire clippers—and the job was done.

Snip! Good-bye, cameras.

Snip! Farewell, alarm.

Still, he moved slowly, carefully, silently. The operation was just beginning. Anything could go wrong.

The target was twelve doors in, on the left. Locked, as they'd expected.

Good thing he had the master key.

The equipment was stashed in a closet directly across the hall, secured behind a NO ENTRY sign, official-looking enough that no one had dared enter. He wheeled out the cart, grimacing at the squeaky wheels. No matter. There was no one to hear. The next security patrol wasn't scheduled for another three hours, thirty-two minutes—and reconnaissance indicated that the night guard almost always skipped his three a.m. rounds in favor of a nap in the front office.

If anyone else approached, the perimeter alert would make sure he knew about it.

He pushed the door open and surveyed the target. It would be close, but they'd get the job done. He crossed the room, taking position by the wall of windows. Thirty seconds with the whisper silent drill, and the lowest pane popped cleanly out of the frame. He attached his brackets to the frame, threaded the high-density wire through, waited for the tug from below and, when it came, locked everything in. That was the easy part.

He turned around, his back to the empty window, and closed his eyes.

Visualization, that was the key.

He'd learned it from the masters. James Bond. Danny Ocean. Warren Buffet. *See* the plan unfold. *Visualize* the details, the problems, and their solutions, the eventual prize in your hand. *Believe* it—then do it.

It sounded like self-actualization, Chicken Soup for the wannabe winner crap—but it worked.

He closed his eyes. He saw. He believed. He *knew.*

And then, with a deep breath, Max Kim got to work.

Once upon a time, there were three lost boys.

One was a Robin Hood, in search of a cause. One a Peter Pan, still hunting for Captain Hook. The third a Prince Charming, bereft of his queen.

There was, of course, an evil prince.

An ugly duckling.

A moat to cross, a tower to climb, a citadel to conquer.

And finally, there was a wicked witch. But we'll get to me later.

Because in the beginning, it was just the three of them: Max Kim. Isaac Schwarzbaum. Eric Roth. The Three Musketeers. The Three Amigos.

Three Blind Mice.

"Janet Pilgrim, October 1956. Betty Blue, Miss November. Lisa Winters, December." Schwarz forced himself to breathe evenly. The familiar litany helped. "June Blair, January 1957. Sally Todd, Miss February. Sandra Edwards, in the red stockings"— *Breathe,* he reminded himself—"March. Gloria Windsor . . ."

He'd almost regained his calm—and then he looked down.

Hyperventilation ensued.

Again.

One hand gripped the edge of the roof, the other hovered over the wire as it ran through the pulley gears, hoisting its load, ready to bear down if anything slipped out of place. But he wasn't worried about the equipment. He was worried about the ground.

His earpiece beeped, and Eric's voice came through, crystal clear. "Another load, coming up."

"Hurry, please," Schwarz begged. "Being up here is not good for my asthma."

"Schwarz, you don't have asthma."

Oh.

Right.

The excuse worked wonders for getting out of the occasional stepfamily touch football game, as Carl Schwarzbaum could barely be bothered to remember that his oldest son still drew breath—much less which bronchial maladies kept that breath labored and far too short for football.

Eric, on the other hand, paid attention. Which made him significantly harder to fool.

"You ready to receive?" Eric asked.

Schwarz nodded. "Roger." He drew in a deep, ragged breath, then leaned over, arms outstretched, waiting for the metal cage to appear out of the darkness. Max was still inside, preparing more loads for Eric, who would pack them securely and send them on their journey to the roof.

Where Schwarz waited. Trying not to look down.

It's only two stories, he reasoned with himself. Not bad at all. Not dangerous. Not worthy of a panic attack. Not enough to make him dizzy and short of breath, to make his chest tighten and his palms sweat inside the rough leather gloves.

"Dawn Richard, May 1957," he murmured. "Carrie Radison, pretty in pink. Jean Jani. Dolores Donlon. Jacqueline Prescott, Miss September. Colleen Farrington, in the bubble bath." It helped, like it always did, like a bedtime story he told himself, chasing the monsters back into the shadows. "Miss November, Marlene Callahan, behind the door. Linda Vargas, by the fire. Elizabeth Ann Roberts, January 1958, a very happy new year."

Just two stories. Not a long way down.

He could estimate the height and his mass, calculate the impact velocity, apply it to the standard bone density and tensile quantity of his muscles, calculate the probability of tears, breaks, demolition. Rationally, he knew that two stories was nothing.

But in the dark, the ground was impossible to see.

And it felt substantially farther away.

From the Oxford English Dictionary:

Hack, *noun, most commonly meaning, "A tool or implement for breaking or chopping up. Variously applied to agricultural tools of the mattock, hoe, and pick-axe type." First usage 1300 AD: "He lened him a-pon his hak, wit seth his sun us-gat he spak."*

I just wanted to understand. After it was all over, I just wanted to know what I'd missed, to get why it had meant so much. This didn't help.

Other options:

"A gash or wound made by a cutting blow or by rough or clumsy cutting."

"Hesitation in speech."

"A short dry hard cough."

Most uselessly: "An act of hacking; a hacking blow."

And then, inching closer to paydirt, the seventh usage: "A spell of hacking on a computer . . . an act of gaining unauthorized access to a computer system." First use 1983.

I showed Eric. He laughed. The date was ridiculous, he said.

The definition was useless, he said.

The term hack *had been co-opted—falsely, offensively, clumsily—by the mainstream media, who thought writing about computer hacking masterminds would sell more papers.*

He said.

According to Eric, hacking in its pure form stretched back centuries. It wasn't restricted to a single medium. It was more than a methodology. It was an ethos.

"This is your problem," Eric complained, tapping the computer screen. The Che Guevara action figure perched on top tilted and swayed, but declined to topple. Max had given it to him for his last birthday—"a revolutionary, for my favorite revolutionary"—and while it was intended as a joke, his prized position atop the computer screen suggested that for Eric, the mini-Che was equal parts entertainment and inspiration. "The OED is an outmoded technology." He leaned over my shoulder, his forearm brushing against my cheek, and closed the window. Then, reaching around me with the other hand, so that I was trapped between his freckled arms, he opened Wikipedia and typed "hack" into the search box. "It's dead, like the Encyclopædia Britannica.

A bunch of old white guys sitting in a room deciding what's true—it's a dead end. That's what this means—" He brushed his hand across the top of the monitor fondly, like it was a family pet. *"The end of gate-keepers, the end of the fossilized system that depended on an 'us' and a 'them,' the knowledgeable and the ignorant. Communal knowledge,* that's *what matters now. Not what they want us to know, but what* we *want to know. That's the future."* He glanced up from the computer, up toward me. Behind the glasses, his eyes were huge. *"Information wants to be free."*

"Schwarz is losing it," Eric whispered. Thanks to his improvements, the mics were so sensitive that they picked up his every word. "Let's speed this up."

"Code names only," Max reminded him. "We don't know who might be monitoring this frequency. And whose idea was it to stick Grunt on the roof?"

"Mine. And it was a good one." Eric flipped channels back to Schwarz, hoping he was right. "You still with us up there?"

"Susie Scott, Sally Sarell. Miss April, Linda Gamble. Ginger Young on the bed. Delores Wells on the beach, Teddi Smith, Miss—"

"Schwarz!"

"Ready for Phase Three." The voice was pinched and nasal, with a hint of a whine. As usual. "Can you, um, *please* go faster?"

"We're working on it."

And back to Max.

"Last load," Max confirmed. "Hoist it up, Chuckles, and I'll meet you and Grunt on the roof in five."

Eric began unhooking the metal grips and threading the wires back through, winding them in a tight coil. His cheeks burned in the wind. Unlike Max, he wore neither all black nor a mask for their missions, trusting the darkness to protect him—and, failing that, trusting the intruder alert sensors, which could never fail, because he had designed them himself. Max dressed for drama; Schwarz dressed however Max told him to. But Eric dressed for efficiency, flexibility, comfort, and speed. A gray T-shirt inside out, its faded message pressed to his skin: IF YOU'RE NOT OUTRAGED, YOU'RE NOT PAYING ATTENTION. His lucky socks, sneakers, Red Sox cap, and cargo pants—stuffed with lockpick, RF jammer, micro-scanner set to the police frequency, pliers, extra wire coils, a house key. He carried no ID. Just in case. If he missed something on the scanner, if their detectors failed, and a car pulled into the lot without advance warning, if someone, somewhere, heard something, and a cop appeared, there was always the all-purpose backup plan.

Ditch the equipment.

Forget the mission.

Run.

"Explain to me again why I have to be Chuckles and you get to be Cobra Commander?" Eric asked Max, hooking the line to his belt and giving it two quick tugs. There was a grinding sound, and then the ground fell away beneath him as the mechanism hoisted him up. He grazed his fingers against the brick facade; it scraped and tickled as the wires hauled him up to the roof.

It was nothing like flying.

"Because you always make me laugh," Max replied in a syrupy sweet voice. "At least, your face does."

"You're hilarious."

"Chuckles is a noble leader of covert operations for the G.I. Joe team," Max said. "You should be proud."

Eric snickered. "And *you* should stop playing with dolls."

"They're not—"

There was a pause. Eric hoped he wouldn't have to hear the lecture again, the one about eBay and nostalgia items and untapped gold mines. The one that comprehensively—just not convincingly—explained why Max had a pristine collection of Pokémon Beanie Babies on his top closet shelf.

"Never mind. Suffice it to say, *that's* why you don't get to pick your own code name," Max said. "You don't have the proper respect. Consider this your punishment. *Chuckles.*"

Eric scrambled over the edge and, with a thin sigh, planted his feet on the rooftop. Schwarz had already hurried over to the opposite edge, to get started on Phase Three. "So what'd Schwarz do to deserve Grunt?" Eric whispered.

"*That's* not a punishment. That's a description. Ever catch him with one of those vintage *Playboys* he loves so much?"

Eric made an exaggerated retching noise and flicked off the sound. Now if only, he thought, staring at Schwarz and wincing as he pictured what he desperately didn't want to picture, he could shut off his brain.

Max was the one who finally explained it to me.

"*Hacks. Not pranks. Never pranks. Pranks are for idiots.*" *He had his back to me. I'd interrupted him in pursuit of his other passion, hawking eighties nostalgia crap on eBay. That afternoon he was downloading photos of his latest acquisitions, a full collection of My Little Ponies, complete with Show Stable and Dream Castle. He'd pieced it together for a total of twenty-seven dollars, and planned to resell it for at least three hundred. Just another day at the computer for Max, who believed that if you didn't clear at least a five hundred percent profit on any given transaction, you just weren't trying.*

"Pranks are for amateurs. Live-action jokes with a total lack of sophistication and purpose. Not to mention sobriety." Warming to the lecture, he spun around to face me, skidding across the hardwood floor toward the couch. It was crimson-colored, like everything else in the Kim family's house. I sprawled across it, my feet up on the side, shoes off, to keep Dr. Kim from having a heart attack on discovering I had scuffed his fine Italian leather. Max warned me that my socks would get Maxwell Sr.'s forehead vein pumping just as quickly.

They were a deep, rich, dark, true blue. A crayon blue. An M&M's blue.

A Yale blue.

So I took my socks off too.

"Prankers have no vision," Max complained. "Saran Wrap on the toilet, cows in the lobby, dry ice in the pool, chickens in the gym. . . ." He rolled his eyes. "So what? What's the point? Gives us all a bad name. Even a good prank—even the best prank—is just funny. And then that's it. Over. Forgotten. But a hack *. . . you're playing in a different league. Higher profile. Higher stakes. Higher calling." His eyes glowed. I'd seen the look before, but only when he was talking about money.* Always *when he was talking about money.*

"TP cubed," he said. "Target, planning, precision, and purpose." He ticked them off on his fingers. "That's what we have, and they don't.

Worthy targets, *long-term* planning, *technically sophisticated and* precise *execution—and a noble purpose. You want to make a statement, stand up for the right side. You want to take someone down who really deserves it."*

"And you want to be funny," I added.

He glared at me like I'd just set fire to his My Little Ponies. *"Funny's beside the point. In 1961, the Cal Tech Fiendish Fourteen got sick of the annual invasion of Pasadena by football-crazed morons. So they hacked the Rose Bowl halftime flip-card show. They fooled* two thousand *University of Washington students into flipping over cards that combined to spell out* CALTECH. *There were more than ninety thousand people in that stadium. Millions more watching live on TV. You think they were going for* funny?" *His face twisted on the word.* "It wasn't about making people laugh. It was about achieving greatness."

"Where's the higher purpose in screwing up a halftime show?"

Max sighed, then turned back to his computer. "Forget it. Maybe it's a guy thing."

I glanced toward the stack of My Little Ponies.

He was lucky I didn't have a match.

It took longer than expected, but by two a.m., Phase Three was completed.

Max stepped back, spread his arms wide, and gave the rooftop assemblage a nod of approval. "A masterpiece, boys. We've done it again."

Five rows of small desks and chairs faced an imposing, kitchen table–size desk and padded black office chair. Behind it stood one blackboard, complete with wooden pointer and blue chalk. Corny motivational posters hung from invisible walls—rows of fishing line strung at eye level. And, hanging above them, the pièce de résistance: one oversize, battery-powered clock, so that when Dr. Richard Ambruster, the desperate-for-retirement history teacher and current tenant of the now empty room 131, eventually found his classroom, precisely re-created on the Wadsworth High roof, he would be able to calculate his tardiness down to the second.

In his twenty-two years of teaching high school, Richard Ambruster had found only one thing in which to take any joy: giving detentions. Speak out of turn? Detention. Request an extension? Detention. Miss a homework? Detention. Refer to him as "Mr." rather than "Dr."? Two detentions.

But the crown jewel in his collection of detention-worthy offenses was tardiness. Thirty minutes or thirty seconds late, it didn't matter. Excuses, even doctor-certified ones, carried no weight with him. "My time is valuable," he would tell the unlucky latecomer in his haughty Boston Brahman accent. "And your time, thus, is mine." Cue the pink slip.

Two days before, a bewildered freshman, still learning her way around the hallowed labyrinthine halls, had foolishly asked an upperclassman for directions to room 131. She'd ended up in the second-floor boys' bathroom. Ten minutes later she'd slipped into history class, face red, lower lip trembling, sweat stains spreading under either arm. She hadn't gotten two words out before Ambruster had ripped into her, threatening to throw her out of his room—out of the school—for her blatant disregard for him, his class, his time, his wisdom, and the strictures of civil society. As she burst into tears, he shoved the pink slip in her face and turned away.

And for this, Eric had decided, Dr. Evil needed to pay.

The freshman was blond, with an Angelina Jolie pout . . . and eyes that seemed to promise misty gratitude—so Max was in.

Schwarz didn't get a vote, and didn't need one. He just came along for the ride.

In the morning, Ambruster's howl of rage would echo through the halls of Wadsworth High School, and Eric would allow himself a small, proud smile, even though no one would ever discover the truth about who was responsible. In the morning, Max would try to scoop up his willing freshman and claim his reward, only to get shot down yet again. In the morning, Schwarz would wake up in his Harvard dorm room, which, two weeks into freshman year, still felt like a strange, half-empty cell, and wish it was still the middle of the night and he was still up on the roof with his best friends. Because that was the moment that counted. Not the morning after, not the consequences, not the motives, but the act itself. The challenge. The hack.

The mission: accomplished.

So what was I doing while they were scaling walls and freezing their asses off for the sake of truth, justice, and bleached-blond high school freshmen?

I was raising my hand, I was doing my homework, I was bulking up my résumé, I was conjugating French verbs, chairing yearbook meetings, poring through Princeton Review prep books, planning bake sales, tutoring the underprivileged, memorizing WWII battlefields and laws of derivation and integration, exceeding expectations, sucking up, boiling the midnight oil, rubbing my brown nose against the grindstone. I was following the rules.

As a matter of policy, I did everything I was supposed to do. And as far as I was concerned, I was supposed *to be valedictorian.*

Except I wasn't.

At least, not according to the Southern Cambridge School District. Not when Katie Gibson's GPA was .09 higher than mine by day one of senior year. All because in ninth grade, when the rest of us were forced to take art—non-honors, non-AP, non-weighted, a cannonball around the ankle of my GPA—Katie's parents wrote a note claiming she was allergic to acrylic paint.

I got an A in art.

Katie got study hall.

My parents threatened to sue.

And, only once, on the way into the cafeteria, because I couldn't stop myself:

Me: "Is it even possible to be allergic to acrylic paint?"

Katie: "Is it even possible for you to mind your own business?"

Me: "Look, I'm not saying you lied, but . . ."

Katie: "And I'm not saying you're a bitch, but . . ."

Me: "What's your problem?"

Katie: [Walks away]

By the second week of senior year, the truth had sunk in. I wasn't going to be the Wadsworth High valedictorian. Salutatorian, sure. Number two. Still gets to give a speech at graduation. Still gets a special seat and an extra tassel. Probably even a certificate.

But still number two. Which is just a prettier way of saying not number one. Not a winner.

Then, in late November, something, somewhere beeped. A red flag on Katie's record, an asterisk next to the entry for her tenth-grade health class, indicating a requirement left unfulfilled, a credit gone missing. She could make up the class, cleanse her record, still graduate—but not in time for the official valedictorian selection. She was out.

I was in.

The rumor went around that I'd given the vice principal a blow job.

Eric held out his hand, palm facing up. "Give it."

"What?" Max's beatific smile didn't come equipped with a golden halo, but it was implied.

"Whatever you've got in your pocket," Eric said. "Whatever you took out of Ambruster's desk."

"What makes you think I—"

"Excuse me?" Schwarz said, his voice quaking. "Can we get down off the roof now?"

"You can go," Eric said. "But *he's* not leaving until he puts it back."

Schwarz stayed.

Max rolled his eyes. "You're crazy."

"You're predictable."

"Clock's ticking," Max said, tapping his watch. "If the guard shows up after all and catches us here . . ."

"It'd be a shame. But I'm not leaving until you put it back." Eric stepped in front of the elaborate pulley system they'd rigged to lower themselves to the ground. "And you're not either."

"You wouldn't risk it."

"Try me."

Schwarz's skittery breathing turned into a wheeze. "I am sorry to interrupt, but I really do not think we should—"

"Schwarz!" they snapped in chorus. He shut up.

Max stared at Eric. Eric stared back.

And after a long minute of silence, Max broke.

"Fine." It wasn't a word so much as a full-body sigh, his entire body shivering with disgruntled surrender. He pulled a folded-up piece of paper out of his pocket.

"Next week's test questions?" Eric guessed.

Max grunted. "And the password to his grading database. You know how much I could make off this?"

"Do I care?"

Max sighed again and began folding and unfolding the sheet of paper. "So how'd you know?"

"I know *you*," Eric said.

"And just this once, couldn't we . . ."

Eric shook his head. "Put it back where you got it."

"You're a sick, sick man, Eric," Max said. "You want to know why?"

"Let me think . . . no."

"It's this moralistic right/wrong bullshit. It's like you're infected. Don't do this, don't do that. Thou shalt not steal the test answers. Thou shalt not sell thine term papers and make a shitload. Thou shalt not do *anything*. It's a freaking disease."

Eric had heard the speech before, and he finally had his comeback ready. "Oh yeah? I hope it's not an STD, or I might have given it to your *mother* last night."

Schwarz snorted back a laugh, and Max, groaning, shook his head in disgust. "First of all, I think the term you're looking for is *yo mama*," he said. "Second of all . . ." He pulled out his cell phone and pretended to take a call. "It's Comedy Central. They say don't quit your day job."

"Put the test answers back, Max."

Max glared at Eric, but slid the paper back into Ambruster's desk. "If you'd just get over it, we'd be rich by now."

"If I didn't say no once in a while, we'd be in prison by now."

"Excuse me?" Schwarz began again, timidly.

Once again, the answer came back angry and in unison. "What?"

Schwarz spread his arms to encompass their masterpiece, the orderly silhouettes of desk after desk, the inspirational posters blowing in the wind. "It is beautiful, isn't it?"

It was.

Three proud smiles. Three quiet sighs. And one silent look exchanged among them, confirming that they all agreed: Whatever the risk, whatever their motives, whatever the consequences, this moment was worth it.

"Now can we *please* get off the roof?" Schwarz led the way down, holding his breath until his feet brushed grass. And a moment later, the three of them disappeared into the night.

It was their final dry run, their final game in the minor leagues. Max was the only one who knew it, because Max already had the plan crawling through his mind, the idea he couldn't let go. He hadn't said anything yet, but he would, soon—because up on that roof, he decided it was time. The hack on Dr. Evil had gone so effortlessly, with almost a hint of boredom. It was child's play, and Max was getting tired of toys.

He knew the idea was worthy.

He knew the plan was ready—and so were they.

I wasn't there, of course. But I've pieced it together, tried to sift the truth from the lies, eliminate the contradictions. And I've tried to be a faithful reporter of the facts, even the ones that don't make me look very good.

Maybe even especially those.

The three of them agreed not to broadcast what they'd done. But much as I know now, close as I've gotten to the center of things, I'm still not one of them, not really. And that means that I never agreed to anything. I'm not bound. I can do what I want—and I want to speak.

So like I say, this isn't my story to tell, but it's the one I've got. And all it's got is me.

THE PLAN

October 7
THE BET

October 15
CAMPUS VISIT

October 19
SATs

November 17
THE GAME

November–December
THE APPLICATION

December 31
APPLICATION DEADLINE/NEW YEAR'S EVE

February 3
THE INTERVIEW

March 10
ADMISSIONS COMMITTEE DELIBERATIONS

March 15
D(ECISION)-DAY

PHASE ONE

October 7
THE BET
Objective: Agree on terms, select an applicant

October 15
CAMPUS VISIT
Objective: Preliminary reconnaissance

1

If you were going to hint plausibly that any American college is a sex haven, you'd hint that it's Harvard.

—Nicholas B. Lemann '76, "What Harvard Means: 30 Theories to Help You Understand," *The Harvard Crimson*, September 1, 1975

"It's not a living wage if it means you're stuck living in a box!" Eric yelled, slamming the latest issue of *Mother Jones* down on the kitchen table. His father didn't even look up.

"The term *living wage* is a false construct," he said mildly, turning the page of his *Economist*. "Part of the delusion that income is somehow owed, rather than earned."

"You don't think the guy who empties your office trash can every night has earned the right to health insurance and food for his family?"

His father still didn't look up. "Don't exaggerate. It's sloppy."

Eric sighed, his mind still foggy from the previous night's rooftop adventure. It wasn't a good morning for an argument, even one he'd had a hundred times before. Even one he'd started himself. "It's not fair. They should—"

"It's not a question of fair, it's a question of what the market will support," his father snapped. "I thought I taught you that much, at least, before you abandoned the discipline to play with your toys. Maybe you need to reread your Adam Smith."

Toys. That's what his father called the gears and wires that lay strewn across Eric's room, the devices—alarm clocks, batteries, telescopes, then later, Wi-Fi–capable walkie-talkies and pencil-size image scanners—that Eric used to show off, before he knew better. As far as his father was concerned, engineering was a game. Whereas economics, according to Howard Roth, Harvard University's Ellory Taft Memorial Professor of Economics, was a discipline. Eric's father had never gotten over the fact that his prodigy son, who used to sit in the back of the grand lecture hall doodling supply and demand curves on the pages of his Rugrats coloring book, had moved on to what Professor Roth insisted on calling "playtoys" and so Eric, in return, pointedly referred to as "real science."

There had been a time when Eric had dreamed of attending Harvard, studying under his father, creating a Roth family economics dynasty . . . but then, there had also been a time when Howard Roth insisted on biking to campus, when his sweaters were hand-knit by his wife, when family dinners spurned meat in support of the rain forest, grapes in support of mistreated migrant workers, and, for a brief period, pork in support of the good karma Howard Roth believed he might accrue from the local rabbi and, on the off chance he was paying attention, God. Now Professor Roth drove the five miles to campus every day in a Lexus SUV, preferred Armani to Brooks Brothers, though he would wear Hugo Boss in a pinch, and ate whatever was put in front of him at his latest Republican fund-raiser.

Times changed.

"Maybe *you* need to reread Adam Smith," Eric argued, "because you don't know what you're talking about."

That made his father look up from his journal. "Remind me. Which one of us is the architect of the current national economic policy? And which of us hasn't been to a lecture on the subject since he threw a temper tantrum at age nine?"

Eric had plenty to say on the subject of the current national economic policy, and his father's architectural skills, which had proven about as effective in Washington as they had two years before, when he'd tried to replace a loose gutter and ended up punching a three-foot-wide hole in the roof. But his cell phone rang with a message from Schwarz.

911

Saved by the *Battlestar Galactica*–themed ringtone.

"I'm out of here." Eric jumped up from the table, grabbing a slice of bacon to go.

"Wearing *that?*" Howard Roth looked pointedly at the message running across his son's T-shirt.

NICE HUMMER.

IT LOOKS GOOD WITH YOUR TINY PENIS.

"They let you go to school like that?"

"It's Saturday," Eric pointed out.

"You should change."

"So should you," Eric muttered. But only once he was already out the door.

Eric burst out of the Harvard Square T station, ran through the Yard, and slipped into Stoughton Hall using one of the spare entry cards that Schwarz had manufactured for his friends. There was no sign of a crisis. And when Max opened the door to room 19, he was beaming.

"So what's the big emergency?" Eric asked.

Max just swept him into the room, his smile growing wider. "You're not going to believe this one."

Schwarz was sitting at the head of his extra-long twin mattress, pressed up flat against the wall, his face pale and ashy, his eyes twitching behind his oversize glasses. He looked like a little kid convinced that there were monsters under his bed, and Eric had to remind himself, yet again, that Schwarz was a college freshman.

A sixteen-year-old freshman who had been homeschooled by his mother for the past two years and had yet to start shaving, but a college man nonetheless.

"Tell him what's going on, Professor," Max said, flicking something across the room. It was pink, and it spiraled as it flew, slapping down squarely on Schwarz's upturned face. It was a bra.

Schwarz squeaked.

"Get it off!" He gave his whole body a mighty shake, but the bra caught in his thick cloud of tight curls and hung there like an oversize earring, flopping back and forth as he shook his head so violently, his glasses flew off. "Please!"

Max ignored him and sank to the floor, convulsing with laughter. So Eric grabbed the bra, gave it a sharp yank, and pulled it off of Schwarz, who shuddered. *If only the girls at Wadsworth High could see him now,* Eric thought, suppressing a smile. Poor Schwarz, who hadn't even shown his face in Wadsworth's hallowed halls in the past two years, had accrued quite the reputation as a sex maniac, his punishment for the alleged sin of installing a micro camera in the girls' locker room. No one had believed that Schwarz built the camera for the purest of purposes—to see if he could—and was only persuaded to give it away to the *actual* Peeping Toms (three lying morons from the lacrosse team) because, well, it was impossibly easy to convince Schwarz to do anything.

No one knew that Schwarz had been nodding along to Max and Eric's wild schemes since he was a precocious six-year-old with a *Star Trek* fetish and the ability to recite pi to the 77th digit—in bases one through twelve. They didn't know that he believed it impolite and inadvisable not to say yes to pretty much everyone and everything— and thus would give his camera away to his new lacrosse buddies just as easily as he would, and had, agreed to help Max and Eric slime their second-grade after-school gifted counselor or rewire their fourth-grade teacher's phone to receive all—and only—incoming calls to the local twenty-four-hour psychic hotline. They didn't know Schwarz, and so they didn't realize that the five-foot-tall genius who'd skipped two grades and probably should have skipped two more, the one with the *Playboy* collection lovingly categorized and laminated in the back of his closet, avoided the beach every summer because, though he would never have admitted it, real live girls in real live bikinis freaked him out.

They didn't know Schwarz, and so they didn't ask questions, they just found the camera, believed the lying lacrosse morons, and called his mother in to the principal's office, and within a week Schwarz was spending his days poring through international topology journals on his own time, at his own alarming pace, in the security of his own home, while Elaine Schwarzbaum hovered and fussed, wondering how to cure her son of his supposedly perverted proclivities, and Carl Schwarzbaum, when he remembered to stop by for a visit, winked at his son for a job well done.

If they could see him now, cowering from a bra . . .

Not that Eric could completely blame him. The bra—and all it implied, the secret power it seemed designed to amplify and contain—was an intimidating thing. Eric had seen bras before, but only his sister's and his mother's. And that didn't count. He turned it over in his hands. Pink, sort of satiny, with an almost fuzzy lining and a collection of snaps and clasps that looked like they belonged on a medieval corset, and the tiny flower in the center was—

"Would you put that down and find the rest of them!" Schwarz yelled.

Eric dropped the bra.

"I mean . . . please?" Schwarz sighed and let his head fall back against the wall with a *thunk*. "They are everywhere."

"What's he talking about?" Eric asked.

"Invasion of the bras." Max pointed to the dresser, where a lacy black strap poked out of the top drawer. "It's heaven."

"It is *Hades*." Schwarz moaned and plopped his face into his hands. "I opened my desk to get a pencil, and there it was, just . . . just *sitting* there. A . . ."

"Bra?" Eric said helpfully.

Schwarz grunted. "It is them. The girls upstairs. They think it is funny to torture me."

"The girls upstairs?" Eric asked. "You mean—"

"Ste-pha-nie," Max sang out, grabbing the pink bra off the floor and plucking another one out of a math textbook, "a.k.a. lovergirl."

"Shut up." Schwarz buried his face in his pillow—then squeaked in disgust and tossed it on the floor. Max bent down and retrieved a white bra that had been tucked inside the pillowcase.

"Face it, Schwarz, she *wants* you," Max taunted.

"If she wants me so much, why is she trying to—"

"Distribute her deliciously *sexy* underthings—which are, I might add"—Max grabbed a lacy black bra out of Schwarz's sock drawer—"dripping of *sex*—throughout your bedchamber?" Max's bullshitting abilities were legendary, but even *he* couldn't quite pull off the non-chalant act in the face of the lingerie onslaught. He could play the lecherous lothario all he wanted, but Eric had seen his last attempt to make conversation with a real live hot girl—if you could call four hopelessly cheesy pickup lines punctuated by a knee to the groin a conversation.

Eric pelted him with the pink satin B-cup. "Any chance at all you could take a five-minute break from being you?"

"Any chance? I don't know, let's ask the probability king." Max turned to Schwarz. "Oh great mathemagician, what sayst thou?"

There was another sigh, a long one. "Zero percent probability." Schwarz hung his head. "Can you please find the rest and remove them?"

"Only if you explain to me how you can be scared of a bra," Max said. "Those girls just turned your room into the promised land, and you're acting like you're in hell."

"Eric, please, can you—"

"Hey, don't look at me." Eric held up his arms in protest. "I hate to agree with"—he jerked his head toward Max—"*that*, but what's the deal? I know your precious Playboy Bunnies don't have too much use for bras, but that's no reason to be afraid of—"

"I am not afraid!" Schwarz said hotly, squirming away as Max dangled a bra in his face. He jumped off the bed and crossed to the other side of the room, giving Max a wide berth. "I just . . . I do not need to see that stuff."

"Bras," Max said.

"That is not why I like the magazines," Schwarz added. "I keep telling you that. It is not about . . . you know."

"Sex," Max said.

"The girls are beautiful." Schwarz blushed. "They are perfect. It makes me think about . . ."

"Sex," Max said, louder this time.

"Numbers," Schwarz said, a dreamy look coming into his eyes. "An equation that draws all the elements together into one simple, unified system. All the irrelevant chaos falls away. The universe resolves itself into order. That is how you recognize a good equation. There is an imperceptible elegance. Perfection. Beauty."

Max thudded his fist against his forehead. "You're hopeless. You're hoarding a copy of every *Playboy* issue ever printed and you want to talk to me about the beauty of *numbers?*" He raised his eyes to the ceiling. "A decade of friendship, and he's learned *nothing* from me? I've failed. Failed!"

Eric clapped Schwarz on the back. "Ignore the drama queen. But, Schwarzie, I gotta tell you, even perfect, beautiful girls wear bras. So I've heard."

"Can you just . . . just take them away?" Schwarz pleaded. "I have three problem sets due, and I cannot get anything done. Not when they could be anywhere."

Max and Eric exchanged a glance. "I think that can be arranged," Max said, smirking as he stuffed the black bra into his backpack for safekeeping, and began the hunt.

After all, what are friends for?

"Excuse me, but I really do not think this is a good idea," Schwarz said again, but they were already at the top of the steps.

"Sorry, my friend, but even child prodigies are wrong sometimes," Max said, his arms overflowing with bras. "And this is your time."

It had taken more than an hour, but they'd ransacked Schwarz's room and found each and every bra, including the red satin one stuffed in his laundry bag, the purple cotton one hiding beneath the Tums bottles and Bactine from Mrs. Schwarzbaum's latest care package, the miracle push-up one lodged between the June and July issues of *Journal of Dynamic and Differential Equations*, and, most sacrilegious of all, the lime green double D slipped into the box holding Schwarz's *Playboys*. Now, Max had decreed, it was time to return the merchandise.

Eric raised his hand to knock—then froze. The door was almost entirely covered by brightly colored condom wrappers.

"You can get them for free in the common rooms and the health center," Schwarz said sullenly. He sounded like a man facing the death sentence. Doomed. "They collect them and then stick them up here. They call it art." He smiled hopefully. "So does that mean we can leave now? Please?"

Max gazed at the door in admiration. "Oh, we are *so* not leaving."

Eric knocked. Schwarz cowered.

The girl who opened the door was wearing a zip-up hoodie and baggy sweatpants, but the loose cotton couldn't disguise the fact that she was built like a model, long and leggy and lean. The silky blond hair didn't hurt. Eric glanced back at Schwarz, who shook his head slightly.

No, then. This wasn't the amazing Stephanie, goddess among women.

But it was still a college girl.

Make that college *woman*.

"I assume these are yours?" Max asked, dumping his pile at the girl's feet. He gave her an oily grin. "We *especially* loved the little one with pink hearts all over it." Max glanced not-so-subtly down at the girl's ample chest. "Though I'm guessing that one wasn't yours."

The girl burst into giggles and turned her head over her shoulder. "Steph, I think the skanky freshman is hitting on me!"

Behind her, the room exploded into laughter.

"Baby, I'm not a freshman, I'm a senior," Max said indignantly.

"Yeah, right. You're a—" The girl's eyes widened. "Oh, God, you're one of Schwarzie's little high school friends, aren't you?" She choked out a laugh so forceful that a light spray of spittle flew out and misted Max's nose.

"Ask Schwarz how he liked his surprise!" a girl's voice yelled out from behind her.

The girl in the doorway peered over Max's shoulder. Schwarz gave her a weak wave. "He's even redder than we thought!" she called back into the room. "He looks like his head's about to explode." And before the boys could say anything else, she scooped up the armful of bras and the door closed in their faces.

"You forgot one," Max snapped, still dangling one last bra from his fingers. He whirled on Schwarz. "Please tell me *that* wasn't your precious Stephanie."

Schwarz shook his head and leaned back against the banister, trying to catch his breath.

Max rolled his eyes. "Since when did they start letting bimbos into Harvard? I mean, she may be hot, but—"

The door swung open. Another girl's head poked out, this one framed by wavy, shoulder-length brown hair and a pair of thin, rectangular, black glasses. Her cheeks glowed red, like they'd been battered by the wind. "First of all, she's not a bimbo, she's a two-time national forensics champion and all-American rower. Second of all, *I'm* not a bimbo, and I could give you all the reasons why, and I could do it in any one of the three languages I speak, but I'm not going to, because third of all, you're still in high school. And fourth, I believe *this*"—she plucked the final bra out of Max's hand—"is mine."

The door closed before he had a chance to react.

Schwarz sighed. "*That* was Stephanie."

Max slid open his front door. *Twenty-two bras,* he thought, hoping the happy memories would insulate from what came next. *I touched twenty-two bras today.* He patted the outer pocket of his backpack, which held a lacy black treat. *Plus one to grow on.* And there was plenty more where that came from.

Imagine the financial possibilities, he thought gleefully. Schwarz was sitting on a lacy goldmine, and didn't even know it. Certainly, Max's regular eBay customers—the ones who knew he was the guy to satisfy their every craving for mint condition Transformers, Micro Machines, Hot Wheels, Cabbage Patch Kids, or that rare and beautiful find, a

Snoopy Sno-Kone Machine in full working order complete with three synthetic flavors of polyurethaned sugar crystals—would have no use for an anonymous coed's unwashed, stretched-out cotton lingerie. But there was an untapped market for such things out there, Max was sure of it: horny losers hungry for tangible evidence that real girls— and their undergarments—actually existed. Max might not want to *befriend* anyone who would buy stolen bras off the Internet, but he had no compunctions about *supplying* them, not if it would bring in the cash. If Schwarz could be persuaded to go along—and who was he kidding, Schwarz could be persuaded to do anything. . . .

But it was no use. Even a get-rich-quick guarantee couldn't buoy his spirits. Stepping into the Kim household was enough to deflate any mood. It was like an allergy—every time he came home, he felt his chest tightening, his throat closing up, his lungs gasping. But it wasn't the air. It was the color. That deep, dark bloody red.

Crimson.

Everywhere. Crimson rug, crimson couch, crimson flag waving over crimson mantel . . . and, worst of all, crimson walls.

The Kims had no art hanging in their home. Most of the space was taken up by framed photos—many of the twins, Nikki and Vikki, proudly accepting a variety of trophies, dancing in recitals, delivering speeches, accepting diplomas; a smattering of relatives, always staring head-on at the camera, stiffly posed, a rigid smile across their face as if somewhere beneath the frame, a gun was prodding them to "smile, or else," and, dominating every room, a photographic record of the childhood of the Kims' only son.

In the entry hall: Max bundled up in a red snowsuit, stuffing a fistful of snow into his sister's mouth.

Over the couch: Max in a high chair, spaghetti streaming down his face.

In the kitchen, hanging above the row of pots and pans: Max, uncomfortable and unhappy in a starched crimson suit, seated on the lap of the John Harvard statue.

Only one wall in the Kim house was photograph-free, and this was the wall on the far end of the living room, opposite the door to the kitchen, visible from almost every point on the ground floor. This was the wall of achievement and, in flowery script bordered by heavy, solid wood frames, it reported the following:

Maxwell Kim, BS in chemistry,
Harvard University, class of 1980

Maxwell Kim, PhD in chemistry,
Harvard University, class of 1985

Victoria Kim, BA in history, BS in biology,
Harvard University, class of 2004

Victoria Kim, LLD,
Harvard Law School, class of 2007

Nicole Kim, BS in biology,
Harvard University, class of 2004

An empty spot awaited Nikki's forthcoming diploma from Harvard Medical School, only a year away.

Another gaping hole toward the center of the wall had long been reserved for Max Jr.

Twenty-three bras, Max told himself, his lips moving. *The black lacy one. The pink one with the tiny flower, the—*

He was starting to sound like Schwarz. Things were even worse than he'd thought. Probably for the best that there was no more time for quiet contemplation—or, more accurately, self-pity. It was six forty-five. Which meant time for dinner.

And yet another round of The Conversation.

It was always the same one, and had been ever since Max had made his big announcement.

"But why?" Maxwell Sr. asked yet again, digging into a heaping plate of kimchi. "Just make me understand."

"It's a once-in-a-lifetime opportunity," Max said, as he always did. "And it's now or never."

His father shook his head. "Another will come along. It always does. If you work hard, if you go to college—"

"I *will* go to college." Max reminded himself to keep his voice calm and level. Maxwell Sr. didn't believe in yelling—at least when it came to voices other than Maxwell Sr.'s. "I *told* you. I'll go at night, take classes at BU or something—"

"BU?" He turned to his wife. "You talk to him. Tell him not to ruin his life."

"We just want you to be happy," Ellen Kim said, giving her son a hesitant smile. "Just look at your sisters—look how far they got with a good degree."

Look at your sisters. Look at your sisters. Max had been looking at—up to—his sisters since he was a helpless toddler, forced to play the role of Baby in their interminable games of House (and later, School, Prison, Wild Frontier, and his personal nightmare, Fairy Princess Tea Party). Now they were finally out of the house, yet he was forced to stare at their cap-and-gown photos and framed summa cum laude diplomas every day of his life.

"Harvard isn't the only measure of success in the world, despite what you think." Max scraped his kimchi over to the side of the plate, revealing the familiar VERITAS crest embossed in gold at the center. The Kims ate exclusively from Harvard commemorative china. "I don't need a Harvard degree on the wall to prove how smart I am. And I definitely don't need it to get rich. Not when this company—"

"Zipco? Zero?" His father snorted. "It's not a company. It's three guys in a basement. You think you're going to be the next Bill Gates working in a basement?"

God, I hope not, Max thought. Eric could—and did—worship Bill Gates's path-blazing philanthropy all he wanted, but to Max, Microsoft would always be the evil empire, with Bill at the helm, a Palpatine determined to co-opt or destroy every last Jedi. Microsoft, Harvard, they were just different faces of the same monster, Max thought, massive Death Stars that exterminated any and all obstacles in their paths. He would *not* be turned to the dark side.

"It's *XemonCo*," Max retorted. "And they won't be in a basement forever. They're just starting up. That's why it's called a start-up."

"I know what it's called. Don't talk to me like I'm an idiot. Not when you're the one who's throwing away his whole life to work for free. Only an idiot would *volunteer* for indentured servitude."

"It's not for free."

"So they're paying you a salary now?"

Max looked down at his crimson, white, and gold commemorative plate, molding his kimchi into a tidy pile directly over the gold VERITAS. "You know they're not."

"So what, then? *Monopoly* money? Maybe they're still on the barter system, they're paying you in pizza and potato chips?"

Max sighed. He'd explained the deal to his father, too many times. In exchange for the data-grinding algorithm he'd designed, XemonCo—the cutting-edge start-up that was, if its plans came to fruition, poised to unseat Google—had offered him full-time employment and a significant chunk of company stock. The latter was contingent upon the former, which meant forgoing his all-but-certain admission to Harvard in favor of the working world.

Though, as his father was always quick to point out, you couldn't really call it work if you weren't getting paid.

"This is it, Dad. The big score. You're the one always saying money is power. As soon as the search engine is done, it'll lubricate the cash flow. . . ."

"And what are you going to do until then?"

Max looked up from his kimchi pile in confusion. "Until then?"

"Are you expecting your mother and me to support you? While you lie around playing video games all day and taking kindergarten classes at night?"

"My search algorithm is not a video game, it's—"

"You think we're rich?"

"Rich enough to pay Vikki's and Nikki's tuition for fifteen years," Max pointed out. "And, like you tell me every night, rich enough to send me to college, med school, law school, and oh yeah, when I get around to it, to get my PhD."

"Only if you want, of course," his mother said.

"Right." Max tried valiantly not to roll his eyes. "So I just assumed . . ."

"College. Yes. Harvard. Yes." His father stood up, pushed his chair in, and looked over Max, fixing his eyes on the framed portrait just above his head, one that featured Maxwell Sr. on a crimson-splashed stage, accepting a degree. "Money for your future, yes. But money for you to make this kind of mistake? No."

Maxwell Sr. grabbed a roll from the basket at the center of the table and pressed it down firmly in the center of Max's kimchi tower, mashing the mountain into a lake of greenish-red sludge. "The free ride ends with graduation," he said. "You go to Harvard—or you go it alone."

2

Your child can contribute to her school and community by pursuing what she enjoys and sharing it with others.

—Eva Ostrum, *The Thinking Parent's Guide to College Admissions*

The car skidded to the right, then veered left, dodging a turbo-charged flamethrower. A hail of gunfire exploded from the alleyway, and the windshield shattered into a storm of glass, but he pushed forward, the tires squealing, and he was almost safe, a smooth getaway, free and clear—when the roadside grenade blew out his tire. The front wheels jerked off the ground, and the car tumbled down an embankment, smashing and crashing its way to the bottom. There was a sickening crunch of metal. And then the car exploded into a ball of fire.

Eric tossed aside the controller in disgust. It was his third try, and this time he'd lasted only three and a half minutes before getting toasted. Other than his new Wii—which even his brain-dead sister had agreed was "more addictive than crack, not like I've tried it, because I'm not a total skeeze, but you know what I mean"—Eric steered clear of hand-eye coordination games. He stuck to the world of digital role-play, which, as far as he was concerned, took brains, style, finesse—and had a significantly lower humiliation factor. Besides, at least as a dragon slayer, he was doing some good in the world. Okay, maybe not *his* world, but it still had to count for something that he'd rescued six villages, 237 peasants, four maidens, an orphan, and a deposed prince from rampage, destruction, and certain death. World of Warcraft trained you to fight the good fight, so that when the *real* fight came to you, you'd be ready. All RoadKill 7 trained you to do, as far as Eric could tell, was pick up hookers and repeatedly drive your car off a cliff. Though he was willing to admit the possibility that he was playing it wrong.

"Do you guys need a remedial tutorial on the meaning of 911?" he asked as Max grabbed the controller. "Last week it's some kind of bra emergency, and now you drag me back here for what? PlayStation crisis?"

"Patience, young Jedi," Max said, leaning closer to the tiny TV in an effort to see whether the fuzzy figure approaching his car was a prostitute or a cop. "All good things come to those I deem worthy."

Schwarz, who was at his desk, legs kicked up on the nineteenth-century wood, the "authentic Harvard chair" (with the gold seal to prove it) digging into his back, looked up from his notebook. "Professor Kempel is giving a lecture on homological algebra and the computability problem at five, so if this is perhaps not that important . . ."

"It's important," Max said, eyes still fixed on the screen.

Schwarz nodded, and turned back to his homework. "Okay."

Eric threw himself down on the roommate's bed, which had

gone unused since the first week of school, when Schwarz's room-mate, one Marsh Preston, of the Upper East Side Prestons ("Maybe you've heard of us?"), had tossed his CK boxers, Paul Smith shirts, and six jars of Kiehl's moisturizers and bronzers into a Harvard athletics duffel bag and taken off for Canaday Hall, where his high school girlfriend had a single. "I could be at a rally right now," Eric said. "People Against the Encroachment of Civil Equality. PEACE."

"That's not PEACE, that's PA-ECE," Max said. "And you hate rallies."

"Fine." Eric sucked in a breath through gritted teeth. "So I could be home playing World of Warcraft. What's the difference? This is still a waste of time."

"This is a time to cherish," Max chided him. "A time to treasure the moments of your lives with the people who truly—"

"A time to cut the bullshit," Eric said. "Why are we here?"

Max hit pause. He stood up and turned to face his friends. "Why are we here? A good question. An excellent question. Why *are* we here? Are we just marking time?"

"I am actually trying to understand the decomposition of symplectic manifolds," Schwarz said, pausing to blow his nose on one of the aloe-infused tissues that had just arrived in another baked-goods-free care package from home, "and their relation to Lagrangian barriers and—"

"We're squandering our God-given talent on lame stunts and schoolboy pranks," Max continued. "It's time to ask ourselves what we want. What we *really* want. Fame? Fortune?"

"Speak for yourself," Eric muttered.

"Or is it something less mundane, more powerful, more *meaningful*?" Max asked, his voice rising and falling in ecstatic preacherlike swells. "We always *say* we want to poke holes in the system, deflate the big heads, unseat the tyrants—but what do we do? Nothing."

Eric hopped off the bed. "It's not *nothing*," he said. "It's . . ."

But what was it?

More than a joke, maybe, but . . . how much more? He looked down at his T-shirt, which today read: WAR IS A STATE OF MIND—BRAIN DEAD.

"What we do *matters*," he insisted. "It's subtle, but it's necessary. We poke holes in the system. Weaken its foundation. Like Borat. Like Michael Moore. Like—"

"Like children," Max said. "Flooding out school board meetings. Sealing the school shut." He snorted. "Kid stuff. Time is slipping by, and all the while, we've been ignoring the real prize. Our perfect score. Our Everest." He waited expectantly, but this time, there were no interruptions, just two blank stares. "I'll give you a hint, boys and girls. When it's not flipping you off, it's sticking its massive fingers into everything. It's gobbling up everything around it like a chocoholic at a Hershey's convention. It *owns* us. All of us." More blank looks. Max shook his head. "Here's a hint, geniuses. Without it, Eric wouldn't eat. Schwarz wouldn't graduate. And my father . . . well, we all know the only thing in life Maxwell Sr. truly loves."

"You want us to pull a prank on *Harvard*?" Schwarz asked, in the same tone he'd used in the fifth grade when Max ordered him to climb up on the roof and field-test their homemade parachute.

"Not a prank, Professor Schwarz," Max replied, with the same mix of confidence and wheedling that had persuaded Schwarz to jump. "A *hack*. And not just any hack, but the greatest hack we've ever done. Our coup de grâce. Our magnum opus." He began pacing back and forth. "Who's with me?"

"With you for what, exactly?" Eric asked.

Max stopped in front of the window and turned his back on the two of them, staring out at the lush green of Harvard Yard. "We're going to take the biggest loser we can find—the least ambitious, least intelligent, least motivated, most delinquent and drugged-up slacker we can get our hands on—and we're going to sucker this school into letting him in."

There was a long pause. "And?" Eric finally asked.

"And what? That's not enough for you?" Max said incredulously. "Look at this place." He jerked his head toward the window. A group of students draped in black sat in a circle listening to their silver-haired professor. A guy on a silver scooter whizzed down the diagonal path that cut through the Yard, veering around a tour group that whipped out cameras and cell phones to capture the authentic slice of Harvard life.

A couple groped under a tree.

Three jocks in crimson sweats whacked each other with lacrosse sticks.

A red-haired kid in a FOREVER JUNG T-shirt juggled milk bottles.

"Appalling." Eric rolled his eyes. "Definitely needs our immediate attention."

"Can't you see it?" Max grimaced, and pulled down the blind. "It's all a scam. And they're the suckers who bought it. My father—"

"Right. Your father," Eric said. "Who I'm sure has *nothing* to do with this. I'm not getting arrested just so you can prove to him that—"

"Forget Maxwell Sr.," Max snapped. "I have." He strode to the other side of the room, ripping a Harvard pennant off the roommate's side of the wall. "And no one's getting arrested. Not if we do this right." He crumpled the pennant and shot it toward the trash can, where it bounced off the rim and rolled a few feet away. Schwarz grabbed it off the floor and, with a nervous glance at Max, laid it on his bed and began smoothing it out.

Max began pacing again. "This isn't about my father. This isn't even about Harvard—or not *just* Harvard. It's about all the bullshit they've been feeding us since preschool: Do your homework, be good, fall in line, do what we say, and maybe, if you're lucky, you'll get the golden ticket. We're supposed to act like the only thing that matters is getting into college—getting into *this* college—and so most of the people who do get in are the ones who buy into the bull-shit so completely that they've never done anything for any other reason. It doesn't matter what they want, what they like, what they care about, who they are—they don't even know anymore, because they're trying so damn hard to be the people Harvard wants them to be. In the end they're not even real people anymore. They're zombies. No offense, Schwarz."

Schwarz gave him a half-shrug.

"And what about all the people that *don't* get in?" Max continued. "The ones who let some stupid letter from some stupid school tell them what they're worth as a person. Harvard says they're nothing, and they believe it."

Alicia Morgenthal, Eric thought, before he could stop himself. He preferred not to think about her at all. It was easier that way. Not because he felt guilty—though he did. But because when he thought about her, he couldn't help thinking about what had happened that day, and he couldn't help thinking about what had happened the night before. He couldn't help wondering whether he could have stopped her.

Or what might have happened that night after she kissed him— if he hadn't let her run away.

It was easier not to wonder at all, but maybe she deserved better than that. Maybe she deserved some justice.

Eric sat down on the edge of the bed and tapped his finger against the bridge of his glasses. "You want us to get someone into Harvard who doesn't belong here—"

"Who *Harvard* thinks doesn't belong," Max clarified.

"To prove that there's something wrong with the admissions system," Eric said. "To prove it's not perfect."

"Or even functional," Max added, rocking gently from his heels to his toes.

"And that it shouldn't be the way you measure your worth as a human being." Eric nodded. "I like it. I don't know if we could do it—"

"Of course we—"

"But I like it."

Everyone knew that the college admissions system was screwed up—not just at Harvard, not just in the Ivy League. Everywhere. Too many people for too few slots, too many kids with overpaid college counselors writing their essays for them, too many over- achievers with too many expectations that the system would be fair and they would win the future they deserved, too much stress, too much misery, too many lies. Eric figured it was bad all over, but in Cambridge, with the shadow of Harvard looming over them like a crimson mushroom cloud, it was unbearable. Everyone knew it.

But no one did anything about it. Because they thought it couldn't be done.

"I would prefer not to get expelled," Schwarz said hesitantly.

"You'll be fine," Max said. "You're doing it."

Schwarz sighed. "We will not get caught?"

"We will not get caught."

"Okay." Schwarz closed his eyes for a moment, and his lips moved as if in silent prayer—but Eric knew better. Those weren't prayers. They were names. Names and months and the occasional color of fishnet stockings. But for Schwarz it was all the same thing. Finally, he opened his eyes and nodded. "I am in."

Max sat down on the floor and grabbed the PlayStation controller. "So it's all set." He tossed one to Schwarz. "Head-to-head action?" Schwarz nodded, even though there was no chance he would win against the RoadKill master, and the thunder of digital engines filled the room.

"Forgetting something?" Eric asked.

Max sent his car flying over a heap of burning tires, then skidded into a U-turn to collect an extra weapons cache. "You're right—case of bullets. See? You're not so bad at this game after all."

"*Me,*" Eric corrected him. "I haven't said I'll do it."

Max shrugged. "You will."

"And you know this because?"

"This shit's right up your alley," Max said, bouncing on his knees as his car raced Schwarz's toward an abandoned overpass. "Taking down the system, power to the people, rage against the machine, all your bullshit."

"It's not bullshit," Eric said hotly.

"Exactly. And this is your shot, so man up."

"*If* we do it, we do it my way," Eric said. "Nothing too illegal. And we stay out of their computer system—it's crude."

"Also a felony," Schwarz pointed out.

Max nodded. "Terms accepted."

"*And* you tell us what's in it for you," Eric added.

"I already told you," Max said. "It's the ultimate hack. And all that crap about the admissions system being screwed up. You may be the righteous avenger and all, but that doesn't mean the rest of us can't get pissed off by all the bullshit once in a while, right?"

"What's in it for you?" Eric pressed.

"Nothing."

Eric crossed his arms. Max continued to stare at the TV screen.

"Pause that game and tell me."

Max didn't answer.

Eric leaned over Schwarz. "Can I see that for a second?" he asked, nodding at the controller. Schwarz handed it over.

Eric rammed his car into Max's, and they both exploded.

Game over.

"What the hell!" Max tossed down the controller. "What's wrong with you?" He turned on Schwarz. "What's wrong with *you*? Why'd you give it to him?"

Schwarz shrugged. "He asked."

Max didn't just roll his eyes, he rolled his whole head.

"What's in it for you?" Eric asked again, now that he had Max's full attention.

"Nothing."

"Try again."

"I made a bet, okay?" Max shouted. "Happy now?"

"Is that the truth?"

"You can't *handle* the truth," Max said in a bad Jack Nicholson impression. Then he shrugged. "Yeah. It's the truth. Just a small bet. No big deal."

"Then no. I'm not happy." They didn't do bets. It was too much of a risk—not just because they didn't have the cash to spare if they lost, but because it meant involving more people in the plan. People you couldn't necessarily trust. More to the point, it went against the whole spirit of the hack.

True hackers didn't hack for money. They did it for pride of ownership, for the challenge, for the principle of the statement. They did it to take a stand—to expose corruption and complacency, and to do it in style.

They didn't do it for cash.

Even Max, who did everything—and anything—for cash, had always understood that. Until now.

"A bet with who?" Eric asked.

"You don't want to know."

Eric gave him a mirthless smile. "Let's pretend I do."

Max looked away, picking up the controller again. Eric yanked it out of his hands. *"Max,"* he said warningly.

Max cleared his throat. "Turns out they're not so bad, once you get to know them. Good cash flow, impeccable credit. I really think—"

"Max! Who is it?"

Max winced. "The Bums."

Eric felt the moan pool in the pit of his stomach, churning through his intestines and slithering up his throat to finally spill out of his mouth in a guttural roar.

"Why?" he asked, when he'd regained the power of speech. "Why would you do that?" The Bongo Bums—so named in honor of scientist, bongo player, infamous prankster, and egomaniac Richard Feynman—were two juniors from Boston Latin High School who gave hackers everywhere a bad name. For them it was all about bets and bragging rights—and they'd won more than their fair share of both. But they knew they were only the second best in the Boston area, and so did everyone else on the hacking circuit. The Bums had always wanted an epic rivalry; Eric, Max, and Schwarz just wanted to be left alone.

"Why not?" Max shrugged. "It's just a hundred bucks, and we can do this—you *know* we can do this—so where's the risk? Why not let the Bums pay us for our trouble?"

"Just a hundred?" Eric didn't buy it. Max's philosophy was that every penny counted—at least when he was the one collecting the payoff—but a hundred bucks wouldn't have been enough to make him break protocol and cut a deal with the enemy. Or at least, it *shouldn't* have been enough.

"Just a hundred . . . each."

Schwarz hiccuped.

"But that just means more money for all of us when we get the job done," Max said quickly. "Which we will."

Schwarz looked pale, but Eric knew he would do whatever Max wanted.

Max knew it too, and looked at Eric. "So what do you say?"

He wanted it. There was something about the idea—maybe the challenge of the execution, maybe the thrill of the payoff, the knowledge that it would actually *mean* something—that felt right.

And yet, there was the bet. There were the Bums. There was the inescapable feeling that, as usual, Max was keeping a crucial detail to himself.

"I need some time," Eric said.

"Of course you do. Take all the time you need. At least until tomorrow, at eight thirty a.m."

"And what happens then?" Eric asked.

"We choose our lucky loser," Max said. "The Bums are meeting us outside the school to approve the selection and cement the final terms. Clock's ticking—applications are due in three months. So if we're going to do this, we start now."

"And if we're not going to do it?"

Max raised his eyebrows and gave Eric a knowing grin, then smoothed back his hair—the cowlick on the top of his head popping up again as soon as his palm had passed over it—and popped a breath mint. "Get your ass in gear, Schwarz. Hillel dinner starts in ten minutes, and I want to get a good seat."

Schwarz groaned. "I do not want to take you back there again. Everyone knows you are not Jewish—"

"Hey, there are Korean Jews, I could be one of them—they don't know!"

"There are approximately one hundred and eleven Korean Jews, and you are not one of them."

"First of all, you know you made that statistic up. Second of all, it doesn't matter, because no will ever have the nerve to call me on it," Max gloated. "That wouldn't be PC, now, would it?"

Eric glanced back and forth between the two of them. "Do I even want to know?"

"You know the girl who plays Ariel-7 in *SpaceQuest*?" Schwarz asked. "The one with the, um, you know, silver all over her . . ."

"Yeah, what about her?"

"She is a freshman here," Schwarz said.

"A *Jewish* freshman," Max added. "A very devout Jewish freshman who eats in Hillel every night." He glanced at his watch. "Which means we're late, Schwarz. Up. Now."

Schwarz jumped up and grabbed his coat, shooting Eric a *rescue me* look on his way to the door.

"Remember, eight thirty a.m., on the steps outside the school," Max said, gazing at his reflection in the back of his iPod.

"Maybe," Eric said. "Maybe not."

Max dropped his voice two octaves. "'I'm trying to free your mind, but I can only show you the door. You're the one that has to walk through it.'"

"*SpaceQuest*?" Eric guessed, trying to place the quote.

Max smacked his forehead. "*The Matrix*. Do you live in a cave?"

"I live in a permanent state of denial that I voluntarily spend my time with you," Eric said. "And that time generally involves a lot of darkness and bad smells—is that cavelike enough for you?"

"Eight thirty a.m.," Max said again, tugging Schwarz out the door. "You know you can't resist. This one's too sweet."

Eric hated it when Max played the mind reader, acting like Eric couldn't possibly think, say, or do anything that Max hadn't already anticipated.

He hated it even more when Max was right.

3

October 1 · THE BET
Objective: Agree on terms,
select an applicant

Colleges are always on the lookout for students who love to learn
and whose passion takes them to the highest level of challenge and
achievement.

—Peter Van Buskirk, *Winning the College Admission Game*

Elton Broussard wore a hat made out of aluminum foil to school
every day. On Mondays, Wednesdays, and Fridays, without
fail, he added a matching aluminum foil belt and suspenders. On
Tuesdays and Thursdays, he wore a white T-shirt and white pants,
completely covered, toga-style, in reams of flesh-colored Saran Wrap.
On the first Tuesday of junior year, he had arrived wearing *only* flesh-
colored Saran Wrap, and had subsequently disappeared from school
until that October, when the first white T-shirt and pants ensemble
made its debut. No one knew why Elton Broussard dressed as he did,
largely because whenever anyone ventured to *ask*, Elton growled.

Which is not to say he responded in a growl-like manner.

He growled.

Low and guttural, like a dog chained to a stake who knows from past experience that it can't leap far enough to bite its target but is willing to try again, believing that, just this once, it might snag a mouthful of flesh.

And, ever since the debut of the aluminum foil hat and Saran Wrap toga junior year, that growl was the first and last sound anyone had heard Elton Broussard make.

"Veto," Max said firmly. "Not a chance in hell."

From the front steps of Wadsworth High, it was possible—if you could stand the nicotine haze—to watch the student body roll in like the opening credits of a bad teen movie. Freaks, geeks, punks, rich girls pulling up in Daddy's Jag, Game Boy warriors with their heads down and their thumbs flying, PDA couples sneaking in one last hookup before the bell, nobodies who thought they were somebodies, slackers, stoners, misfits, and the rest, a faceless mass of Abercrombie and American Eagle swarming up the stairs, unmemorable masses greeting another unmemorable day.

Max, Eric, and Schwarz perched at the top, scouting their prey. Beside them sat a pair of gangly sixteen-year-olds with spiky brown hair, tragically hip emo T-shirts, E PLURIBUS MODEM buttons, and identical sneers: the Bums. One was named Gerald, the other Ash; both were assholes.

"What do you care who we pick?" Ash asked. "It's not like you're going to be able to pull this off, whoever you end up with."

"*Foetes ergo vincimus,*" Gerald sneered.

At Max's questioning look, Eric leaned in with a whispered translation. "'You stink, therefore we win.'" He leaned back against the concrete wall, tipping his gaze up and away from the depressing procession into the school.

So he wasn't looking when Gerald pointed across the parking lot and, with a steely certainty, announced, "Him."

Eric looked down again, following Gerald's extended middle finger. The first thing he took in was the car. It was a '94 Buick LeSabre with a scuffed maroon paint job, the driver's side door painted black. Rusty hubcaps, tilted fender, mud-spattered windshield, a broken left taillight, and a lavish skull and crossbones painted across the hood. Its owner, wearing oversize jeans so worn that they'd lost all their color and so low that a thick strip of black boxers shadowed the waistline, was a perfect fit. His expression said *Fuck off,* just like his T-shirt. Watching the guy climb out of his car, lean against the hood, light a cigarette, and run a hand through his oily black hair, Eric's face went pale.

"Veto." It came out nearly inaudible, a wheeze. He sucked in a deep breath. *No fear,* he thought, furious with himself. *"Veto."*

"Sorry, three strikes and you're out," Ash jeered. "You used up all your vetoes. Either take him or forfeit."

Forfeiting would mean paying the Bums a hundred bucks—each. More than that, it would mean giving up before they'd even tried. But accepting would mean . . . Clay Porter.

I'm not afraid of him, Eric told himself.

This wasn't third grade. He wasn't some twerpy eight-year-old too chicken to stick up for himself. He was Eric Roth, a guerrilla warrior who had scaled buildings, evaded cops, cracked safes, caused chaos, made mayhem, defeated danger, all in the name of righteousness, destabilizing monolithic systems, striking a blow for the underdog. Clay Porter was no longer his tormentor; he was just another enemy, just another easily squashable cockroach in the house of justice.

And *that* was why Eric couldn't agree to be his ally.

Not because of all the times Clay had left him bruised and humiliated in the muddy patch beneath the jungle gym, or the day he'd watched Eric gulp down his juice for several minutes before mentioning, "I peed in your thermos." Not because of the time he'd called Eric a turd-eating shithead and stuffed a fistful of dirt in his mouth. Not because of the wedgies or the flushies or the recess when Clay had pantsed him, then laughed as Eric, running away with his jeans flopping around his ankles, tripped, wiped out, and skidded headfirst across the basketball court, his bare legs and arms grinding into the cement, his Pikachu-covered ass in the air.

Not because, ten years later, he was still afraid.

"What's in it for me?" Clay leaned back against the low brick wall that bordered the far edge of the parking lot, took one last drag on his cigarette, then squeezed the burning tip between his thumb and forefinger and tossed it over the edge.

"A college education?" Max suggested, in the same whisper-tight voice he'd used to lay out their proposition. Schwarz and Eric hovered a couple feet behind, Schwarz's face pale, Eric's fists clenched tightly and shoved into his coat pockets.

"More school?" Three alarming, low-pitched barks issued from Clay's mouth like machine-gun fire. He gave his thigh a sharp smack, and the band of thick metal links around his wrist clanged against the chain strung from the pocket to the waistband of his low-slung jeans. It took everyone a moment to realize that this was the Clay Porter version of laughter. "Think I'm crazy?"

"More like psychotic," Eric muttered. Max kicked his instep.

Clay's wolfish smile shrank down. "What'd he say?"

"Nothing," Max said quickly. "Nothing. So school's not your thing. Fine. Great. How about bragging rights?" The used-car-dealer sheen seeped back into his voice. "You'd be free to tell your story—I'm seeing morning talk shows, *SNL* skits, a *New Yorker* profile—"

"You want *me*"—Clay's lips turned upward again—"to brag about hanging with *you*?"

"Well, for obvious reasons, we'd prefer to stay anonymous," Max said. "But once we expose the hack, you'll be free to—"

"Pass." Clay slid off the wall, his baggy jeans sliding even farther down his waist as gravity took over. "Later."

"Running late to flush someone's head in the toilet?" Eric asked under his breath.

"What?"

"Nothing," Max said. "Ignore him. I do."

Clay fingered the chain hanging from his waist, wrapping the metal links around his knuckles. He glared at Eric. "You wanna say it to my face?"

"I *said* . . ." Eric paused. He took a deep breath. "Nothing. Forget it."

Clay cleared his throat, leaned over, and hocked up a wad of spit. It splashed on the ground a few inches from Eric's feet. Then he straightened up and pulled out a pack of cigarettes, slipping out one for himself and—as an afterthought—one for Max.

Max gripped the slim white cylinder like a pencil. Clay flipped open a black lighter and held it out, but Max waved him away.

"Trying to quit," he said, holding the unlit cigarette to his lips. "I just like the taste of them. You know how it is. The, uh, feel of it in your hands and all that."

"Been there, man."

A moment of solidarity. Max grabbed it. "Look . . . man. What'll it take to get you in on this with us?"

"You want me to, like, take tests and shit? Dress up like some geek and act like I care? No offense." He was staring at Schwarz, who hastily shook his head. *None taken.*

Max glanced at Eric, waiting for another muttered retort, but Eric was silent, his eyes fixed on the ground.

"It's just not my thing. Later." Clay shrugged and began to shuffle away, the frayed cuffs of his jeans brushing the pavement.

Max looked queasy. If they lost Clay, they lost the bet. There was one last resort, a doomsday measure that went against everything Max believed in, but desperate times . . .

"Cash!" he finally yelled, sounding like he was in pain.

Clay froze, though he didn't turn back. "How much?"

"Five hundred."

Eric flinched, Schwarz paled, and Max ignored them both. "You in?" he asked Clay.

"A hundred up front."

"Fifty."

"Seventy-five."

Max extended a hand. "Done."

Clay didn't shake. "You for real?"

"Would I lie?" Max asked. "To *you*? Trust me, I'm smarter than that—as maybe you've heard."

"I say yes, that means we got a deal. That means you pay up—no matter what." Clay took several steps toward him, stopping only when Max's nose was an inch or so from his chin. "You smart enough to get what that means?"

Max, all 630 of the underdeveloped muscles in his body clenched, could barely nod his head. But it was enough.

Clay shrugged. "Then I'm in."

"Great!" Max exclaimed as Clay walked off. "Cool. Good to be working with you, man. So we'll be in touch, right? Yeah. Okay. Talk to you soon!" He was still babbling as the car door slammed, the engine roared to life, and the LeSabre roared out of the lot.

"Congratulations," Eric said sourly. "You just made a deal with the devil."

"No thanks to you!" Max snapped. "What the hell was that?"

"What?"

"More like psychotic," Max simpered, his Eric imitation sounding more like a ten-year-old girl. "Were you *trying* to screw this up for us?"

"I just want him to know what he is," Eric said.

"And that would be?"

"A bully."

Max sighed. "Look, that shit he pulled on you was a long time ago—"

"I'm not talking about me!" Eric took a deep breath, and when he spoke again, his voice was calmer. Slightly. "This isn't personal. This is about the principle of the thing. He picks on people who are weaker than him."

"Picked," Max said. "Past tense. He's on our side now. I know

you're the king of the grudge-holders, but just this once, let it go?"

Eric made a whooshing sound and flourished his hands like a magician. "All gone. Happy now?"

"I'll be happy when we win and I've got a big lump of cash in my pocket."

"Um, speaking of our most assured victory," Schwarz said nervously, "can you just clarify something for me, please?"

"Anything, Professor Schwarz!" Max said expansively, his mood on the rebound. "Perhaps you'd like a lesson in the sublime art of bullshitting? Sorry to say, what you've witnessed here is less of a learned skill and more of a . . . let's say a gift." His head dipped in mock humility. "But it's one I'm only too happy to share with my brothers, for the sake of the mission. Of course, if you should feel the need to thank me, tokens of appreciation are never declined. House policy."

"It is not the prevaricating," Schwarz said. "It is the five hundred dollars. We are paying Clay Porter five hundred dollars?"

"Not us . . . exactly." Max fiddled with the silver Harvard key chain on his backpack, a "gift" from Maxwell Sr. "The Bums."

"And how do you figure that?" Eric asked.

"Seventy-five up front, we can handle that. The rest, we pay him out of our cut, when we win."

"Schwarz, you're the one who won the International Math Olympiad," Eric began.

Schwarz blushed. "Second place."

"Whatever. Why don't *you* explain to Max how it's mathematically impossible for us to pay Clay five hundred dollars of our three-hundred-dollar cut?"

"Excuse me, Max, but it seems like if we each get a hundred dollars, then—"

"It's possible the bet may be *slightly* bigger than you think," Max admitted.

Eric gritted his teeth. "How much?"

"You know what they say, size doesn't matter. It's not like we'll ever have to pay. We're going to win."

"How much?"

There was a pause.

"Twenty-five hundred."

"Dollars?" Schwarz yelped.

"No, pesos." Max rolled his eyes. "Of course dollars."

"You bet those goons *twenty-five hundred dollars?*" Eric pressed his hands to the sides of his head, like he was trying to prevent his brain from leaking out of his ears. "I don't have that kind of money—and I *know* you don't. Just tell them to forget it. Bet's off."

"I guess I could, but . . ."

"But what?"

Max gestured at the skid marks Clay's tires had left behind. "You heard our friendly neighborhood thug. Do *you* want to be the one to tell our new best friend that he doesn't get his money?" He smiled, scenting victory. "Your funeral. But you better leave me your sound system in your will."

4

Apparently, a whole lot of people got together one day and decided they would pick the prom king and queen of higher education.

—*Ten Things You Gotta Know About
Choosing a College*, ed. SparkNotes

The admissions officer's pit stains were growing larger by the minute.

"Of course there's no magic formula," he drawled, pulling a handkerchief from his breast pocket and wiping it across his forehead. Outside, winter had already arrived, with the first pre-Halloween snow Boston had seen in years. But in the wood-paneled conference room, which was stuffed well beyond its capacity, the heater burped and hissed, leeching moisture out of the stale air and turning wool sweaters into a distinct sartorial liability. "We examine each applicant's file and base our evaluation on any number of factors, ultimately"—he paused again, this time using the same handkerchief to blow his nose—"ultimately striving to create a balanced, unique, well-rounded freshman class that can most fully take advantage of the incredibly opportunities we have to offer."

Twenty-eight pairs of eyes tracked his every move, noting the color of his socks and the part in his thinning hair, boring into him like they could, through sheer force of will, dissect his Harvardian brain and uncover the secrets that lay inside. Twenty-eight hands scribbled down every word on twenty-eight well-worn notebooks, frantically flipping pages, preparing to fly into the air as soon as he uttered the magic words: "Any questions?" And twenty-eight nervous overachievers turned their questions over and over in their minds, massaging the phrases, polishing them until they reeked of erudite desperation, certain that this would be their one shining chance to make their mark.

Then there was the twenty-ninth hand, which was idle. The twenty-ninth pair of eyes, which, as often as possible, flicked away from the gray-suited admissions officer and scanned the room. The twenty-ninth mind, which, instead of rehearsing a pointless question, was comparing each face with the dossiers he had at home, the folders of stats, surveillance data, and skeletons in the closet he had spent two weeks compiling.

There was plenty of work to be done, but Eric had been charged with the first and perhaps most important task: spying on the competition.

It was a special session for Cambridge-area students, half of whom came from Wadsworth High. Cambridge kids had a somewhat better chance of getting in than the rest of the country—it never hurt to butter up the locals—but that meant twice as many of them applied.

And since applicants were evaluated by region and by school, local competition mattered, to the school, to the applicants—and to Eric. His MP3 player's microphone was taking everything in, while his cell phone was perfectly positioned to snap periodic shots. But no digital photos could reflect the full flavor of the meeting, and no recording could take the full measure of the competition. That was all up to Eric. So he watched. He listened.

He tried not to throw up.

Bernard Salazar had snagged a seat at the conference table and was typing everything he heard into a shiny new Sony VAIO. According to Eric's research, Bernard had a 3.6 GPA, mediocre SAT scores, and a father who'd just gotten out of prison for embezzling funds from his bankrupt public relations firm. The file didn't note Bernard's shifty eyes, chewed nails, and proclivity for eating—not gnawing on, but *eating*—pencils, but Eric had made a mental note of it all.

Bernard, who usually dressed like a gangsta rapper but today was decked out in a Harvard-appropriate three-piece suit, never missed an Ivy League info session. Rumor had it that his father had offered him a Lexus SUV if he could get into Harvard.

Poor Bernard was going to have to make do with his used Beemer, Eric decided. And not just because most of the Salazar assets had been impounded by the government. The problem wasn't with the cash flow (there was still a hefty chunk stashed away in a variety of off-shore accounts), it was with Bernard. He was devious and determined, but he just wasn't a contender.

The rest of Wadsworth High's usual suspects were there too. Scott Chang, who did everything that was expected of him—nothing more, nothing less—and was more bland than vanilla nonfat pudding. Katie Gibson, of course, who at that point still planned to be valedictorian. "Last year, more than a thousand high school valedictorians were rejected," the admissions officer had announced. Katie put a hand over her mouth to cover her smirk, assuming the warning didn't apply to her. Everyone's an exception in their own mind.

Ella Stryker and Hannah Dwight sat next to each other, as usual, in two of the folding chairs set up behind the conference table. Each wore a giant green ribbon, denoting their commitment to the cause of the week, whatever it was. They had already interrupted the presentation twice to press the admissions officer on university recycling policies. Behind them hovered Finn Webber, who wore a black leather choker and fishnet stockings and claimed to hate the world—and who hoped no one would ever find out that, every afternoon, as soon as she got home, she slipped into jeans and a J. Crew cardigan, then plopped on the couch just in time for *Oprah*.

Carl Dishler was a Serious Musician—or, at least, that's how his Ivy Bound college counselor had advised him to package himself at their last $500-an-hour session. Simone Pallas wrote bad poetry about tar-covered penguins. Seth Hunter—whose family had changed its name from Humper—did Model UN and preferred to be addressed, at all times, as "the representative from Argentina." Just to stay in character. Kurt Weiler was the second-best soccer player in the state, and would get in anywhere even if he filled out his applications in crayon.

And then there was Alexandra Talese. Most likely to succeed, and most likely to run you over with a bulldozer to do it, then smile and say have a nice day. Eric's eyes, which had skimmed over the other faces, needing nothing more than a checkmark confirmation that everyone he'd expected was there, hesitated, passing over her face, and then, like a stutter, dipping back for a second glance, then a third. She was prettier than she looked in her class pictures, though that still didn't make her *pretty*, exactly, just above average. He had seen her in person before, of course. They'd shared plenty of classes, and even a lunch table one year, though there had been a good three feet of empty space separating him from the yearbook–honor society–key club crowd at the other end of the long table; close enough that he could hear their laughter, far enough away that he couldn't know it was the half-stilted, half-manic laughter of a group always one heartbeat away from awkward silence.

Her hair was that blondish, brownish, beigeish color that always looks dirty, but it was stretched back, smooth and glossy, into a neat ponytail. She was the kind of girl whose socks always matched her outfit—and the kind of girl who wore "outfits," not in the cover girl sense, but more like someone whose mother still dressed her (though Alexandra's did not). Eric was too far away to see the color of her eyes, which were a grayish hazel flecked with yellow and could only wonder whether the speckling of discolorations across her nose were freckles or zits.

He knew from the file he'd assembled that she excelled at both the sciences and the humanities—though "excelled" only within the limited constraints of the high school curriculum. (She was, for example, acing AP calculus but would have been lost in the upper-level courses Eric was already auditing at MIT.) Yearbook editor, key club vice president, student council representative, debate team champion, president and founder of Hugs for the Homeless, candy striper—generic, he thought to himself. A dime a dozen. Nothing that should unduly interest him.

And yet, he didn't look away.

Not until he caught Alexandra Talese—caught me—looking back.

5

Just as no one chooses a car without a test drive, no one should choose a college without a test visit.

—Zola Dincin Schneider, *Campus Visits and College Interviews*

"I saw you," I said to Eric, falling into step beside him as we followed the student guide on a "thrilling tour of Harvard's storied past and stunning present." "Watching me."

He pitched forward, his foot catching on an invisible rock, pinwheeled his arms through the air, and caught himself moments before hurtling to the ground. "Dntkemnwatytenabert," he mumbled.

"What?"

Eric scowled. "Don't. Know. What. You're. Talking. About."

"This is actually the second Harvard Hall," the tour guide confided to us, walking backward so she could face the crowd. She gestured toward a large redbrick building on the edge of the Yard, just inside the towering steel gates. "The first burned in 1764."

He wasn't attractive, not conventionally, not by any stretch of the imagination. If he was cute, it was in a three-legged-puppy kind of

71

way. Pitiful and lopsided, but, whether confronted by a Chihuahua or a pitbull, still ready to fight.

"You were staring at me," I insisted. "All through the meeting. I saw you."

"Nothing to see," he said, keeping his eyes fixed on the tour guide. "You must have been imagining it."

"The fire destroyed every book in Harvard's original library collection," the guide continued, with a beauty pageant grin that seemed to say, *Burning books? Bring on the marshmallows!* "Only one book survived, because the night before, a student had illegally taken it out of the library so he could continue to read through the night."

"So you're calling me paranoid?" I asked.

Eric finally looked at me. His eyes looked like he was smiling, even though his mouth was fixed in a frown. "Either that or an egomaniac. Take your pick."

If we'd been a few years younger, I would have crossed my eyes and stuck out my tongue. Instead, I had to settle for the eyebrow raise and half smile. Message: Utter disdain. "Oh, so that's your thing."

"What?"

"Yeruhjrk."

"What?"

"You're. A. Jerk."

Now I had his attention. "So I guess your thing is that you're a—"

"What?"

"Forget it."

Like I hadn't heard it plenty of times before. "I'm a . . . ," I prompted.

"I'm *trying* to listen," he said, turning back to the tour guide.

"Fine."

"Fine."

"Legend has it that after the fire, the student took the stolen book straight to the president of the College, who accepted it with deep gratitude—and then expelled him." The tour guide giggled, and, after a beat, the crowd of students laughed heartily along with her. "Of course, disciplinary measures aren't quite as strict anymore—unless you steal a book from the library!"

More laughter.

We followed along after her in silence for another few minutes.

"What makes you think I have a thing?" Eric finally asked.

"What?"

"You said my thing is that I'm a jerk. Why do I have to have a thing?"

"Excuse me, but I'm actually *trying* to listen," I said snottily, and tried not to smile.

"Fine. Forget it."

We both turned back to the guide. But I could see him out of the corner of my eye, simmering.

"The statue of John Harvard is nicknamed 'The Statue of Three Lies.' Does anyone want to guess why?"

We didn't need to guess; everyone had memorized the admissions brochure. But only one person was lame enough to raise a hand.

"It's not John Harvard," Bernard Salazar explained proudly. "That's one. Two: John Harvard wasn't actually the founder of Harvard University. Three"—he pointed to the date inscribed below the stone puritan—"the university wasn't founded in 1638." He rubbed his hand on faux–John Harvard's foot and gave the tour guide an oily grin. "But even so, millions of tourists every year rub it for luck."

"And every year, hundreds of drunk freshmen piss all over it and then laugh their asses off at the tourists," Eric whispered, and when I tried to suppress my laughter, it turned into an oh-so-attractive snort.

I decided to give him a break. "You never talk." The group paused to watch an a cappella group doo-wopping their way through a Justin Timberlake song. I suppressed the urge to jam my fingers into my ears.

"You just told me to shut up," Eric pointed out. "You're trying to listen, remember?"

"No, I mean in school, you never talk. Whenever I see you, you're always sitting in the back, or on the edge of the group, not saying anything. You're a lurker. Sometimes it seems like you want to talk, but you never actually do. You just lurk. So I've always figured you were either shy or a jerk."

Eric raised his eyebrows. "Seems like *you're* the one who's been watching *me*."

"See? Definitely a jerk." But I laughed—and, after a moment, so did he.

"Maybe I'm neither shy nor a jerk," he said. "Maybe there's just rarely anyone worth talking to."

I grinned triumphantly. "Only a jerk would think that way," I pointed out, although it was something I often thought myself. "Maybe you just don't give people enough of a chance."

"I don't know—one could argue I'm giving you more than enough of a chance, Alexandra."

I must have flinched.

"Surprised I know your name?"

"We've gone to school together for six years, *Eric*. If you didn't know my name by now, I'd have to seriously question that whole genius reputation you've got going."

"Remind me again how it is that I'm the jerk in this conversation, *Alexandra*?"

I've always hated that name. "My friends call me Lex," I said. It wasn't true, but I wanted it to be. Lex sounded like someone a little daring, cool, edgy, someone who deserved to have an *x* in her name. A Lex might even cut class, if she had a good reason to do it. Alexandra would never even show up five minutes late.

Not that I needed to impress him. It was just that I had already decided that the college me was going to be Lex; she deserved a trial run.

"Okay, your friends call you Lex. So what am *I* supposed to call you?"

"The jury's still out."

The Justin Timberlake song ended, but just as I thought we'd been saved, the group bop-bop-bopped their way into a Beyoncé medley. It wasn't pretty.

Eric tilted his head to the side, like I would make more sense from an angle. "Well, I'd say it's nice to meet you—"

"Remember the part about how we've known each other for six years?"

"We've never actually *spoken*," Eric said. "As you pointed out. Remember the part about how I've been too busy lurking?"

"Fine. You win. It's nice to meet you."

"Not necessarily the adjective I'd choose, but . . ." He reached out his hand and, after a beat, I met him in midair. We shook. It was stiff, formal, and not a seventeen-year-old thing to do, but somehow it seemed appropriate. "Let's just say it's not un-nice to sort of meet you." And even though his arm was skinny, his grip was strong. "Lex."

"This campus sucks," Eric tugged his coat tighter around himself as the wind picked up. Neither of us had actually suggested sticking together after the tour ended, we had just . . . stuck. We were sitting on a bench in front of the Science Center—a brutish gray building whose architecture, in the shape of a Polaroid camera, was supposedly as innovative as its name was mundane. It didn't look like much of a landmark of design to me, though. More like a clumsy stack of building blocks—or a prison. I was waiting around for my appointment with someone from the chemistry department, in hopes of, as one of my books recommended, "personally demonstrating my passion for the discipline." Or in my case, inventing a passion believable enough that they'd buy it. Eric was just waiting. I hadn't asked him why, and he hadn't volunteered.

"It's not so bad." The trees were half-bare, and the Yard was strewn with dead leaves, but if you squinted, you could almost imagine the green idyll that they showed in all the pictures.

"It's hideous."

"It doesn't have to be pretty," I argued. "It's iconic. It's *Harvard*."

"And that's why you want to go here?" He grabbed a soggy fry from the carton we were sharing and popped it into his mouth. "'It's *Harvard*?'"

"It's the best," I pointed out. "Do I need another reason?"

"It's only the best at getting people to think it's the best." He shrugged. "But it's your life."

"Is it hard work to be this rude, or does it come naturally to you?"

"I'm not rude," he said. "It's just difficult for me not to point out the obvious."

"Like?"

"Like there's not a single math teacher in our school who could tell you what Poincaré's conjecture is or whether it's been solved. Like my sister's sleeping with her asshole boyfriend, even if she's got my parents fooled into thinking she's a nun. Like you're just acting the way they want you to act, buying into whatever they say, and convincing yourself it's what you really want."

"Sorry, but that's bullshit." I stood up, grabbed the half-empty carton of fries out of his hands, and tossed it in the trash. "Who's *they?*"

"You know. They."

"No, I don't know. Neither do you. It's just something people say when they want to make something up and have it sound rebellious and nonconformist. Choosing a college isn't like picking a breakfast cereal. And I'm not some zombified toddler drooling at the screen, going 'Ooh, Harvard, that's pretty, I want.'" I started to stride away, then paused after a couple steps. It wasn't the way I had intended things to go.

When I turned around, Eric was standing behind me.

"Look, that's not what I meant," he said.

"Whatever."

"I just . . ."

"Yeah." We sat down again. Not that there was anything left to say.

"So," I began finally. Lamely. "You're into the green thing?"

"What?"

I nodded at his T-shirt, which had a black SUV printed across the chest. The caption below read: WEAPONS OF MASS CONSUMPTION. "You know, save the world? An inconvenient truth? All that?"

He looked down, like he'd forgotten what he was wearing, then shrugged. "Yeah, I guess."

"You've never come to one of our Endangered Earth meetings," I pointed out. I was the vice president. Which, as far as responsibilities went, meant only that I was the one who took attendance.

Eric shifted in his seat. "Yeah, well. I don't really do the group thing."

"Why not?"

"It doesn't matter."

But the way he said it, I knew it did.

I checked my watch: Ten minutes until I had to go inside the gray building and put on a show for the chem professor. My résumé was tucked into a faux-leather portfolio, and I had a whole speech planned out about how I'd read this biography of Mendeleev that had inspired me to be a chemist and, ever since, I'd been slaving away in any lab I could find. I would tell them how Bunsen burners thrilled me, how litmus tests were my life.

And while I waited, I would make conversation to keep my mind off of how sickened I was by the idea of spending the next four years seeing the world through a pair of safety goggles.

"Why *not*?" I asked a second time.

"You'll just call me rude again," he complained.

"Sticks and stones may break your bones, but names—"

"Fine." He took off his glasses for a moment, so he could rub the bridge of his nose. His eyes looked smaller without the lenses, but also lighter. I could see flecks of gold within the rings of deep brown. "All those groups at school, Endangered Earth, Amnesty International, World Affairs—they're not for people like me. They're for . . . you know, people who only do stuff so they can put it on their college applications. They don't actually care, they just want to look like they care, even though all they really want is to get into—" He stopped abruptly, looked at me, blushed, then looked away. "You know."

"People like me," I said quietly.

"Told you it would sound rude."

"No, not rude," I said, almost sweetly. Then I went in for the kill. "Hypocritical."

"I am *not* a hypocrite," he said, jumping to his feet.

"You're here, aren't you?" I pointed out. "You hate Harvard so much, but here you are with the rest of us, and—"

"Please. I don't care about Harvard enough to hate it. It's the whole thing, the applications, and this stupid idea that there are only five or six schools in the whole country that you can go to, and if you don't get in, then your life is over."

"Alicia Morgenthal," I murmured, almost to myself. I hadn't been there when it happened, but I'd heard. The whole school had heard. Alicia Morgenthal, superstar senior, who had it all: perfect SAT scores, perfect GPA, perfect life. And then, one day, the perfectly pleasant rejection letter from Harvard University. A perfect match to the letters from Brown, from Princeton, from Yale, from every school she'd applied to. No one knew where she'd gone that night, after getting the news. But everyone knew what happened the next morning. Twenty minutes into first period, she'd climbed up on her desk and started screaming. She didn't stop when they sent her to the nurse's office. She didn't stop when they carted her off to McLean, the two-hundred-year-old asylum on the hill that had housed Sylvia Plath and every other Cambridge intellectual—not to mention all the pseudo-intellectuals—who'd lost the ability to cope. For all I know, she's still screaming.

I would be.

"What'd you just say?" he asked.

"Nothing."

I don't know why I lied, maybe because I didn't want him to realize how easily her name came to mind, how often I thought about her. How much I worried that we weren't that different. Eric didn't push it.

"It's not like it's your fault," he said. "It's not just you, it's the schools, and the parents, and the guidance counselors, and all the people who will give you a job someday just because your college football team played in the Ivy League—it's the whole damn system. And we just keep buying into it, every year. Because what else are we supposed to do?"

"So since you've got it all figured out, what are you doing here?" I asked. "With the rest of us chumps."

"Oh. Well . . . I'm probably not applying here, I'm just . . . you know . . . looking around. I'm going to MIT."

"Right, because MIT's not an elite university that most people go to for the name recognition," I said. "You've *totally* defied the system. Congratulations."

"It's not like that," he protested. "I've been doing research for this professor there, and their engineering program is amazing, and . . ." His body sagged, just a little. "Yeah. So maybe I am a hypocrite. A little bit. But . . ." He shrugged. "At least I've got a reason. I didn't just pick MIT because it's at the top of some list." When he spoke again, it was almost too softly for me to hear. "I don't think."

"You're not a hypocrite," I told him. "You're . . ."

But I couldn't think of the right adjective, and the silence stretched on, and then it was too late and the moment had passed.

Eric tapped his watch. "You should probably go," he said quietly. "Your appointment."

On impulse, I reached out my hand for him to shake. "Good talking to you, Eric Roth."

He grabbed my hand. "You too. Lex." He held on one beat too long, and it felt, for a moment, like we were holding hands—not normally, but in a frozen, formal way like someone had erected a stone monument to good manners. Then it ended, and, realizing my hand was sweating, I went to wipe it on my skirt, but then stopped—I didn't want him to think I was wiping him off.

He gave an awkward wave and began to turn away.

"I have a reason," I blurted out.

"For what?"

I chewed on the edge of my lower lip. It was a habit, and I'd always thought it was a cute one, until my one and only boyfriend Jeff told me it grossed him out. Of course, this was before Jeff hooked up with the sandwich girl at Au Bon Pain and became my one and only ex. But I still believed him about the lip thing. "For this. For Harvard. I mean, I have lots of reasons. And whatever you say, Harvard *is* the best. But . . . a lot of it is about my grandfather."

Stop talking, I told myself. *It's not too late.*

"He went here?" Eric asked.

I laughed. "Not quite. He *worked* here. It was when he was young, right after he married my grandmother. The students treated him like shit. So did the professors. They all thought they were so much better than him, just because he was mopping their floors. He used to really hate it here—and then he met this guy, a history professor. I guess they started talking, and eventually they got to be friends. When my grandfather was done working for the day, he'd go to this guy's office and they'd have a drink together. And that professor told him that he shouldn't waste his time hating Harvard—he should *beat* it. He should prove to everyone that he was just as good as they were. That he was *better*. And, eventually, that professor helped my grandfather get a better job, where he didn't have to wash floors anymore—but when my mother got into Harvard, he still couldn't afford to send her. So now it's my turn. And I'm not going to let him down."

Eric looked like he'd run over my puppy. "I, uh . . . I didn't know."

"Well, now you do." I shrugged. "No big deal. I just wanted you to know—I have a reason."

I was a good liar.

Not that I didn't have a grandfather, but he hadn't worked at Harvard. He had gone there. (A lot of good it would do me, since according to the admissions brochure, it wouldn't qualify me as a legacy applicant and so wouldn't help me in the least.) He didn't care about the place—didn't love it, didn't hate it, didn't have any opinion on whether or not I should follow in his footsteps. He thought of college as just one of those things you have to get through—like a dentist's appointment, or the Korean War—and didn't care where I ended up, as long as it was somewhere. Which was my parents' party line too, although I knew better.

And I did have my reasons—real reasons. They might not have been as picturesque as a dead grandfather and a family legacy, but they weren't the superficial, society-imprinted, consumerist nonentities that Eric had implied either. I had done my research, pored over every page of my Fiske guide, memorized all the inane what's hot/what's not lists in my Princeton Review; I had made my pro/con charts, carefully weighed all the options, and chosen a winner. There was a reason Harvard had a reputation for being the best, I'd decided, and the reputation was self-fulfilling, because it meant Harvard *got* the best—the best students, the best professors, the best resources—which meant I wanted it to get me. I wanted to get lost in the country's biggest college library; I wanted to learn Shakespeare from a grand master while staring up at a ceiling carved hundreds of years before. I wanted to sunbathe on the banks of the Charles and imagine Emerson, Thoreau, Adams, all lying in the same place, centuries earlier, dreaming up the ideas that would build a nation. I wanted to be in awe of the school, the teachers, the history, the legacy—I wanted to be terrified I wouldn't measure up. I wanted to prove that I could.

I had my reasons.

So why lie?

It wasn't because I wanted to impress Eric, convince him that I wasn't just some mindless overachiever—I didn't care if he judged me. He obviously judged everyone. And I had no need to prove myself, not to him.

But I had to make him stop thinking of me as a target to acquire or a photo in a file. That was step one, and a lie was the surest way to accomplish it.

I don't like lying—but I'm good at it. And I'll do it when necessary.

This time, it was.

Because Eric wasn't the only one with a plan.

6

There is no formula for gaining admission to Harvard.
—Harvard University admissions brochure

"You should have warned me the nerd herd was coming over today," Eric's sister complained as Eric led Max and Schwarz down to the den.

"I know you wish you'd had time to get all dolled up, Lissa." Max gave her a sickly sweet smile. "But we love you just the way you are. In fact, I was just telling Schwarz what a junior hottie you are. Right?"

Lissa Roth's mouth twisted like she'd bitten into rotten fruit. "Are you *trying* to make me puke?" She glared at her brother. "They're *not* staying for dinner. Sarah and Hallie are coming over, and it's bad enough they know I'm related to *you*. I'm not subjecting them to Thing One and Thing Two."

Eric glared right back. "*Subjecting?* Big talk from Little Miss 420 Critical Reading." He clutched his chest like he was having a heart attack. "Don't tell me you've actually been . . . studying?"

"It was 520," she snapped back. "And everyone knows the PSATs don't mean shit. Some of us have better things to worry about. Like, you know, our *lives*. But I guess you wouldn't know about that kind of thing. Having a life."

"Bite me," Eric said, slamming the den door in her face.

"How'd I luck out and get such a great big brother!" she yelled from the other side. "I should go thank Mom and Dad . . . for *ruining my life!*"

She stomped up the stairs, and the guys were finally alone. Max flung himself on one of the beat-up couches that the Roths hid in the den so no real company would ever see them. "I hate to say this, Eric, but your sister's a total bitch."

"She's not that bad," Eric said. "She's just . . . misguided."

"She is full of excrement," Schwarz countered, pulling a thick blue binder out of his backpack.

"Full of *shit*," Max corrected him. "What's with the no-cursing thing these days, Schwarzie? Trying to look more virginal? Because trust me, it's not necessary."

"'Profanity and obscenity entitle people who don't want unpleasant information to close their ears and eyes to you,'" Schwarz quoted. "So says the master, Kurt Vonnegut. So says I."

Max shook his head. "Lissa's right. You really are a nerd."

Eric raised his eyebrows, nodding toward Max's T-shirt, whose bright red slogan read GO AHEAD, MAKE MY DATA! "Pot? Meet kettle."

"Point taken." Max shrugged. "In that case, I guess I call this meeting of the 'nerd herd' to order. Reports?"

Eric laid out the basics of the competition, supplementing the facts and figures with anecdotes from his info session surveillance. "Not too much real competition," he concluded. "Sam Gutierrez looks good, and Aron Merrow has the tuba going for him, so we should keep an eye on him. Also Sasha Dwyer and Alexandra Talese—"

"What was that?" Max cut in, leaning forward.

"What?"

"When you said her name, you sort of . . ." Max narrowed his eyes, trying to put his finger on what had caught his attention. "Say it again."

Impatient but eager to move on, Eric obeyed. "Alexandra Talese?"

"See?" Max asked.

"Obviously I don't."

"It's like . . . a hiccup."

"I didn't hiccup," Eric said.

"No, not a real one. But it's like your face did. Like it lurched a little, and then reset itself."

"My face did not hiccup!"

"Schwarz?"

Schwarz gave Eric an apologetic smile. "Excuse me, but it did."

Max grinned. "Go on, say it again."

"What? No!"

"See!" Max jumped off the couch, pointing at Eric's face. "You did it again, just thinking about her." Eric rolled his eyes, and Max dropped back down to the couch, looking into the distance. "She's not bad," he decided, nodding. "I mean, kind of uptight for my taste, and the soulless grade grubbing is a turnoff, but she's got that goody-goody thing going for her. You like that."

"You're being ridiculous," Eric snapped.

"Not much going on in front," Max continued, ignoring him, "but that's not everything, right? And you've seen her in that green skirt, the one with the slit on the side? Not bad. Not bad at all."

Eric could feel the heat pulsing in his face. "I wouldn't know."

"But I bet you can imagine. Maybe you are right now. . . ."

"Shut up."

"No need for embarrassment, a little healthy fantasizing never—"

"I'm not fantasizing about Alexandra Talese!" Eric shouted.

"Methinks he doth protest a little too much."

"He protests exactly the right amount," Eric insisted.

"Schwarz?"

"It is a little much," Schwarz admitted.

Eric grabbed a pillow off the couch and threw it at Schwarz's head. "Do you have to agree with *everything* he says? Try thinking for yourself once in a while."

"I *am* thinking for myself," Schwarz said indignantly. "And I am just saying, there is nothing wrong with being in love. It is . . ." He sighed, and his face dissolved into a stare so dreamy you could almost see pink cartoon hearts bubbling out of his head. ". . . something."

"In love?" Eric asked incredulously. "Is that what you're calling it? So I guess Stephanie's not making you rub her feet anymore?"

"Well . . ."

"And she's not whining about how she can't keep track of all her guys?"

Now Schwarz was blushing. "I did not say—"

"And she's stopped treating you like her little sister?"

"She never—well—she does not mean to—I—"

"Ain't love grand," Eric said sourly.

"Oh, stop picking on him," Max said. "No need to be cranky just because you're not getting any."

"And what is it, exactly, that *you're* getting?" Eric asked, knowing full well that Max's last two—only two—relationships had never gone past the IM stage.

"We're talking about you here," Max said.

"And that's the problem." Eric grabbed a thick blue binder and waved it in Max's face. "We're supposed to be talking about the hack. Or have you forgotten?"

"Hey, fine with me," Max said. "Back to work. *I'm* not the one who can't stop talking about Alexandra Talese."

"Are you kidding me? I was not—" Eric slammed the binder down on the table and cleared his throat. "Fine. Back to work. Like I was saying. Other than Sasha Dwyer and Alexandra Talese—"

"Hiccup," Max coughed.

"What?"

Max shook his head. "Nothing. Tickle in my throat. Please, continue."

Eric kept talking, but the damage was done. As he gave his report, his mouth ran on autopilot. Because inside his head, he was stuck in a feedback loop.

Alexandra Talese, he thought, turning the words over in his mind.

Alexandra Talese.

Alexandra Talese.

It was all Max's fault.

Alexandra Talese.
It certainly didn't mean anything.
Alexandra.
It didn't matter at all.
Lex.

By the time they heard the knock, they'd made it through the day's business and moved on to debating the merits of fantasy baseball versus fantasy football. Still, they fell silent, years of experience teaching that, regardless of conversation topic, it was always safest not to be overheard. Eric assumed the knock would be his mother. Not because his mother was in the habit of checking in on him when his friends were over—that she'd stopped once she'd confirmed those friends weren't related to anyone she needed to impress—but because there were no other likely suspects. Lissa would rather drop dead than voluntarily interact with her brother more than once in the same day. His father was on a consulting trip in New York, helping the rich get richer.

But maybe, Eric thought, his mother had joined some kind of Committee for Concerned Parenting and was reviving her long-dormant maternal tendencies. Or maybe there was a fire in the kitchen and she'd remembered that she had a son long enough to warn him to evacuate.

Whatever the reason, he climbed the stairs without a hint of fear, not realizing that, to anyone watching the scene, this would have been the moment when the hero takes one foolishly confident step after another toward certain doom, his hand pausing on the doorknob while the audience shouts at him, "Turn the hell back!" but instead of doing so, he pushes forward, and, with painfully slow inevitability, twists the knob. Swings the door open. Drops his jaw in frozen horror.

And screams like a girl.

At least in his head.

"'Sup?" Clay Porter asked, pushing past him. "Your sister let me in. She's scorching, you know? Sure you're related?"

Eric gave himself ten seconds to catch his breath. Then he eased the door shut and slowly descended the stairs, focusing very intently on balancing his weight on one foot and then the other as he thudded down, step by step by step. By the time he made it to the bottom, Clay had already settled in next to Schwarz and snatched Schwarz's notebook out of his hands. Schwarz lunged for it, but not quickly enough. A slim magazine that had been tucked between the pages slipped out and fluttered to the floor. Clay scooped it up. Schwarz squeaked.

"You actually *buy* this shit?" Clay asked, flipping immediately to the centerfold. "You know you can get it for free online, right? *Good* stuff, not this posing-by-the-fire shit."

"It is not, uh . . . excrement," Schwarz protested in a thin voice, trying to grab the magazine away. Clay held tight—it might not have been the "good stuff," but it was apparently good enough.

"Damn right it's not excellent. I said it's *shit*," Clay repeated. "Look at how she's sitting, you can't even see—"

"It is not about that," Schwarz said quickly. "It is just . . ."

Eric plucked the magazine out of Clay's hands and tossed it into Schwarz's lap.

"Leave him alone."

Clay held up his hands. "Hey, chill, I got no problem with the little man."

Eric didn't feel like chilling. "How did you know where I live?" His voice cracked, and he swallowed hard. "How did he know where I live, *Max*?"

Max ignored him. "Greetings, salutations, and heartfelt appreciation for gifting us with your presence, Clay."

Clay pulled out a pack of cigarettes. "Okay if I smoke in here?"

"No," Eric said.

"Sure," Max said at the same time, louder. "It's cool." He grabbed the blue binder, which had a weathered *Star Trek* sticker peeling off the front and a small *Playboy* insignia stuck to the spine. "Care to do the honors, Professor?"

Schwarz took the binder and shoved his glasses higher up on his nose. "As noted within, I have secured work-study employment in the admissions office, where I am conducting a survey of the admissions archives and a statistical analysis to determine the potential likelihood of varying traits impacting the application decision. I have compiled an algorithm, operating on a variety of axes with an effort to minimize internal contradiction—"

"Schwarz!" Max barked. He closed his eyes and feigned a snore. "Speed it along. In English, preferably."

"Excuse me, but the math on this *is* quite fascinating," Schwarz retorted. "But if you insist . . ." He handed Clay the binder. "I call this the Binder of Power. It contains all the information you will need for the hack. Names, dates, places, specifications, everything you will ever need to know."

"Yeah, whatever." Clay took it, but didn't bother to look inside.

Eric suddenly wondered if the Neanderthal even knew how to read.

"Um, if you turn to page two, you will see what we have in mind," Schwarz continued, reaching over to flip open the binder. "Wardrobe, image, lines, a daily schedule. You will be the tortured artist type, brilliant but angst-filled. A painter, willing to do anything for your art."

Clay took one last puff on his cigarette, stubbed it out against his knee, leaving a perfect sphere of ashy residue in the worn denim. "You want to turn me into a pussy?"

"Not *pussy*," Max said, overemphasizing. *"Painter."*

"Same difference." Clay kicked his feet up on the coffee table. A spray of dirt showered down on the glass. "I failed art. Twice."

"Welcome to the wonderful world of modern art," Max said. "Artistic talent not required. Check out pages twelve through seventeen." He leaned over Clay's shoulder, pointing at a series of images as the pages flipped past. One showed a white canvas with a thick red stripe down the middle. Another showed a black canvas with a light blue border. A third was a photograph of four sticks, assembled into a square.

"'A spare interpretation of the deforestation of the planet and the social constraints imposed on modern man,'" Max recited from memory, "'using naturalistic materials on an artificial backdrop to synthesize the contradictory yet symbiotic elements of twenty-first century life into a free-flowing yet structured whole.' Nice, huh? I wrote a program that'll spit as much of that crap out as we need. We should have the art professors eating out of your hands—they'll be *begging* the admissions crew to let you in."

"You're going to call that shit art?" Clay asked dubiously.

Max nodded, smirking. "So I guess that makes you the shit-artist."

Clay shrugged. "For six hundred bucks, I'll be anything you want."

"Five," Max reminded him. "We said five hundred."

"And now I'm saying six." Clay waved the Binder of Power in the air. "You want me to do all this shit, it's gonna cost you."

Eric blew out sharply. "You can't just—"

"Eric, I got this," Max said. He glared at Clay. "Five hundred."

"Six."

"Five."

"I'm out of here."

Eric lurched off the couch.

"Fine. Six hundred," Max said quickly. "But no more. Agreed?"

Clay leaned over and squeezed his hand. Hard. "So what's first?"

"First, I make sure we can put together enough cash up front to set everything in motion, Schwarz installs his surveillance cameras in the admissions office . . . and Eric shows you how you're going to ace the SATs."

"I *what*?" Eric yelped.

"You're the one who designed the equipment," Max hissed to Eric. "You're the one who shows him how to use it."

"I told you I don't want anything to do with him," Eric whispered.

"Scared?"

"No!" Eric stood up. He stood unafraid. "Fine. Whatever. You go, and I'll show Clay what he needs to do."

Max hopped off the couch, his face plastered with a maddening smirk, and dragged Schwarz up the stairs.

"You'll be fine!" he called back down to Eric, just before slipping through the door. "You're a big boy now."

Only one problem, Eric thought. Clay was still bigger.

The sign hanging outside Circuit Surplus read WE GOT IT. YOU WANT IT?

And they definitely had it. All of it.

Resistors, capacitors, toggle switches, radar display indicators, yards of twelve-gauge wire, hydraulic pumps, planimeters and insulators, coaxial switches, hermetically sealed relays, pin modulators, altimeters, even a vintage U.S. Army Signal Corps generator. Amidst the rows of dusty shelves cluttered with semifunctional parts, Eric had, over the years, found everything he'd ever needed, and done so with a quiet but determined relish that cemented his position in the community of gearheads who floated through the aisles high on solder fumes, bickering over the last universal potentiometer, kneeling in reverence before a sixty-year-old oscilloscope that still had its original knobs and display screen. It was everything an aspiring engineer could ever want, and everything Boston's top hackers would ever need. It was also the one place Eric felt completely at home.

So he had been understandably reluctant to bring Clay Porter along. This was *his* place. It had always been a refuge, a place to hide from problems like Clay Porter. They were two worlds that should never have to collide.

Just tell him what he needs to know and get rid of him, Eric told himself. *No fear.*

"So like I said, you don't need to do anything, it'll be all set up," he said, pulling out a pair of thick-rimmed glasses. The camera was lodged in the black bridge between the two lenses, with a pair of nearly invisible wires running along the frame to a Wi-Fi transmitter that would be hidden behind Clay's left ear. "On the morning of the test, you just have to press this button, and—"

"Dude, this place is awesome," Clay cut in. He plunged a fist into a nearby box of resistors and pulled out a handful. "Fifty cents each? Sweet."

Eric wondered whether he thought they were bullets of some kind. Or maybe he just liked shiny things.

"I'm retooling my speaker system," Clay said, veering toward a discounted coil of copper wire. "Amping it up, you know?"

"Uh-huh." Eric almost asked what his plans were, whether he'd built his own system or was just supplementing something store-bought, whether he'd had the same problem with the filter frequency that Eric had struggled with the year before. But this was Clay Porter, he reminded himself. "Amping up" probably meant giving the speaker a kick and waiting to see what happened.

They walked through the next aisle in silence until, finally, Eric found what he was looking for, the final thing he needed to make the SAT plan work. The thermoswitch controller cost thirty dollars, and, as he counted the bills out at the register, he hoped Max meant what he'd said about having a solution to their money woes. Expenses were piling up. "So you get what you have to do?" He handed Clay the glasses, along with a transparent molded earpiece that would relay the test answers.

Clay stuffed them into his pockets as if they were loose change, rather than delicately designed mechanisms Eric had spent two weeks perfecting. "What's your problem?" he growled, scooping his resistors off the counter and slipping them into his other pocket.

"With what?"

"With me." Clay stepped outside the store and leaned against the wall, his bloodred shirt fading into the brick.

"No problem," Eric said, half-hoping Clay wouldn't buy it.

And then what? he thought, disgusted. *I punch him? He punches me? I run away?*

Third grade didn't feel so very far away. Back then, in his mind, Eric had been a hero, defending the even smaller kids against the brutish giant. Defending himself. But his body had always been a coward. It shook. It ran. It stumbled. One memorable day, it had peed its pants just at the sound of Clay's laugh.

It was pathetic. And now his legs were trembling. "I've got to go," Eric said. "I'm late."

"For what?"

"None of your business." *Late for not getting my ass kicked,* he thought in sudden alarm as Clay grabbed his forearm—and part of him wanted it to happen. At least then it would all be out in the open, and he could finally fight back. He could prove that at least one of them had changed.

"What the hell is your problem? You're acting like I screwed your sister." Clay looked thoughtful for a moment. "I didn't, did I?"

Just let it go. But that was Max's voice in his head—a voice Eric had long ago learned to ignore.

"You don't remember me, do you?" he asked. "Samuel Adams Elementary?"

"What, you went there too?" Clay narrowed his eyes and peered closely at Eric's face. "I don't know. Maybe. Kind of short, with big-ger glasses? Or, like, a smaller head. Why? You remember me?"

Eric paused. "Not really." What was he supposed to say? *Yes, I remember every hellish moment?* "Maybe. Who knows. It was a long time ago."

So there was the truth: Clay Porter's reign of terror was one of the most important memories of Eric's life. He'd shaped everything. But apparently Eric was just a blip on his radar.

Not even that.

"I really don't have a problem," Eric said, offering a hand for Clay to shake and willing it to be true.

"Cool." Clay slapped his hand, rather than shaking it.

"Yeah. Cool. It's all good."

It was something he'd often heard Lissa say to her friends, usually after one of them had made the mistake of pissing her off and she was in that stage of feigning forgiveness before taking her revenge.

It's all good meant *watch out—soon it will be.*

7

Tired people are not good test takers.

—*The Princeton Review: Cracking the SAT*

'Twas the night before test day, when all down the block,
Not a creature was stirring, not even a jock.
The prep books were stacked on the desks with great care,
In hopes that—

Okay. So I guess you can see why I was marketing myself as a chemist, not a poet. But if Rimbaud, Baudelaire, and Conor Oberst could wring poetry from the damp towel of desperation, why couldn't I?

And it was definitely desperation. Tortured, sleepless, sweat-drenched, red-eyed, heart-pounding, stomach-churning desperation. Nine hours until the test that could determine my fate, and what was I, Alexandra Talese, model student, professional test-taker, soon-to-be valedictorian, doing?

Certainly not sleeping.

Not memorizing vocab or drilling math problems or assembling a list of generic literary allusions that would work with any essay topic, and certainly not cramming in one last piece of crucial advice from one of the eleven prep books lined up on the shelf over my desk.

I was lying in bed, my eyes wide open, because when I closed them, all I could see were rows and rows of tiny bubbles. And in the quiet, I imagined I could hear a clock ticking down the seconds. *Message: Your time is running out.* My eyes locked on to the Harvard sticker I'd foolishly stuck on the corner of my window three years before, in the afterglow of a month at Harvard's high school summer program. At the time it had seemed my unquestionable destiny to return there, triumphant, as a "real" student. But now the sticker just haunted me, the first thing I saw every morning, the last image I blocked out every night, mocking me and my ignorant, long-gone certainty. *Alexandra Talese, Harvard material?* It seemed to say. *I don't* think *so.* And in my slowly-losing-its-grip-on-reality mind, the sticker often seemed to have the same haughty Boston accent as the not-so-friendly neighborhood admissions officer who, when I'd cluelessly introduced myself to him in Starbucks that freshman summer, had given me a once-over, decided I wasn't worthy of a twice-over, and gone back to his cappuccino.

I had one chance to prove him wrong. One morning, one test, one shot.

Sleep was not an option.

The following sentences test your ability to recognize grammar and usage errors. Each sentence contains either a single error or no error at all. No sentence contains more than one error. In choosing answers, follow the requirements of standard written English:

1. If you screw up the SATs, you will be totally screwed.
     A   B   C   D

   No error
    E

2. Everyone is expecting you to get a perfect score.
     A   B   C

   But no pressure. No error
       D   E

3. The SATs have been scientifically designed to measure
              A

   your intellectual aptitude, and, therefore, you should
          B

   feel free to interpret your score as a measure of both
               C

   future earning potential and inherent self-worth.
                                  D

   No error
    E

Answers:
1. B (Trick question. You may think *If* is a usage error, and that it should be *When*, but that's actually a factual error. As in: "*When* you screw up *on* the SATs.")
2. D (This is a sentence fragment. And also a lie.)
3. E (This sentence is 100 percent accurate.)

I had taken the test three times already. Once sophomore year, for practice. Twice junior year, each time scoring higher than the last but neither time attaining my goal. The elusive, mythical perfect score.

It wasn't the golden ticket. I got that. Every year, Harvard rejects hundreds of students with triple eight hundreds. But it's what my parents were expecting, and it's what I was expecting. So I was taking it again.

This was my last shot.

The week before, it was all anyone could talk about. I'd heard rumors that somewhere, there were clumps of seniors who honestly didn't care, maybe even some who weren't taking the test, for whom Saturday was going to be just another day. But if there was a subset who wasn't obsessed with test scores and college applications and planning out every detail of the future before graduation hit, if they weren't just a rumor, some mythical species like unicorns, dragons, or bad boys with a heart of gold, they were staying out of sight.

Everyone *I* knew was scarfing Adderall by the fistful or coasting on a Red Bull high. And then, of course, there was the couldn't-care-less crew who were playing it cool and pretending that one test couldn't determine the course of their entire life, an attitude that, if you ask me, was more dangerous than a bottle of Ritalin and about as genuine as my father's ten-dollar Folex watch. My drug of choice? Preparation. Test-prep books, to be specific. And I'd just about overdosed.

They called it drill and kill. Practicing day and night, until you'd seen every type of question that had ever appeared on any version of the test, until you'd developed an allergy to dangling participles, you'd drowned in hexagons and octagons and pentagons and the formulas for determining the volume of any and all regular solids, and you'd memorized all eleven hundred potential vocab words along with the statistical likelihood of their appearing.

I turned my nose up at the classes. Let the masses sweat their way through a Princeton Review course, jotting down the ramblings of some BU freshman like they were gifts from the College

Board gods. The classes were a crutch—an annoying one that dug into your armpit and gave you a rash. I'd decided to go it alone.

Just me, my brain, my number two pencil . . . and a six-foot-high stack of practice books, each promising the top-secret, copyrighted, foolproof technique for outsmarting the SATs. It was unclear to me why colleges would put so much stock in a test that, according to the books, bore no relation to any form of learning, problem solving, or information processing that any normal human being would need to use in any other stage of life. But that's one of the first things the books taught you:

Don't question.

Don't try to understand.

Just accept the instructions.

Just do it.

It wasn't just a test-taking technique. It was a way of life.

Schwarz crunched down on his Twix bar—a necessary nightly ritual when you weighed ninety-six pounds and the dining hall food tasted like rat poison—and turned up the volume on his computer. On screen, admissions officer and 24/7 surveillance target Samuel Atherton III was leaning back in his desk chair, his feet propped on a trash can, complaining about his wife's cooking. Atherton had been assigned to handle all the applications from Wadsworth High—and Schwarz had been assigned to handle *him*.

It was like the world's most boring reality TV show, and yet Schwarz watched it compulsively, putting it on in the background whenever he was in his dorm room, ostensibly to learn as much as he could about the admissions process, but actually because he'd grown addicted to watching the officers scurry back and forth, trash-talking their bosses, picking their noses, sucking up, sneaking cigarettes, and doing whatever else it was they did when they were supposed to be working.

This is what normal people are like, he told himself. *This is what they do.*

There was something familiar about the feeling, something that took him back to his childhood, and the worn red *Star Trek* jumpsuit he'd worn to school every day for a year, pretending he was an alien observer of human life. Let Eric have his misguided *Battlestar Galactica* obsession—for Schwarz, it had always been, would always be *Star Trek*, without question. *BSG*, as Eric insisted on calling it, may have had the superior special effects and may have, as Eric argued, captured the messy realities of human frailty, but Schwarz wasn't in the market for messy. The *Star Trek* universe was clean, it was rational, it was law-governed, all actions and interactions overshadowed by the Prime Directive—it made sense. Vulcans acted like Vulcans, Klingons acted like Klingons, and Captain Picard (for it was only the Picard Enterprise that interested Schwarz, never the shabbier original ship commanded by the lusty and increasingly bloated Captain Kirk) always had the perfectly pithy prescription for how the conditions of humanity should be fulfilled. Picard understood humans in a way that the ship's android, desperate as he was to blend in, never would. Poor Data watched, he emulated, he smiled when it was time to smile and frowned when it was time to frown and assumed that if he watched long enough, the rules would become clear. Schwarz was no robot, but *that* was behavior—observation, fascination tinged with desperation—that he could understand. Because, like Data, he had watched.

He'd watched—just like he watched now—trying to figure out

why people said the things they said and did the things they did, trying to come up with some theory that would explain away human behavior the way the Navier-Stokes equations turned the chaos of fluid flow into an elegant, predictable, *comprehensible* system. He'd done what he was told, assuming that everyone else must have known what he didn't. He'd watched, he'd obeyed, and he'd waited for his overgrown brain to figure it out. To finally say, with the same satisfaction that came with penning in the QED at the end of a proof, *This is why they do what they do.*

And then he'd discovered Kurt Vonnegut—and suddenly it all became clear. "All people are insane," the master wrote. "They will do anything at any time, and God help anybody who looks for reasons." Human behavior would never make sense, Schwarz realized, because *humans* never made sense. They were inherently flawed, inherently illogical, inherently broken. It was why—except for the occasional vacation in electronic voyeurism—he preferred numbers. Numbers and photographs. Beauty distilled, perfection trapped on the page. Vonnegut taught that humans would always disappoint—but you could only be disappointed if you allowed yourself to set expectations.

Schwarz, with the rare exception, set none.

And then the exception walked through his unlocked door and he slammed the lid of the laptop shut, his palms sweaty, his face red, and his throat clenched.

"Oh—sorry to bother you," Stephanie said, leaning against the door frame and not looking sorry at all. "You busy?"

"No!" He shoved the laptop onto the desk and threw a pile of papers on top of it for good measure. "I was not doing anything of any importance."

"Good." She threw herself on his bed, rolling over onto her back and kicking her legs up against the wall. "I'm bored."

You are beautiful, he wanted to say.

She had the eyes of Miss September, 1967, and the glossy blond hair of Miss December, 1974. But her smile was something he'd never seen in any of his magazines. It was generous and impatient at the same time, like she was willing to grant any request—but only until she got bored and moved on to something else.

She flipped over on her stomach and made the half-whine, half-grunt that he recognized as the *Give me a massage* command. Schwarz sat down on the bed, his fingers trembling.

He didn't want to touch her.

He *wanted* to touch her.

"You're sitting on my hair," she said.

"Sorry!" He hopped up again, and she swept her hair away.

He had a take-home exam due by nine the next morning, and he'd barely gotten started. But that didn't seem to matter. Not with Stephanie lying across his bed, her hair splayed out on the "sensible" navy plaid comforter his mother had insisted on buying.

She turned her face toward him and patted the side of the bed. "Come on."

Schwarz sat down again. His fingers hovered over her shoulders. Finally, his heart thumping, he pressed his fingertips against her back and began to knead. His fingers kept slipping on her T-shirt.

What if she takes it off? he thought and, for a moment, feared that his imaginary asthma had come to life because he couldn't suck in enough air to fill his lungs.

"Ever wonder why they let you in here?" she asked suddenly.

Schwarz barely heard her. He was too focused on the smooth curve of her back and the slim band of bare skin peeking out just above her jeans.

"You know, do you ever think you were a mistake?"

"Um, not really," he said.

"Me neither." She took a deep breath, then let out a sigh. "Cassie's always angsting about whether she really belongs here and why she got in, like she thinks she doesn't really belong, and I just don't get it." Cassie was Stephanie's roommate, the rower. Schwarz was a little afraid of her. "I never think that way. I know I belong here. Do you think that makes me some kind of narcissist? Like I just assume that I should get whatever I want?"

Stephanie was taking intro psychology and had been diagnosing herself—and her dorm-mates—all semester.

Schwarz shook his head, forgetting that she couldn't see him. Not that she was waiting for a response.

"Except I don't even *know* what I want. You know, my dad wants me to be a lawyer, like him. You should have been there when my brother told him he was going to film school. Insane. You don't get a physics degree from Princeton and then spend the next thirty years fetching coffee for some Hollywood nutjob, right? But at least he knows what he wants. He's got this passion, this *thing* that he's going for, and sometimes I think I'm never going to have that—I mean, I like my classes, and yeah, I could be a psych major, or social studies seems cool, but if I'm never going to really *love* any of them, maybe I should just forget it and go to law school and make a million bucks. If you can't be happy, be rich, right?"

"Stephanie, maybe you should—"

"I know, I know, we're only freshmen, but it's not like I can just stop thinking about this stuff until graduation. I mean, that's fine for Cassie, she'll probably just get her degree and move back to Indiana and be a doctor or something, but that's not what I want. I want to be . . . I don't know. It sounds stupid to say it out loud, but I really feel like I could be . . ."

"Great?" Schwarz suggested.

Stephanie pushed his hands away and sat up. "Exactly! So you do know what I mean." Then she shook her head. "What am I saying? Of course you know what I mean. You're the prodigy, right? You're already great. You probably have no idea what it feels like not to know who you want to be—you've got math, you're set for life."

He wanted to tell her that he did understand, and that he was confused, just like her. But it would have been a lie.

"You will figure something out," he said instead.

"You really think you can do it?" she asked.

"What?"

She pointed at the poster of a bushy-haired Einstein that was hanging over his bed. "Fulfill your dream. Be *him*."

Schwarz could feel his cheeks heating up. "What makes you think I want to be him?"

"Well, you obviously want to be a famous scientist—"

"Mathematician."

"Whatever. And, you've got the hair thing in common—"

Schwarz touched his puffy curls self-consciously. Max, who called it his Jewfro, always begged Schwarz to shave it all off. Maybe it wouldn't be the worst idea.

"Plus, the socks," Stephanie added.

"What socks?"

"You never wear them. Just like him."

Schwarz couldn't believe she'd noticed—or that she'd figured out the reason.

"What?" she asked, seeing his look of shock. "Everyone knows Einstein didn't wear socks. It was his thing. Like it's your thing." She looked triumphant.

He had stopped wearing socks when he started at Harvard—partly because it was one less thing he had to wash, but partly because, as Stephanie guessed, he thought it might bring him one step closer to greatness. She was the only one who'd noticed.

"So, he's your hero, right?" She laughed. "I'm a little disappointed, you know. The whole Einstein thing's kind of a cliché."

"He is not really my hero," Schwarz said quickly. He glanced up at the poster, saying a silent apology to the great one. "I mean, yes, he was remarkable, but it is not like I worship him."

"Okay, then who?"

"Why does it have to be anyone?"

Stephanie leaned toward him, and he realized her eyes weren't the pure, emerald green he'd imagined them to be. They were more washed out, with a little brown mixed in. There was a tiny discoloration just below her left eyebrow. Some kind of raised red bump. Not a zit, he thought. Her skin was too creamy smooth for that.

"Come on, play along. Let's say you could be one famous scientist—"

"Mathematician."

"Whatever. Who would it be? I'll tell you mine—Mozart."

"He is not a scientist."

She shoved him, hard enough that he nearly tipped onto his side.

"That's not the point. I *mean*, if I could be anyone from history, anyone *great*, it would be him. They say he just heard music in his head, constantly, like it was in the air—like all the songs he wrote already existed in some perfect form—and all he had to do was write them down. Amazing."

Schwarz eyed his violin case, which had lain untouched under his desk since the first day of school. "Do you play something?"

She laughed. "Can't even read music. But I can imagine. . . ." She gave herself a little shake. "Okay. Your turn. Famous guy—or girl—you'd want to be. Go."

He pretended that he had to think about it. But he didn't, not really. "Descartes."

"'I think, therefore I am'?" She nodded, and tapped him on the chest. He tried not to flinch. "So deep down in there lies a philosopher? I like it." Her smile popped out again.

"No, not that," Schwarz said. "That is all anyone remembers now, but that is not what made him truly great." He couldn't believe he was talking about this, talking about it with a beautiful girl. A beautiful girl who was sitting on *his bed*. "It was his math—it was his *system*. Before Descartes, people were always trying to explain the universe like it was alive. The math never made sense, but they just ignored it, because they did not believe the numbers could reveal essential physical truth. Then came Descartes. He eliminated the human element. He boiled the universe down into something that was clean and pure and mechanical. Bodies in motion, every movement determined by a mathematical rule. It was the first purely mechanical system. It was the first system that made *sense*." He suddenly noticed that Stephanie was staring at him. "What?"

"Well, for one thing, that's the most you've ever said at one time. And for another, you're like . . . glowing."

"Like I am radioactive?"

"No, like you're . . ." But she didn't finish the thought, just kept staring, like she was trying to figure something out.

Then her cell phone rang, and instead of ignoring it, like he'd hoped, like he would have prayed if he didn't believe that praying was pointless and illogical, she answered.

And turned her back on him.

"What? I'm—oh. Yeah. Of course—now? Okay." Stephanie flipped the phone shut and stuffed it back into her pocket. "Gotta go."

"Now? Where?" Schwarz hoped he didn't sound like he was whining.

"That was Anders. He's lonely." She rolled her eyes. "He's such a little baby, always whining about something."

"He is the lacrosse player?"

She snorted. "No, that's Jack. That was last week's disaster. Anders is the one from my gov class, the hot one with the girlfriend back home—though I think he's getting ready to break up with her. She called when we were hooking up last night, and he didn't even try to pretend I wasn't there. It was kind of pathetic." She tipped her head back and ran a hand through her hair. "Listen to me, I sound like a total bitch."

"You do not sound—"

"And I know, I know, if he's cheating on her, what makes me think he wouldn't cheat on me?" She sighed. "He's just so freaking hot—yesterday, he came over straight from the gym, and he was just all—" Her cell phone rang again, and she glared at it. "I'll get there when I get there!" she complained, pressing a button to silence the ring. "Guys are such babies, aren't they? Or maybe I just need to find myself one who doesn't suck."

Schwarz could have pointed out that she'd found one—and she was the one walking away.

He could have stood up, rushed across the room, and answered her with a kiss.

He could have railed at her for being bossy and vain and rubbing her love life in his face, and then tossed her out of his room.

He could have declared his undying love and begged her not to go.

But instead he chose E.

None of the above.

Max tossed down the controller in disgust. "I give up. Tell the truth. You don't do anything but play with your Wii, practicing to beat me."

Eric rolled his eyes. "You got it. That's my main goal in life. Beating you."

"Beating off is more like it," Max shot back.

"Who am I, Schwarz?"

Max snorted. "Everyone has his or her own special talents," he said in a saccharine, kindergarten teacher voice. "And Schwarzie's are legion."

"I don't know," Eric said, with fake skepticism. "You know what he always says."

"Yeah. Right. Kid's got a collection of six hundred *Playboy*s because he just likes to 'appreciate the perfection of the female body.' And I'm sure he reads the articles, too."

Eric handed him back the controller. "Not everyone's as obsessed with their Wii as you are."

"What did I tell you about making jokes?" Max asked.

"What?"

"Don't. It's embarrassing, and painful for those of us with an actual sense of humor."

"Are we playing another game, or are you ready to surrender to my inevitable superiority?" Eric asked.

"Much as I'd like to wipe that ugly smirk off your ass—oh, excuse me, face, I get confused—I can't." Max jerked his head toward the long hallway that stretched toward his parents' room. "Time for me to pretend to be asleep."

"It's only eleven," Eric pointed out.

"I didn't say *sleep*, I said *pretend* to sleep. As you so astutely point out, it's almost eleven, meaning any minute now, Maxwell Sr.'s going to come out here and 'invite' me to breakfast with him and his alumni cronies tomorrow."

"And you know this because . . ."

"The man runs his life like he's in the army. Comes home at precisely six forty-five every night. Eats dinner at seven on the dot. Does the crossword puzzle in thirty minutes—unless it's Sunday, when it takes him forty-five. He probably craps on a schedule too. Every Saturday morning he has a liquid lunch with his Harvard buddies, and every Friday night he reads a week's worth of Crimson sports pages, makes his West Coast fund-raising calls, and then darkens my doorstep to try to suck me into his cult."

"I take it he's still not down with your brilliant no-college-Internet-millionaire scheme?"

"Is that a note of sarcasm I detect, young Roth?"

"You're a big boy. Old enough to do what you want"—Eric pursed his lips—"even if it is a dumbass idea."

"Stick around—you and Maxwell Sr. will have a lot to talk about." Max grabbed a folder from his desk and handed it to Eric. "My Harvard application. He's already filled it out for me. All I need to do is attach an essay and sign my name. The man's delusional."

"Your father's fifty years old and still goes to keg parties," Eric pointed out. "You're only just now realizing he's delusional?"

"Two hundred and twelve days," Max said fiercely. "Just two hundred and twelve days to graduation, and then I'm out of the nut-house and on my way." He gave himself a violent shake. "Forget it. We ready for the big day tomorrow?"

"The equipment's set."

"Clay knows what he needs to do?"

Eric shrugged. "I explained it to him, twice. As for whether he gets it . . ."

"You underestimate him."

"He's a moron."

"He'll be fine," Max said. "I've got a good feeling about this."

"Must be nice," Eric muttered.

"Do we have a problem?"

"I just don't like this."

Max pressed his hand over his eyes and began to massage his temples. "Look, I know you and the moron have a history, but—"

"It's not about that," Eric said. "I mean, yes, I have a problem with him, given that he's a thug with an ugly soul—"

"*Was!*" Max exclaimed. "When he was *eight!*"

"As I was saying, it's not about the thug and his ugly soul. It's about tomorrow. The SATs."

"I'm guessing I don't want to hear this."

"You know how I feel about cheating," Eric began.

Max blew out an angry burst of air. "It's not cheating! The terms of the bet state very clearly—"

"I'm not talking about cheating on the hack, I'm talking about cheating on the test." Eric waved his hand toward the file cabinet where Max kept his supply of term papers. "I know you don't care, but I don't like it."

"Don't remind me," Max groaned. "If you didn't have your pathological obsession with honesty, do you know how much money—"

"Spare me the lecture, I know all about my 'disease.'"

"Look, it's not cheating," Max argued. "Not in this case. Not really. If Clay was some wannabe Ivy Leaguer who couldn't quite make the cut, like Bernie Salazar, and we were helping him scam a better score, that would be cheating, right?"

Eric nodded.

"But he's not. Clay won't be using his perfect score for evil. He'll be proving a point. Our very worthy point, remember?"

"I know we've got to do it, and we'll do it. I just—" Eric pressed his lips together tightly for a moment. "I just wish there was another way on this one."

"But you do know there isn't, right?"

"I know." Eric headed for the door.

"And you'll be there tomorrow?"

Eric paused in the doorway and gave Max a wry grin. "Would I ever let you down?"

"You haven't yet," Max admitted.

"Then there's your answer."

◆ ◆ ◆

Two trains are on a collision course. Train A leaves point A at 4:20 p.m. Train B leaves point B at 4:35 p.m. Point A and point B are twenty miles apart. For the first ten minutes, train A travels twice as fast as train B. Then both trains continue on at the same speed. At what time will the collision occur?

A. 5:00 p.m.
B. Dinnertime
C. When hell freezes over
D. Not enough information to determine an answer
E. Plenty of information to determine an answer, but you're too dumb to know it

Sometime after midnight, I finally gave up on falling asleep. Lying in bed with impossible questions and nightmare scenarios whizzing through my head just wasn't cutting it. So, wide awake and too jittery to lie still despite a weeklong moratorium on coffee and chocolate, I got out of bed and, without turning the lights on, felt my way over to the computer to check my e-mail and research the fear of taking tests which, if you can believe it, is actually called *testophobia*.

I'd only been on for ten minutes when the IM popped up on my screen.

GodwinAdama: your up late
Glassgirl: who is this?
GodwinAdama: maybe it's a secret
Glassgirl: maybe I'm gone
GodwinAdama: wait
GodwinAdama: eric roth
Glassgirl: how did you know this was me?
GodwinAdama: i know everything.

I had to laugh. The kid was even cockier in writing than he was in person. *It would serve him right if I just shut my laptop and went back to bed*, I thought.

But I didn't.

GodwinAdama: whats w/the name? you don't wear glasses.

Glassgirl: glass, not glasses. as in, half empty

GodwinAdama: ha (i don't do lol)

Glassgirl: you don't laugh out loud?

GodwinAdama: don't write it. that's for 12 yr old girls.

Glassgirl: think U mean grrls. as in, omg! Lmfao, U grrls R so kewl!

GodwinAdama: ha x2

Glassgirl: what about your name?

GodwinAdama: figure it out.

Glassgirl: bite me

GodwinAdama: godwin=an anti-revolutionary revolutionary. thought he could build a better human.

Glassgirl: so you think you're god?

GodwinAdama: GodWIN

Glassgirl: v. profound. kinda pretentious. and adama?

GodwinAdama: fictional character

Glassgirl: let me guess.

Glassgirl: star trek.

GodwinAdama: NO!

Glassgirl: star wars

GodwinAdama: what kind of total geek do you think i am?

```
Glassgirl: no one's a total anything.
GodwinAdama: v. profound
GodwinAdama: kinda pretentious
Glassgirl: funny. who's adama?
GodwinAdama: he's from bstar galactica
Glassgirl: oh, you're THAT kind of
   total geek.
GodwinAdama: so which kind are you?
```

Before I could write back, my inbox dinged with a new message, one that I almost junked as spam before realizing who it was from.

```
Good luck tomorrow. Don't forget what
you need to do. We'll be watching.
```

It was exactly the reminder I didn't need, not eight hours before the test, not while I was talking to Eric, not when I'd almost convinced myself to forget what I had agreed to do the next day. But maybe that made it exactly the reminder I *did* need—because, I warned myself, I couldn't afford to forget. I stared at the e-mail for a long time, then finally clicked delete. There was no need to reply; there was nothing left to say.

```
GodwinAdama: didn't mean to be rude again
GodwinAdama: shouldn't u be asleep or
   something?
GodwinAdama: for tomorrow?
GodwinAdama: hello?
GodwinAdama: maybe ur asleep
GodwinAdama: ok. good luck
GodwinAdama has signed off.
```

PHASE TWO

October 19
SATs
Objective: A perfect score

Use your laser thinking. . . . You can cut through the fog and illumi-
nate each question. Focus directly and completely on the task in
front of you—the test.

—Mimi Doe and Michelle A. Hernandez, *Don't Worry, You'll Get In:
100 Winning Tips for Stress-Free College Admissions*

"B" Schwarz whispered into the mic. "D. C. A, A, A, C, B." This was
child's play. There was something almost fun about whipping
through the remedial math problems, watching the numbers fall
effortlessly into place. After years of visualizing and fracturing complex systems, juggling multiple variables in a multidimensional
space, contorting surfaces and interpreting possibility matrices, it
was thrilling to face a problem whose answer was simply: 7.

There was a simple beauty to the Pythagorean theorem, and a
glee in plotting the most basic $y=2x$ curve on a 5 x 5 graph.
Although . . . if you tipped that curve along its axis and expanded
it into a third and fourth dimension, then substituted a different
function for y and assumed x was an imaginary number—

"I think there was a problem like this on the Putnam last year!" he said excitedly. Schwarz hadn't been eligible for the annual college math challenge before, but he was already preparing for this year's contest. "But you are not looking for the dimension of the real vector space, you are just trying to analyze the—"

"Schwarz?" Max cut in. Like the rest of them, he was lying on his stomach beneath the bushes, his head propped up in his hands, his eyes fixed on the tiny monitor. "Personally, when I'm wallowing in the dirt, there's nothing I love more than hearing a lecture about imaginary numbers, but I think our friend Clay is less than enthused. . . ." He nodded toward the screen, where page three of the first math section was being slowly but surely obscured by something fleshy and pink. The image soon resolved itself into a middle finger.

"Um, maybe I will stick to the test problems," Schwarz said. "Sorry, Clay. Number twelve is D. Then E. B. C. C. . . ."

Giving a little wave at the camera hidden in his glasses, Clay went back to shading in the correct bubbles. Five minutes later, they'd finished the section.

Things were going as planned, the questions captured by Clay's camera and sent out to the guys, who were huddled under the bushes outside the school's western wall. Clay and his secret weapons breezed through the sections, racking up the right answers, penning an essay on the topic: "Do the Ends Always Justify the Means?" There was nearly a scuffle at that point, when Max lunged for the headset, eager to tell the College Board exactly how he felt about their means and his end. But cooler heads—or, at least, faster hands—prevailed. Schwarz held Max down as Eric dictated six bland paragraphs on corporate malfeasance, foreign affairs, and baseball, adding just the right counterintuitive twist. Of the thousands of essays arguing for moderated means, Eric knew that "Clay's" incisive defense of righteous ends would stand out as a masterwork of eloquent inanity, just what the doctor ordered.

And then, as Max and Eric eased into the sentence completions, debating the subtleties of *chasm* versus *schism*, it happened.

The screen went dark.

"Hello?" Eric whispered, trying not to panic. "Clay? You there?" Silence.

Max gave him a sour look. "The microphone only goes in one direction, brainiac."

They froze, staring at the screen, willing it to blink back on. Ten seconds passed. Then twenty. Still nothing.

"What the hell's wrong with it?" Max asked.

Schwarz checked his watch. They had twenty questions and eighteen minutes left—not to mention two sections still to come. Eric checked the connections at every port, measured the current, confirmed the signal broadcast.

"Sixteen minutes," Schwarz said.

"Would you fix it already?" Max snapped, his voice sliding toward higher registers. "We're running out of time. Come on. Come on!"

Eric bit down hard on his tongue, trying to drown out Max's voice. Focus. He unplugged the transceiver from its portable power source, pulled out a fresh set of video cables for the monitor, reset the whole system. Held his breath. "This should do it." He flipped everything back on.

Max clapped him on the back. "Finally! Never doubted you for a second."

They stared at the screen, which flared white, then faded back to a dull, fuzzy gray.

They waited for an image to emerge.

The fuzz danced across the screen in a static waltz.

"Come on," Eric muttered. "Come on, come on, you can do it."

"Fifteen minutes," Schwarz said in a doomsday voice.

"We get it!" Eric shouted. "Clock's ticking, thanks."

"I am just trying to help."

"Help would be figuring out what the hell is wrong."

"What's wrong is that your equipment failed," Max said.

"It did *not*. Everything's working perfectly."

Max tore loose a clump of grass and threw it at the screen. It fell several inches short of its mark. "Yeah, I can see that." He let himself fall flat onto his stomach, plowing his face into the grass. "We're screwed."

Schwarz gave Eric a cryptic look. "Eric, we could still . . ."

"Yeah." Eric sighed. "But I *know* I can fix this."

"Fourteen minutes," Schwarz said quietly. "Maybe we should . . ."

"What the hell are you two blabbering about?" Max asked, his voice muffled by the ground.

"*If* it's actually broken," Eric said, "we do have a backup plan."

Max sat up, bumping his head against a low-hanging branch. "We do? Who, exactly, is this *we*?"

Eric and Schwarz exchanged a glance, and Schwarz timidly raised his hand. "Him. And, um, me." He began rummaging through his backpack, pulling out a clunky, misshapen ball of wires and alligator clips, the new thermoswitch at the center. "Thirteen minutes," he reminded Eric.

"Yeah. Yeah, fine." Eric hung his head, defeated. "Hit the boiler room."

Schwarz hopped up and ran off.

"Where's he going?" Max asked, scrambling up as Eric swept away the equipment and crawled out from under the bushes. "Where are *you* going? And since when do we have a backup plan?"

"Since always," Eric said, raising his binoculars in time to spot Schwarz at the nearest fire exit. By the time he'd disabled the alarm, picked the lock, and slipped inside, Eric was off and running.

"So why don't I know about it?" Max panted, trying to stuff the monitor and headset into his bag as he raced alongside Eric.

"Because you were so proud of your little plan—I didn't want you think I'd lost faith in you," Eric said.

"My *plan* worked perfectly. It's your *equipment* that screwed us up."

"Fine," Eric said. "Then I didn't tell you about it because you would have wanted to know why I expected the equipment to break down."

"And that would have been so stupid, except, oh wait, funny coincidence, *it did break down.*"

"Not my fault," Eric insisted.

"Except that you saw it coming, and—"

"And this is exactly why I didn't tell you."

"How about you tell me where we're going, then?" Max asked, gasping for breath as they rounded the south side of the school.

"We're already there." Eric stopped him and, counting silently, pointed to a second-story window midway along the wall. "Eight windows in. Room 207. SAT central for last names *O* through *Q*."

"Damn, you're right. I can see that greasy hair from here."

"What?" Eric shook his head. "Not possible. They're sitting alphabetically. Which puts him third row down, two seats from the wall."

"Nooo," Max said slowly. "He's right next to the window. There's his greasy hair, there's his leather bracelet, and there's his stupid earring blinding me every time the sun hits it."

Eric took a closer look. "Shit."

"Why am I suddenly getting the feeling we need a backup plan for our backup plan?"

"It's nothing."

"You're such a crappy liar. Haven't I taught you anything?"

Eric pulled out a high-powered scope and a Megalaser 15mw OEM laser pointer. "This has a thousand-yard range and an adjustable filter. The scope has precision setting capability—I've already programmed in all the angles, I've hidden reflecting panes in the classroom, the calculations all work out, and as long as we're standing right here"—he pointed down to the shallow X he'd carved in the grass the day before—"we'll have a perfect view of the questions, and we'll be able to beam back the answers with the laser pointer. I customized it so we should be able to project the letter right onto the page."

"Won't the window glass refract the beam?"

"Schwarz is in the boiler room as we speak, turning up the heat to exactly eighty-five degrees."

"Not hot enough to shut down the building, but just hot enough to—"

"Open the window," Eric said as the windows began to rise.

"The perfect plan B." Max grinned. "Impressive."

"Yeah. Genius."

"So why aren't we smiling?"

"Because you had it right the first time. We're screwed." Eric pointed toward the window again. "Everything depends on Clay sitting in the right seat. The seat three rows back and two seats from the wall. Without that? We can't get a line of sight from here, the mirrors in there are useless—and we're screwed."

"Unless . . ." Max took a quick look around. The Wadsworth south lawn was framed by a grove of low-hanging trees, which, according to the school's official history, had been planted by Henry Adams. According to unofficial rumor, the school's first principal had had a wannabe landscaper wife—she'd planted the trees just before walking out on him and moving in with her fertilizer supplier. Both explanations seemed equally unlikely, but there must have been some reason why the scabby, stooped grove hadn't been put out its misery long ago. "'Military tactics are like unto water,'" Max intoned, staring at the trees. "'Water shapes its course according to the nature of the ground over which it flows.' Sun Tzu, *The Art of War*."

"Is that supposed to mean something to me?"

"Successful strategy has to be flexible enough to take the context into account," Max non-explained. "And the successful strategist knows how to use his context to get the job done. In other words, plan C."

Eric stared back blankly.

Max sighed. "You're the engineer, you tell me: Wouldn't that branch give you a perfect sight line to Clay's desk?"

Eric looked up—and suddenly it seemed way up—to the narrow, twisted limb Max had chosen. "Give *me* a perfect sight line?"

"It's your backup plan, Inspector Gadget. And a brilliant one it is." Max checked his watch. "Eight minutes and counting. Climb safe."

"Maybe you should come too. I might need help with some of the answers."

"With an IQ like yours? Doubtful." Max gave him a none-too-gentle whack on the shoulder. "You can get an eight hundred in your sleep. As long as"—he glanced up at the tree again, his eyes following the trunk up, up, and up—"well, as long as you don't fall out."

"I'm not afraid of heights," Eric muttered, hugging the trunk. "*Schwarz* is afraid of heights. I'm fine. This is all going to be fine."

And then, later.

"I'm going to kill Max. If I don't kill myself. Max is dead."

One foothold after another, bark stains running up and down his jeans, his muscles—disgruntled at being called upon for the first time in a decade—screaming in complaint. And then, without warning, he was there, shimmying out onto the branch, his heart thudding and his entire body trembling. Slowly, carefully, he shifted to the left to get a glimpse at his watch.

The climb had lasted only four minutes.

Feeling especially sorry for himself, Eric lodged his body into the crook between the trunk and the branch. He drew in a deep breath, then, very slowly, pulled the scope and the pointer out of his carpenter's belt and got to work.

But first he looked down.

Way down. Max gave him a silly grin and a thumbs-up.

Eric gave him the finger.

Four minutes left in the section, twenty questions to go.

He put the scope to his eye. Max had been right: The angle was perfect. The resolution was so sharp that he could see the wax in Clay's ear, the zit on his nostril, the space between his front teeth, and the rhythm his fingers tapped out as he waited for some signal of what to do next.

Eric could also see the test booklet and the next question. He flicked on the laser pointer, took aim, and a bright red D popped up at the top of the page. Surely not the first time Clay had seen such a thing—but still, he jerked in surprise, nearly knocking the booklet off his desk. He shot his head to the left and right, looking for the source.

"Come on, you psychopath," Eric muttered. "Figure it out. Answer the damn question."

Through the scope, he could almost see Clay's brain struggling through its thought process.

"Come *on.*" Eric gritted his teeth as the seconds ticked by. He waved the pointer around, so that the glowing D danced across the page, landing on Clay's answer sheet atop the appropriate bubble. "Put it together."

It took twenty more seconds, but finally, with a relieved smile and an eager nod, like he'd just solved Fermat's Last Theorem, Clay did. Bearing down hard, he filled in the bubble.

One question down, nineteen to go—with three minutes left.

Piece of cake.

There's no success like failure.

　　　　　　　—sample SAT essay prompt; Linda Metcalf, PhD,
　　　　　How to Say It to Get Into the College of Your Choice

I t was over.

All that studying, all that cramming, all those torturous nights lying awake, juggling equations, memorizing Latin roots . . . and it was over. I'd pulled out my number two pencil (one of seven sharpened ones in my bag of supplies, just in case), carefully bubbled-in my name, half-afraid, as always, that *Alexandra Talese* would prove too tediously long for the space provided, and then—no. I couldn't think about the "and then." I wouldn't. Not now, when it was too late to change it, when the booklets were closed and the envelopes sealed and the Scantron warming up to determine my fate. Not when it was over.

The crowd of students flooding out of the school fell into two categories: the triumphant and the destroyed. It took only a single glance to figure out who fit where.

Triumph was complex: a half-suppressed grin, a strained combination of modesty and pride, fingers twitching in a caricature of a body too stressed, too sleepless, too driven for too long. They raced for the parking lot or wandered lazily, savoring the long-awaited feeling of having nowhere in particular to go. A couple even flung themselves down in the grass, arms stretched out, faces tipped toward to the sun, as if needing physical confirmation that, beyond the sterile realm of number two pencils, the world was still there.

Destruction, on the other hand, was simple: misery. Tears, welling or gushing. A dead look of abandoned hope. Some of the destroyed sat on the steps of the school, as if reluctant to leave. Leaving would put the final seal on the day, admitting there was no turning back and no hope of reprieve.

That's where Eric found me. And he was the only one bold enough to ignore the *Stay the hell away* vibes and sit down—next to me, but not too close.

Just not too far away.

A car honked, and someone shouted at him from the driver's side window. He waved them away. The car peeled out of the lot. Eric stayed.

"Hey." He was looking straight ahead, not at me. Maybe because he was nervous; maybe because he knew I preferred it that way.

I nodded. "Hey."

I wasn't crying.

"So, how'd it go?" Eric asked quietly.

"You don't want to know." I pulled my hair out of its ponytail and shook it down, hiding behind the long shaggy strands that fell in front of my eyes. "*I* don't want to know."

"Just because you think you messed up, doesn't mean . . ." He shrugged. "People always think they've done worse than they actually—"

"Give it up," I snapped. "I know how I did. I was there."

There was a long pause.

"Sorry." Eric began to stand up. "I probably shouldn't have—"

"No. Wait. *I'm* sorry. You were just trying to . . ."

"It's okay." He scratched the back of his neck, then buried his chin in his chest, twisting his fingers into a tangled knot. "I just wish it had gone better."

I spit out a laugh. "Now I know things are bad."

"Why?"

"You're being *nice*."

He smiled. I didn't. And then neither of us said anything for a long while.

Most people would have tried to perk me up, tell me everything was going to be okay, that I could take it again, that it wouldn't matter that much, whatever. They would have spouted platitudes and probably, worst of all, tried to touch me, do that awkward shoulder-touching or back-stroking thing that people think is actually going to make you feel better, even if you're almost strangers.

Eric just sat there, waiting for me to make a move.

"I don't really want to talk about it," I said after several quiet minutes had passed.

"Yeah, I got that." His eyes darted toward his watch.

"You got somewhere to be?"

"No," he said quickly. "I was supposed to meet up with—well, it doesn't matter. They'll deal."

"Who?"

"No one." He stood up and brushed off the butt of his jeans. "Want to walk?"

I shrugged. But I stood up, too. We walked down the stairs together, me quickly and him a little slower, so that no one watching would have realized we were together. Not that we were. Together, I mean. We were just walking toward the same place, which was nowhere.

We walked for about an hour. It was one of those New England fall days that make tourists drool. You know: brisk air, clear sky, a sun so bright that looking out the window you would guess it was seventy degrees rather than forty, and plenty of foliage. That's what we call it here, thanks to the tourists. Everywhere else in the country, you've got trees, with leaves that change color and eventually fall off, all crusty and dead. Here, we have *foliage*.

We walked down Mass Ave, through Harvard Square with its chain stores dressed up in colonial garb. As if Starbucks doesn't count as an evil harbinger of globalization if it's tucked behind a facade of three-hundred-year-old brick; like no one's going to recognize a Barnes & Noble if you print the logo delicately small under the giant HARVARD COOP sign. Back when we were kids, Harvard Square had all these little stores and restaurants that were famous just for being in Harvard Square—greasy diners and skanky bars and funky thrift shops. Then the rent rose too high, they went bankrupt, and got replaced by B&N, Starbucks, Baskin-Robbins, and Abercrombie. I guess some people have this idea of Harvard Square as a quaint little college town, because that's the way they make it look in movies— but these days, in real life, it's more like Disney World.

You know how Disney World has that fake Main Street? On the outside, the buildings look all old-fashioned, like Ye Olde Chocolate Shoppe and Smitty's Apothecary—but then you go inside and they're all selling the same crappy Donald Duck dolls and Mickey Mouse ice-cream bars? Well, just substitute tacky crimson sweatshirts and Starbucks lattes, and you'll have a pretty good grasp on Harvard Square.

But I didn't say any of that out loud.

We walked through Kendall Square, which is much more "real" (in the J Lo sense, as in keepin' it that way), even though it's got a campus of its own. Which isn't necessarily a good thing: I'm not sure all those creepy alleys and empty warehouses are any better than Starbucks.

We didn't talk until we were halfway across the bridge, with less than a quarter mile of brownish river separating us from Boston proper.

"182.2 smoots," Eric said, stopping at the railing so abruptly that a jogger almost rammed into him.

"What?"

"The bridge is 364.4 smoots across—well, technically, 364.4 and one ear—and we're halfway." He pointed down at the faint yellow inscription reading 182.2 SMOOTS. Next to it was an arrow pointing back toward MIT and the words HALFWAY TO HELL.

I'd just spent the last three months of my life memorizing the dictionary, so I could be certain. "There's no such thing as a smoot."

Eric got a weird half-smile on his face. He leaned against the railing, facing out toward the river, half-turning back toward the campus. From the midpoint of the bridge you could see stretches of grass, still green and lush even as the trees were losing their leaves, marble buildings, a gleaming white dome. I'd walked across the bridge plenty of times, but I'd never stopped to look back at MIT. I always looked out at the river, watching the crew boats glide under the bridge and, when it was the right time of day, staring at the reflection of the skyscrapers in the water, all glittery orange from the setting sun. For a few days a year, in that glowing hour of twilight, it was my favorite spot in the city.

"It started as a hack," Eric said, staring down again at the faded yellow writing. It was the first time I heard him use the word. "Well, more like a frat prank. October 1958, the pledgemaster of Lambda Chi Alpha had his pledge class go out and mark the bridge in 'pledge lengths.'" He sounded like he was reading from an encyclopedia. "That way, all the MIT kids crossing the bridge would know how far they'd gone without having to look up into the wind. They picked the shortest pledge: Oliver Reed Smoot, five foot seven. Then they went out in the middle of the night and Oliver lay down on the bridge while the other pledges marked off the distance from his toes to his head in white paint. They did it again, and again, 365 times, all the way to the other side of the bridge. By the end he was so cold and tired they had to drag him." His eyes were shining. "It's one of the most successful pranks in history. They repaint the markings every couple years, so now they're pretty much permanent, and even the cops measure the bridge in smoots. Google Earth lets you measure the *world* in smoots. *That's* making an impression."

I looked down at the markings again, less impressed with the story—which, to be honest, didn't thrill me, a bunch of MIT frat kids painting lines on a bridge, big deal—than with the look on Eric's face.

"So that's why you want to go to MIT?" I teased. "Smoots."

His cheeks flushed pink and he turned away from the campus. "Maybe. Would that be weird?"

"Sort of." I tilted my head and tapped my finger against my lip, as if I were giving the matter deep thought. "Well . . . definitely."

He just shrugged. "So now you know my deep, dark secret. I'm weird. Want to tell me yours?"

"My . . . ?"

"Your secret."

My hands tightened on the railing. "What makes you think I have a secret?"

"You're too interesting not to," he said, then turned pink again. "I mean, you know. Everyone does."

I didn't want to lie. But I couldn't tell the truth. So I picked a harmless one. Although, I guess it couldn't have been that harmless, since I'd never said it out loud before. "My secret is, I'm scared."

"Of what?"

Try everything.

But it was too much. "Of getting pneumonia, if we stay out on this bridge much longer," I said, forcing a laugh. I tugged my jacket tighter and realized that I actually was cold. The sun had disappeared behind some clouds, and the wind raking across the bridge wasn't "brisk" so much as "frigid."

"Oh. Right. Yeah, we should go." He turned abruptly and started hurrying back toward the Cambridge side of the bridge, walking fast enough that by the time we hit the Kendall T station, I was nearly panting. "I've got some stuff to do for that professor I work for," he said, as we paused at the mouth of the station. "So you should prob-ably just . . ."

"Yeah." I did that awkward wave thing where you're not really sure how to say good-bye, so you just end up looking like some frumpy mom sending her kid off to kindergarten. He waved back, looking even less cool. "So thanks for, uh, hanging out, and all," I said.

"Everything works out, you know."

"Is that some kind of law of nature, MIT boy?"

He grinned, and a little of the awkwardness faded away. "Sure. First law of thermodynamics: Energy can neither be created nor destroyed. Whatever happens, the universe maintains its equilibrium."

"Doesn't the second law say that entropy increases and that the universe is just going to keep falling apart until there's nothing left?"

"Well . . . if you're a glass-half-empty kind of girl, then I guess you could look at it that way." We both laughed. "Impressive, by the way."

"What?"

"That you knew that."

"I know a lot."

"Yeah. I'm getting that." He chewed on the edge of his lip, just like I do. Or used to do, before I tried to quit. It wasn't gross; it was almost cute. "So, do you want to, maybe, do this again sometime?"

"Do . . . *this*?"

"Well, we could skip the part where you blow the SATs."

I winced.

"Too soon?" he asked.

"Maybe."

"I just meant, you know. Do something," he stammered, inarticulate for the first time. "Sometime."

"I don't do hypotheticals," I told him. All his blushing and stuttering was giving me a weird feeling, one I'd never really had when talking to a guy—a feeling like I was the one in control. I liked it. "But if *sometime*, you were to actually ask me to do *something* . . ."

"You'd say . . . ?" he prompted.

"I guess we'll find out." I grinned at him and stepped onto the escalator down to the subway. "Sometime."

10

Consider getting into the habit of being honest.

—Marty Nemko, PhD, *The All-in-One College Guide*

There was no errand at MIT.

There was, however, a meeting at Harvard. And Eric was almost two hours late.

"Which part of *rendezvous after the test* didn't you understand?" Max asked as Eric, face flushed and out of breath, flung open the door to Schwarz's room. "Should I use smaller words next time?"

"We were getting worried," Schwarz said, without taking his eyes off the computer screen.

"What are you, his mom?" Max was standing by the window, fiddling with a yo-yo. He made it walk the dog, then threw in an around the world. "No one was worried. Just increasingly pissed. Where were you?"

"Additional surveillance. Checking in on the competition—" Eric broke off, realizing that there was an extra body in the room. Bernard Salazar had taken Eric's customary position, lounging at the foot of the roommate's unused bed. "Competition for the Bot Battle next month," he added quickly. "You know, bunch of guys building robots trying to kill each other, I just want to make sure my bot's the best—"

"You can drop the act," Max said. "He knows everything."

"And by everything, you mean . . . ?"

"The hack," Bernard said eagerly. "Harvard, Clay 'like dirt' Porter, I got the 411 from your peeps."

Eric glared at Max, who looked away, swinging his yo-yo in smooth, lazy arcs. "Say hello to the newest member of Team Max."

Eric looked the interloper up and down. "Nice shirt."

Bernard plucked at the wifebeater. "Made it myself. Gotta dress for success, yo."

"Right." Eric strode across the room and snatched the yo-yo away from Max, tossing it onto the bed. "Oh captain, my captain, I think 'Team Max' needs to have a little team meeting. Yo."

"You bros gotta get down with this shit," Bernard advised, thumping his chest. "Go with the flow, you know?" He patted the heavy gold chains strung around his neck. "Life in the loop is off the *hook*, yo. I mean, I got honeys lined up to get some Bernie-loving, and these ho's are *hot*." Bernard rolled his eyes. "I know how it sounds, gentlemen, but trust me, these high school girls eat it up like candy."

"Bernard's full of bright ideas," Max said, without a trace of sarcasm, his expression warning Eric not to bring up the fact that Bernard, despite his rap-star fantasies, had been an object of ridicule since third grade, his parties well-attended only because he could be counted on to pay for top-shelf liquor. As for the "honeys," it seemed clear they were less attracted to the clumsy faux-hawk, hip-hop delusions and perma-tan than to Bernard's rep for outfitting his admirers with "hot 'n' heavy bling."

"We got tired of waiting, so we replaced you," Max said.

"Funny." Eric didn't crack a smile. He pointed at the door. "We need to talk."

Bernard jumped up and strode across the room, clasping Eric's hand in a firm grip. "Don't worry. From what I hear, you sir, are irreplaceable." He clapped Eric on the back, and despite the ghetto gear, his voice and manner were suddenly pure Donald Trump. "Couldn't be happier working on this with you fellows."

"Eric, meet our new backer," Max said. "Bernard here has agreed to finance the hack."

Eric narrowed his eyes. "In return for what?"

Bernard let out an explosive and thoroughly artificial burst of laughter that sent flecks of spittle spraying across the hardwood floor. "What do you think, bro? You get me in too."

"Information sharing," Max clarified. "We fill him in on whatever we find out about the admissions people—the rest he does himself."

"I like to call that a win-win scenario." Bernard beamed. "My favorite kind."

"I like to call this an exit line," Eric said, and walked out of the room, slamming the door behind him. He stood by the stairwell and waited.

It took less than a minute for Max to appear.

"Well, that was suitably dramatic," Max said, shutting the door behind him. He leaned against the wall and crossed his arms. "You want to tell your fearless leader what the problem is?"

"You—I can't believe—what are you—" Eric flung his arms toward the door. "How could you—"

Max drew in a loud, deep breath, then blew it out slowly, in short bursts, like a Lamaze coach. "Take it easy. Use your words."

"Bernard Salazar!" Eric finally managed to spit out. "You brought in *Bernard Salazar*? What the hell were you thinking?"

"I was thinking we had a cash-flow shortage, and Bernard has a platinum card."

"So you want to sell us out for a few extra dollars?"

"Maybe I'm missing something," Max snapped. "Did you win the lottery lately? Can you fund this? Weren't you the one complaining just last week that you had to dig into your savings for the micro-camera? Bernard will fix all that for us."

"Yeah, but for what?"

"You heard for what," Max said. "We're just going to give him a little extra help."

"We're going to help him *cheat*."

"Lighten up, Eric." Max flashed a smile at the group of girls passing through the entryway. "Think they thought I was a college man?"

"Focus, Max."

"How about *you* focus?" Max shook his head. "What was so important that you had to ditch us?"

"I had stuff to do," Eric said. "I told you. More surveillance."

Max snorted. "I bet. "

"What's that supposed to mean?"

"Look, all I'm saying is, you were supposed to be here, and

instead you were . . . elsewhere. Schwarz and I talked it over, and he agrees with me. Bernard is our best shot at some quick cash inflow. Low risk, high gain."

"Oh, Schwarz agrees with you?" Eric asked. "I'm stunned. Please. If you told him our best shot at cash was rowing out into the Harbor and digging up sunken pirate treasure, he'd agree with that, too."

"Did I hear you right?" Max asked, cocking his ear with mock disbelief. "Are you actually suggesting our most loyal and trusted friend doesn't have a mind of his own?"

Eric slammed his hand against the banister, wincing at the impact. "I'm saying this idea is just as stupid, and Schwarz is too polite to tell you. Bernard can't be trusted. He's a weasel. Or do you not remember the time he turned Kara Winters in for cheating, when *he* was the one who suckered her into stealing a copy of the test?"

"What are you, an elephant? That was like ten years ago."

"That was sophomore spring," Eric shot back. "And he gets worse every year. He's a total fraud—in school he talks like Eminem, and now listen to him, he's Lil' Ken Lay."

"Holding the sins of the father against the son?" Max clucked his tongue. "How very un-Christian of you."

"I *am* un-Christian," Eric reminded him. "And I'm just stating a fact. His father doesn't have anything to do with it, although—"

"He claims his father was set up."

"Oh, really? And how does he explain the six employees who came forward to testify that he'd raided all the retirement funds?"

"We can't all live up to your disgustingly high moral standards."

"You would know."

Max sighed. "You want to share with the class what this is really about?"

"Am I being too *obtuse*? Let me spell it out for you: I. Don't. Trust. Him."

"Who does?" Max asked. "But that's not your real problem. You want to know what your real problem is?"

"I assume this is where you enlighten me?"

"You're having second thoughts."

"No."

"Yes."

Eric rubbed the back of his neck. "This is a good hack. We're doing the right thing."

"But," Max said, with a knowing smile.

"But." Eric paused. "But for every person that gets in, there's someone—a bunch of someones—who get rejected. It was one thing when it was just Clay, but if we're going to get Bernard in too . . ."

"We're just giving him a slight advantage," Max said. "The rest he can do—or more likely, screw up—on his own."

"Even so. Don't you ever think about it? The person, whoever it is, who's going to get rejected because of us?"

"Look, if she's a deserving applicant—"

"He or she," Eric said.

Max smirked. "Whatever you say. If he or *she* is a deserving applicant, he or she will get in, whatever we do."

Eric laughed bitterly. "You know that's bullshit."

"Of course I do—and so do you. That's why we're doing this in the first place, remember?" Max leaned his head back against the wall, spreading his fingertips wide against the bubbling white paint. "And I quote, 'We're bringing attention to a broken system. It's the only way anyone's ever going to fix it.' Know who I'm quoting there?"

"Max—"

"It was a wise man, my friend. A very wise man. Can you guess his name?"

"Max, all I'm saying—"

"It was *you*." Max jabbed his finger toward Eric. "You said it when we started this whole thing, and you were right."

"I know what I said." Eric sighed. "I just don't know if this is the way to do it. Not if someone's going to get hurt."

"The ends justify the means, Eric. Who said that? Oh, that's right—you again. Just this morning. And you were very persuasive."

"We both know the SAT version of critical reasoning doesn't apply to the real world."

"Tell that to the College Board," Max pointed out with a sly grin. Eric didn't smile back. Max ran a hand through his spiky black hair. "Look, nothing's changed. If this was a good idea yesterday—and it *was*—it's still a good idea today. Bernard's just supplying the cash, which we need. Don't we?"

Eric nodded. He'd used up the last of his cash on SAT supplies, and they were still months away from the end of the hack.

"You weren't here, Eric. I was all set to discuss this, but you didn't show—and now it's too late." Max's tone softened. "Look, Salazar knows what we're doing, and if we cut him out now, no doubt he'll turn us in. He's an asshole."

Eric finally smiled. "You noticed, too?"

"I'm not blind," Max said. "Just poor. And now we've got a guy who probably uses cash as toilet paper. We need this. We need *him*. And all he wants from us is a little help. So let's just suck it up, okay?"

"You really think we can trust him?" Eric asked dubiously.

"Are you nuts?" Max shook his head. "But it'll all work out. No need to trust him. Trust *me*."

"Trust you?" Eric grinned, his eyebrows rising to his forehead. "Are *you* nuts?"

Bernard was like a wart.

A painful, infectious, oozing growth that wouldn't go away.

As the hours dragged by, they tried conventional methods, hoping to ease him out the door with subtle, then not-so-subtle, suggestions that it was time to go, but he stuck. Even when Eric logged into World of Warcraft and jumped into battle with a local wizard while Schwarz and Max hovered at his shoulder pretending to care, Bernard stuck around. He lounged on the roommate's bed, his shoes on the pillows, his head propped up on the Harvard sweatshirt that Schwarz's mother had bought him the day after the acceptance letter arrived.

Eric and Max had each, separately, tried making a break for the door, only to be drawn back in by Schwarz's plaintive expression and silent pleading: *Do not leave me alone with him.*

"Your presence, though magnanimous, is also superfluous," Max pleaded with Bernard. "Now that we've concluded the business portion of the day, I'm sure you've got a full social calendar, so . . ."

"Not a problem." Bernard pulled out a ballpoint pen and began drawing a lightning bolt on his left bicep. "We're just hanging out, right? I like to see who's going to be spending my money. . . . Unless you've got a problem with that."

"Of course not," Max said quickly. Schwarz and Eric shook their heads.

He was a stubborn wart, and conventional methods obviously weren't going to do the trick.

Bring on the cauterizer.

It was already dark outside when the door flew open, revealing Clay Porter leaning against the doorjamb, one hand in his pocket, the other propped over his head, resting against the frame. "Ready to go?"

Eric looked at Max, Max looked at Schwarz, and Schwarz looked down at his calendar. "You are off for the night. It says right here—morning, SATs. The rest of the day, nothing."

"So you can go do . . . whatever it is you do," Max added.

"I party," Clay said. "Never aced a test before in my life."

And you didn't do it this time either, Eric thought. *We did.*

"It felt good," Clay continued. "We're going out."

"I have to get up early tomorrow," Eric said.

Max tapped his cell phone. "I've got a few transactions to take care of."

"And I have homework," Schwarz said quickly.

"I'm out too, yo." Bernard leaned toward Eric and lowered his voice to a whisper. "I can't be seen with someone like him—you know, my rep." Then he turned back to the rest of the room. "Yeah, I'll just stay up in here wit' my boy Schwarzie."

"You know what?" Schwarz shut down his laptop and leaped out of the chair. "It is Saturday night. Fornicate my homework."

"Eric?" Max raised his eyebrows.

Eric looked back and forth between his two options.

Both sucked.

He shrugged. "All right. Fornicate the homework it is."

11

Premature senioritis can be disastrous.
—Paulo de Oliveira and Steve Cohen, *Getting In! The First
Comprehensive Step-by-Step Strategy Guide to Acceptance
at the College of Your Choice*

They rode the T into South Boston. The farther Clay led them down back streets and dark alleys, the closer they stuck to him, refusing to meet one another's eyes. They trudged in silence, heads bowed, shoulders hunched against the wind, so no one noticed when Clay stopped abruptly in front of what looked like just another broken shell of an empty house. "Guys!" he called. His voice echoed down the deserted street. "Here."

On closer examination, it wasn't a house. At least not according to the crooked wooden sign hanging over the entrance, its paint faded and nearly illegible.

It was the Yankee Doodle.

"Don't laugh," Clay advised them, when he saw they'd noticed the name. "They don't like it when you laugh."

No one felt like laughing.

A small stairwell led down to the entrance, and at the bottom sat a man in a black T-shirt who was almost as wide as the doorway. He didn't look like he laughed much, either. Max pulled out his wallet, but Clay grabbed his wrist and shook his head.

"IDs," Max whispered. The year before, he had cooked up fake licenses for all three of them, the test run for a business that never got off the ground. They had yet to be used.

"Don't need 'em," Clay said. "Not when you're with me."

He jogged down the stairs and bent his head toward the bouncer, murmuring something too quietly for the rest of them to hear. Then he pointed up toward the boys, and they both began to laugh.

"What's he saying?" Max whispered, squinting as if, through sheer willpower, he could read their lips.

"Maybe 'you hold them down while I beat the crap out of them'?" Eric suggested.

Clay beckoned.

"This is them?" The bouncer laughed even harder as they lined up at the bottom of the stairs. His stomach rippled with every gasping chuckle, but that was it as far as the flesh jiggling went—those arms, nearly as thick as Eric's head, were obviously pure muscle. "Shit, Clay, I thought you were joking."

"Meet Jesse," Clay said, clapping him on the shoulder. "My mom's ex."

"One of 'em," the bouncer added, winking.

Schwarz, whose homeschooling had included a steady dose of maternal etiquette, extended his hand. "Nice to meet you."

The bouncer kept his arms folded. "I don't shake." He jerked his head toward the bar. "Get in there." He burst into another round of laughter. "You boys are gonna have some fun tonight!"

Was his face red?

It didn't feel red. Not any redder than usual, at least. It was hot, but then, he was hot all over, tingling, almost glowing. He took another swig of beer. He liked that. *Swig*. It sounded manly.

His father's face always got red when he drank. That's how Max knew what he was doing every Saturday afternoon at lunch with the boys. Lunch, right, except he came home smelling like he'd taken a bath in gin, his face a radioactive, highlighter pink, wanting to talk about the old days.

What else was new?

For Maxwell Sr., the old days were all that mattered, after all. Four years, four golden years—*crimson* years, Max corrected himself— that mattered more than anything he'd done before or since.

More than his career, his promotions, his research.

More than his wife and family.

More than his son.

Fuck my father, Max thought, and when someone thrust another beer in his face, he grabbed it and choked down the putrid, bitter liquid without even making a face. *He'd hate to see me now.* The thought almost made the beer taste good.

The Yankee Doodle was the kind of place where Maxwell Sr. assumed all non-Harvard graduates ended up. Dank, dark, dirty, crammed with drunken regulars, the bar reeked of thwarted potential, frustrated mediocrity, and stale popcorn. Someone had hung a row of dartboards along the back, because nothing says fun like a bunch of drunks with needle-nosed projectiles.

Three dartboards, a wall of sagging booths, a mahogany bar—where Clay was, at that very moment, turning Schwarz into a Southie Casanova—and one faded, pitted, three-legged, absolutely beautiful pool table.

Not as fancy as the one in the Kim basement, sure.

But when Max beat his father ten games out of ten, week after week, until the old man refused to play anymore, all he got out of it were bragging rights. And bragging wasn't worth anything in the Kim household unless it came complete with a certificate to hang on the wall.

This place was different. Bragging be damned.

Max smelled money.

"She is beautiful," Schwarz said, slumping onto the bar, his head lolling against his shoulders. "Perfect. So perfect. Like . . . like perfect, you know?" The beer had been bitter in his mouth, but he had choked it down, first one mug, then the next, and now it didn't taste like anything anymore. It was just cool. Not like him. He would never be cool. He was a loser. He was miserable. He was alone. He was confused. And he was having trouble pronouncing his words. "I look at her, and it is like in the magazine. Beautiful. Her hair and her eyes and when she looks at me, she doesn't even see me. She just talks, and I am listening, but she doesn't see me. And it does not matter, I don't need her to, I just want to look at her. It's like she is not even real, like I imagined her, but if she was an imaginary number then I could square it and then . . . what?"

"What?" Clay asked.

"What was I just . . . I'm sorry, I lost what I was . . . what?"

"Dude, I have no idea what you're—"

"Oh. Yeah. 'Scuse me, but like an equation? That's what she is. There's symmetry and elegance and on the surface it looks simple but then within it there are multitudes, and an infinity of complexity but it all falls into place and there are rules." Schwarz guzzled down more beer, barely noticing when half of it sloshed onto his jeans. "'S like music. All those different pieces, chaos, and then it all blends together in harmony, everything fits into the system, and that is magnificent, because how can the grass and the stars and the quarks and the footballs all follow the same rules, but they do, everything's vibrating in sync, and everything that's real has an ideal and it's there beneath the surface, and that's what she is, the ideal. Except that she has no rules and no equations and if she were a number she'd make sense but she doesn't. I want some rules!" He banged his fist on the bar. "*Math* has rules. There is always a system. There's always order. And the magazines, the pictures have a system. One a month, always one a month, and it's always the same and she's just there and you know what you're getting, and every chaotic system resolves itself into order, except in chaos theory, and even that has rules and formulas and it all makes sense, but she's real and she doesn't make any for-nic-at-ing *sense!*"

Schwarz buried his head in his hands.

"Dude, you're one messed-up little geek," Clay said.

Schwarz hiccuped.

"You wanna know what your problem is?"

"Yes, please?" He looked up, took another swig. Now the beer tasted like hope.

What does hope taste like? he thought. His mind was floating, like it wasn't attached to anything. Like if he didn't hold on, it would slither down the bar and slip away. *It should be cotton candy. Or Milk Duds. Chocolate. Pizza. I wonder if the bar has pizza.*

"You got that?"

Schwarz looked up. "What?"

"He said you don't understand women," Eric snapped. He was slouched in front of his second glass of Coke, pretending not to listen, acting like he had a stick up his posterior—even more than usual, Schwarz thought.

Clay clinked his shot glass against Eric's Coke. "Right. Whoever this girl is—"

"Stephanie," Schwarz moaned.

"Yeah. Stephanie. She's not perfect. She's not some goddess that's going to rule the universe, or whatever that shit meant that you were saying."

"It's not ex-e-cre . . . excrement," Schwarz said, his tongue tripping over the syllables. "It's math."

"Yeah, like I say, this Stephanie chick's not math, and she's not perfect. You're never gonna get her if you think she's perfect. And even if you do get her, it's not gonna take you too long to figure out that she's not."

"Could you, um, talk slower?" Schwarz asked. He felt like a multivariable calculus student trying to comprehend hypoellipticity of sub-Laplacians.

"Let me break it down for you," Clay said. "Women are just people, okay? You can't be scared of 'em. You can't worship 'em. You have to just treat them like regular people. It's the only way to understand them."

Schwarz moaned.

"Don't panic. I got this." Clay tapped his shot glass against his teeth, then slammed it down on the bar. "Okay, first thing, no more of this 'whatever you say' shit. You gotta start standing up for yourself. Be your own man."

"Okay!" Schwarz slammed his glass down on the bar too, and straightened up. For a moment. Then he slouched again. "But . . . please, could you tell me how?"

Clay rubbed his hands across his face. Schwarz drank more beer. He wondered what it meant that his tongue was getting numb. Or maybe it wasn't quite numb. Maybe it was just bigger. Clumsier. Like a dead fish clogging up his mouth. The thought made him gag. He washed it away with another mouthful of beer. And he listened.

"Okay. You know what? Forget being your own man. Maybe that's like—that's like an honors class, right? You get that? You belong in remedial."

"I'm a genius," Schwarz said proudly. "Everyone says."

"Yeah . . . that's not gonna help. And you need some *major* help. We're gonna take this step by step, got it?"

"Got it."

"Step one. You wanna be tough, but not too tough, you know?"

"Tough. But not too tough," Schwarz repeated.

"They like to *think* you're this bad boy, right?" Clay said, clapping him on the back. Schwarz pitched forward, and caught himself just before his head smacked into the mahogany. "Some tough guy who won't take shit from anyone. But then . . ."

"Then?" *I should be taking notes,* Schwarz thought. Then he giggled. "I think I'm drunk. Do you think I'm drunk?"

"*Tough*," Clay said. "And then you gotta be soft. But just a little bit, and you act all embarrassed about it, like it's this big secret they've uncovered. Like they're the only ones who know the real you, right? The rest of the world thinks you're a thug, but they know you're just a sweetie. They totally get off on that shit, trust me."

"That really works?"

Clay pointed across the bar, where the bartender was bending over to get something off a lower shelf, her tight skirt riding up her thighs. "Worked on her," he said, with an appreciative nod. "Want to meet her?"

"No! I can't—"

Too late.

"Sammi!" Clay called. "Get your ass over here."

The top half of her was even better than the bottom. Schwarz tried not to look.

"You got any friends for my boy here?" Clay asked, giving her a quick kiss on the cheek. "He needs to get laid."

"No, I do not," Schwarz squeaked. "Really. Don't worry about it. I've got Stephanie. I mean, I don't have her, and she's got someone else, but maybe—"

"*He's* your man?" Sammi asked. "Did you join Big Brothers or something?"

Clay grinned. "He's cool. I'm just trying to teach him how to be, you know. Cool. He needs a girl."

"Woman," Sammi corrected him.

"Girl. Look at the kid. He's three feet tall."

Sammi reached over the bar and patted Schwarz on the head— he could barely feel the pressure of her hand through the wiry mop of hair. "Don't listen to this guy," she said. "He likes to play like he's tough, but deep down . . ." She gave Clay a kiss back, first on the cheek, and then somehow—and despite Schwarz's wide-eyed stare, he couldn't figure it out—ended up attached to his mouth, sucking at his lower lip like it was a lollipop. Schwarz felt his lungs tightening at the sight of it—how was she *breathing*? "He's a good guy," she said, finally breaking away. "A real sweetie."

Clay waved good-bye as she was called over to the other end of the bar. His eyes twinkled. "See what I mean?"

"Three ball, side pocket," Max called. He cradled the cue, leaned down toward the table—and almost threw up.

Four beers, six beers, eight beers, he didn't know. He just kept making bets and people kept shoving bottles into his hand. And now the world was listing and tilting and he wondered how the balls stayed so still on the table, when he felt like he was about to roll across the room.

He aimed the cue, commanding his fingers to keep steady. But the tip bobbed and weaved—unless it was the cue ball that was moving, trying to escape the strike.

Pull back. *Stay smooth,* he thought. Take aim. *Nice and easy.* Make the shot. *Now.*

The cue skidded past the ball and slammed into the opposite edge of the table. "Shit!" He whacked the cue against his knee in frustration, waiting for a crack. But there was only a soft thump. And pain.

"Eight ball, corner pocket," his opponent called. It was an easy shot, and a smooth one, and then the game was over. The beefy guy in the Red Sox cap and the army surplus coat had won.

Max had lost. For the fourth game in a row.

"Pay up." The guy had a heavy Boston accent—*Masshole,* Max thought dimly—and an open palm. "I gotta get home."

But Max didn't have the cash; he hadn't planned to lose.

"IOU?" he said weakly. And then threw up on the guy's boots.

"Asshole!" The guy took off his jacket. There was more Red Sox crap underneath, a Johnny Damon T-shirt with hand-drawn devil horns and a red X scrawled over the face. The tattoo running thick around the guy's bicep read BELIEVE. "You fucking owe me all right."

His buddies caught his arms in mid-lunge. "Forget it," one said. "He's just a kid. He doesn't know what he's doing."

"Look at him, he's harmless."

"Kids do stupid shit. Let it go."

Just a kid.

Harmless.

Stupid.

Doesn't know what he's doing.

They thought he couldn't decide for himself. Just like Maxwell Sr. They thought what he did—what he *wanted*—didn't matter. That he didn't count.

They didn't see that he was a man. A better man than his father, even drunk, even broke, even screwed, at least he was doing what *he* wanted to do. He wasn't a kid. He was his own man. And no one was going to take that away from him.

He burped.

He stumbled.

And then he lowered his head, hunched his shoulders, and aimed straight for Johnny Damon's nose.

"Fuuuuuuuuuuuck!" he screamed, bashing into a wall of flesh. It didn't shake, didn't move. There was a soft *oof*, and then iron fingers clamped down on Max's arms and the next thing he knew he was launched off the ground, kicking, flailing, cursing— and then dangling upside down, his ankles locked together in a pincher grip, his arms pinned behind his back. His captor lowered him toward the ground, like a prisoner into a pot of boiling oil, until his face was an inch from the sticky floor. A moment later, a wave of beer crashed down, washing across his face, puddling up beneath him.

"Lick it up, kid." It was the Masshole, cackling above. *"Lick. It. Up."*

Eric didn't get it. Not until Clay emerged from the back, carrying a wriggling Max over his shoulder like a two-year-old having a temper tantrum.

He'd heard the shouts, the curses, a crack, and a thud, and then, moments later, a scream. He'd seen Clay drop his glass and rush toward the back.

Running toward *trouble*, Eric had thought. *Typical.*

And then Clay reappeared with Max, storming through the bar, chased by the herd of brutes, their faces bruised and their fists shaking. "And stay the hell out!" one bellowed as Clay barreled through the door. Eric grabbed Schwarz, who'd spent the last hour weeping into his beer and now clung to Eric like a drowning victim. They made it outside just in time to see Clay deposit Max onto the ground—and then grab him again as Max struggled to escape back inside to finish whatever he'd started.

Clay as hero. Clay Porter as rescuer.

It didn't compute.

Eric was the one who saved Max, and vice versa. It's what they were there for. Clay didn't factor into the equation. At least, not on the side of good.

Except that there it was: Clay had rushed into the fight, Clay had swept to the rescue. While Eric stood on the sidelines, clueless. Worse than that: useless.

"Let go of me, asshole!" Max snarled, still trying to pull free. "Get the hell off."

"So you can go back in there and get yourself killed?" Clay asked, a trace of a smile creeping across his face. "Don't think so. Not while you still owe me six hundred bucks."

"Was doing *fine* until you came along." Max was slurring so much it was hard to understand him. "I'm on my own."

"Whatever." Clay kept his grip.

"Fuck off!"

"Dude, I'm on your side here," Clay said, frog-marching him up the stairs toward the street. Eric and Schwarz hurried after. Not that anyone needed them. "I'm one of the good guys."

Max laughed, a thick, phlegmy gargle that quickly turned into a cough. He doubled over, wheezing and heaving, though nothing came up. "Yeah, a fucking great guy. Tell it to Eric."

"Max, shut up," Eric warned.

"You wanna make me?" Max stumbled toward Eric and gripped his shoulders, his breath hot and sour in Eric's face. "Come on, *make me.*"

Eric pushed him out of the way. "How much did you drink back there? You're a fucking mess."

"That's me, right?" Max slurred, flinging his arms out wide. "A big fucking mess. Not like you, not like Eric, always does the right thing, always follows the rules, always has to be fucking right and too bad he's got such a fuck-up best friend who's always dragging him down, right?"

"What are you talking about? You're not a—"

"Such a freaking hassle for you, right?" Max shouted, stepping blindly into the street. Eric pulled him back just as a car sped past. Max shook him off. "Except you love it, right? You *love* it that you're better than me, that you get to get up on your high—your—you know—the thing, and just look down, and there's Max, in the dirt, and you get to be right again."

"That is *not* what I think," Eric protested.

"But what makes you so great, huh? You talk all this crap about everything, but you don't *do* anything, right? It's all talk, talk, talk. Well, talk now!" He pointed at Clay, his wobbly arm drawing zigzags in the air. "Go on, tell him everything, tell him all about what he—"

"Shut up!" Eric shouted.

"What the hell's he talking about?" Clay asked.

"He's just drunk," Eric said. "He always, uh . . . talks a lot of shit when he's drunk." Max, of course, didn't "always" do anything when he was drunk, having never been drunk before in his life.

"*You* talk a lot of shit!" Max cried. "Just say what you wanna say. Be a fucking man!"

"Something you been wanting to say, Eric?" Clay asked.

Schwarz leaned his head on Eric's shoulder. "Maybe you should tell him," he whispered loudly. "Catharsis is good for the soul."

"Can we just focus on finding a cab and getting the hell out of here?" Eric snapped. He wasn't a crybaby, and he wasn't a pathetic eight-year-old running around with his pants at his ankles. Not any-more. It was ancient history. If Clay didn't remember what he'd done—didn't care—Eric wasn't going to remind him. It had nothing to do with being afraid, Eric told himself. It had nothing to do with being "a fucking man." It just didn't need to be said. "I think we've had enough celebrating for the night."

"You're so uptight all the time, man," Max said, the anger drained out of his voice. He staggered over to Eric and Schwarz and threw an arm around each of them. "My boys," he said, wheezing a blast of beer-stained breath in their faces. "I love my boys. But you just gotta learn to let go a little. *Live.*"

And then he passed out.

12

Whatever you do about girls this fall, remember that it will end badly. . . . They'll tromp on you, boy, they'll pluck your heart out and crack it like an egg. But they mean well, and the fault is yours—you asked for a date.

—David Royce, '56, "Sex and Society: Coming of Age at Harvard," *The Harvard Crimson*, October 8, 1955

Seventeen days passed.

Not that I was waiting for his call.

I had plenty to keep me busy. A typical November day:

Wake up at five a.m. Shower, root around for a sweater that's been worn fewer than three times and isn't covered in cat hair, towel-dry hair because blow-drying takes too long, even if it means wet hair will freeze into mousy brown ice crystals as soon as it's exposed to the elements. Pull on gray peacoat that can't even begin to put up a fight against the November cold, because it looks better than Big Puffer, the red North Face ski jacket with an overstuffed fleece lining that makes me look like a walking tomato. Grab a granola bar—

the kind with chocolate chips and frosting, even though every week I vowed to ditch the junk and start eating the Healthy Harvest Energy Sticks that taste like mulch. Spend an hour in the library, researching Legal Issues paper on *Roe v. Wade*, having ditched original topic—early twentieth-century treatment of sex crimes—after discovery that last year's PTA library committee had banned all relevant books as pornography. Meet with debate team for twenty minutes to strategize arguments for next week's topic: "Resolved: Restriction of civil liberties is a necessary element in any free society." Disband meeting prematurely when the cofounder of the philosophers club calls the president of the Student Republicans a fascist, and the president counters by kneeing him in the balls.

Eight forty a.m., homeroom in the yearbook office, approving layouts and trying to ignore the student life editor who wants my job muttering "bitch" when I veto his spread. Then four AP classes before lunch, with a quick nap while our alcoholic French teacher shows *La Gloire de Mon Père* for the fourth time so she can nurse her hangover in the dark instead of teaching us *le subjonctif*. A quick peanut butter and jelly sandwich by my locker, with a Twix bar for dessert—again, in spite of repeated resolutions to be healthy and satisfied with nonfat yogurt—then back to class for AP chem lab. Three more AP classes, two tests, one pop quiz on a history chapter I hadn't bothered to read. Two forty p.m., key club committee meeting to discuss fund-raising for upcoming convention, along with much debate over who will room together, in which I stay silent and hope not to get stuck with Shirley Penn, who doesn't wear deodorant.

Four to five p.m., read to the blind. Six p.m., cold pizza at the joint student council/senior class council prom planning meeting (pushed back until the evening so the jocks could shower after practice without missing a single scintillating moment of the ongoing "Some Enchanted Evening" vs. "Boogie Nights" theme debate). Seven to midnight, write a response paper on constitutional arguments for and against separation of church and state, read the chapter on Prohibition and discover all my wrong answers on the pop quiz, copy calculus homework answers from the back of the book with just enough scribbling and equations to make them appear legit, conjugate thirty French verbs, and translate a passage from *Les Misérables*. Then bed, and five hours of sleep—or two hours of nightmares, three hours of lying awake, worrying about the next day, the day after that, SAT scores, AP tests, finding a date for prom, and, now that Katie Gibson was out of commission, writing a valedictory speech and convincing the rest of the school that I hadn't traded the vice principal a blow job for the honor.

I drank a lot of caffeine in those days.

On the eighteenth day, I called him.

"Hey. It's Lex."

"Hey." He didn't sound surprised. Or particularly pleased. "What's up?"

"You mean, why am I calling, or how am I doing?"

"Pick one."

"I'm calling because you didn't."

There was a silence on the other end of the phone. "Was I supposed to?"

I wasn't sure what to say. *Yes? Of course not? Only if you wanted to—which you obviously didn't?* "So . . . how's it going?"

"You know. Busy."

"Busy doing . . . ?"

"You know. Stuff."

I hated myself for calling. "Okay, well . . . I should probably go."

"Wait!"

I waited.

"I really have been busy," Eric said quickly. "And I didn't think . . . anyway, uh, how's it going with you?"

"You want the official answer or the real one?" I lay back on my bed, stretching my toes out the way I used to do when I was a kid, pretending to be a ballet dancer. Someone told me once that my feet had great extension, whatever that means. I thought it meant I should be a dancer. My parents thought I was too clumsy, so I took piano instead. And then chemistry.

"What's the difference?"

"Official is what I'll tell the family at Thanksgiving next week. It involves a lot of fake smiling. Real is what I don't tell anyone."

"But you'd tell me?"

"No." I smiled, glad he couldn't see me through the phone. "I just wanted to hear which you'd pick."

"So, Jupiter is pretty close to the earth this week," he said.

"Should I be bracing for a collision?"

"I thought, maybe, you'd want to see it. With me."

"In your spaceship?"

He laughed, haltingly, like he wasn't sure if I was teasing him or making fun of him, but wanted to make it clear, either way, that he got the joke. "I know a place. Uh, Friday night?"

"That's a time," I said. "Not a place. Genius."

This time, his laugh was louder. "Ten o'clock. Should I pick you up?"

"Well, I can't meet you there," I pointed out. "Since I don't know where *there* is."

"Okay. Ten o'clock. See you then."

"This isn't a date," I said quickly, before he could hang up.

"Of course not," he agreed, faster than I might have liked. "Just . . . an astronomy lesson."

"Ready to tell me why we're here?" I asked Eric. He'd spent the whole ride babbling nervously about our AP government teacher, who'd recently given someone a detention for daring to suggest that the U.S. lost the Vietnam War. Since we'd arrived on campus and begun our long, cold walk through the silent Harvard Yard, he hadn't said much of anything.

"Not yet," he said.

"How about a hint?"

"How about a kiss?" he replied, and before I could react, tossed me a Hershey's Kiss. I fumbled it. Which was convenient, because if I was scrabbling around on the ground for a piece of chocolate, he wouldn't see me blush.

I popped the chocolate in my mouth and took a closer look at the wrapper, which glittered under the yellow sodium lights. "Are those . . . polka dots?" I asked, squinting at the dark blue smudges scattered across the silver.

"Jewish stars," Eric admitted. "They're leftover favors from my cousin's bar mitzvah."

I sucked on the Kiss, wanting to take my time and savor the taste, slightly bitter and, at the same time, a little too sweet. Just the way I liked it. "I didn't know bar mitzvahs came with chocolate," I said. "I should've had one."

"Bat," he said.

"Excuse me?"

"*Bat* mitzvah. It's what girls have."

I knew that. Or I should have known that. Seventh grade had been bat mitzvah madness—despite the fact that I was neither Jewish nor, in even the loosest sense of the word, popular, it seemed like every other weekend I was slipping into a ruffled dress, sitting through three hours of incomprehensible chanting, and then posing for a caricature artist while the rest of my class limboed across the dance floor and begged the DJ for a pair of oversize gold sunglasses or giant inflatable shoes. "But you didn't have one," I pointed out. Or at least I hadn't been invited.

"I'm not a girl," he said. "In case you hadn't noticed."

"I mean a bar mitzvah, obviously. You didn't. Did you?"

"Sort of. My parents thought the whole party thing was a 'gross commercialization of sacred tradition,' so instead we went to Israel for a week and I read my Torah portion by the Western Wall. Then we had a falafel dinner with my grandparents. Tons o' fun."

"That sucks."

He shrugged. "Not really—a *party* would have sucked. Dancing?" He shuddered. "Besides, that was back during my dad's religious phase, so at least he bothered to show up. When Lissa turned thirteen, they threw this whole black-tie thing with a band and these hideous Rockette type dancers—and my dad walked out in the middle to deal with a Japanese stock market crisis."

"What happened to the 'gross commercialization of sacred tradition'?"

"Like I said, a phase. Guess they grew out of it."

He was staring at the ground as he walked, and when I glanced over, I noticed the way his right ear stuck out a little from the side of his head. And the way his thumbs were hooked into his pockets while his fingers tapped out a rhythm on his jeans, like he was playing an invisible piano. I told myself to stop staring. I told myself there was nothing cute about his squarish black glasses or the way the corner of his mouth twitched right before he smiled, like an early warning system for his face.

I didn't look away.

"What about you? Did you grow out of it?" I asked, just wanting to say *something*, because if we went back to that comfortable silence, I would have too much time to think. And watch.

"I was never in it."

"You didn't go to Hebrew school or anything?"

"For a while. Max—my friend Max—"

"I know Max," I said, trying to keep the disdain out of my voice.

"He kind of got me kicked out."

"Max is *Jewish*?"

Eric shook his head. "No, but he used to come meet up with me after class, and one day . . . well, it was his idea, but I guess I . . ." He looked like he couldn't decide whether to be embarrassed or proud. "It was kind of dumb, but basically, we, uh, rigged the sound system to start playing 'Rudolph the Red-Nosed Reindeer' during the Hanukkah service—and also we, uh, snuck into the sanctuary the night before and stuck antlers and Santa hats on top of the Torahs."

I started giggling. "So basically, you're going to hell?"

"Not me," he said, tossing me another star-spangled Kiss. "Jews don't really believe in hell. You ask me, it's the best part."

"Why? Because it means next year you can string up some Christmas lights on your rabbi's roof with no divine consequences whatsoever?"

"No, it's not just the no consequences. There are no rewards, either. Or at least, no one talks about them much." We passed under the gate at the edge of the Yard, and in the moment of shadow, his expression faded into darkness, but I could tell from his voice that he wasn't smiling anymore. "That's the thing—in some religions, you're supposed to behave so that you don't get punished after you die, right? Or you're supposed to do good things so that you'll end up in some kind of eternal paradise. But Judaism isn't about what happens next. It's about what happens *here*, in this life. You don't necessarily get rewarded for doing the right thing; you don't get punished for doing the wrong thing. You're supposed be a good person just because that's the right thing to do. Doing the right thing—*that's* the reward."

I choked back a laugh. "You're claiming the universe runs on the honor system?" I thought about the teacher I'd had junior year who left the classroom every time we took a test. It was supposed to teach us honesty and responsibility; after the first test, it taught us that there was no point in studying, since as soon as she walked out of the room we could pull out our textbooks and copy down the answers. "Seems like a system doomed to fail."

"Only if you think human nature is inherently selfish, and that people will always do the wrong thing unless someone's policing them," he said. "I don't."

"Ahhh, so you're a romantic."

"I prefer realist."

"No, *I'm* a realist," I told him. "Because in the real world, people do whatever they have to, if it'll get them what they want. *Especially* when they know they won't get caught."

"Are we talking about 'people,' or are we talking about you?"

I crumpled the Kiss wrapper into a tiny, hard silver ball and rolled it back and forth between my thumb and index finger. Then it slipped out of my grip. I stopped abruptly, knelt down, hunted for it in the dark, partly because I didn't want to litter, but mostly because I didn't want to answer the question. "All people," I said finally, standing up again with the wrapper in hand. "Which includes you."

"I think you're wrong," he said.

"Not possible. I'm never wrong."

"Amazing—something else we have in common."

We ended up in front of the Science Center, where we'd started a month before, and he steered us through the revolving door. The last time I'd been in there—the only time—it had been filled with people, not just the ones going to class or taking a break from their labs, but real, live Harvard students checking their e-mail or eating a nasty-looking Chickwich from the nasty-looking snack bar. I had tried to imagine myself as one of them. *A year from now,* I'd thought, *this will be me.* But I couldn't see it.

At night, the place was deserted. It was like a high school on the weekend, or one of those Bermuda Triangle ghost ships where everything seems normal—lights on, half-full coffee cups on the table, music on the radio—until you realize there are no people. Anywhere. It was more than a little creepy.

Eric led us over the security guard's desk and flashed a student ID. The guard barely bothered to look; he just handed Eric a key and waved us toward the elevator.

"*You* have a fake ID?" I whispered.

He nodded, like it was no big deal that one of Wadsworth High's top five geeks had a fake ID, while I'd never even been to a party where they served beer.

"You have a fake ID, and you use it to sneak into the Harvard Science Center?"

"And what do you use *your* fake ID for?" he asked, in a way that let me know that *he* knew I didn't have one.

"Sneaking out of bad dates," I snapped.

"Good thing I don't have to worry about that." We stepped into the elevator, and he pressed the button for the top floor. "Since this isn't a date."

"What *is* this place?" I asked in a hushed, churchly voice. But *what* wasn't the right word.

The word was *when*.

Up the elevator, down a passageway, up a creaky stairwell, through a rusted door—and as we crossed the threshold, it felt like we'd stepped back in time. Eric led me into a perfectly round room with a domed roof. The walls were covered with glow-in-the-dark paintings of the stars, and in the middle loomed a massive machine, its gears and pulleys climbing up along a tube so wide, I could have crawled inside, and so high that, had I shimmied up its length, I could have pressed my hand flat against the ceiling. An old wooden ladder was propped against it, leading up to a small platform that met the tube at its midpoint.

A viewing platform, I realized.

It was a telescope.

"They built a new one a few years ago," Eric said, running his hand along the metal. "This one's so old, no one bothers with it anymore. Students are allowed to use it themselves, but . . . guess they all have better things to do."

I took a deep breath, nearly choking on all the dust. It felt like we were creeping through an archaeological site—like we'd stumbled on a lair of forgotten ruins, a moment from the past left behind as the future rushed in. "How do you even know about this?"

"Max's sisters used to bring us up here when we were kids. Now I just come sometimes on my own, whenever . . . well, it's a good place to get away from stuff." He was drumming his fingers on the lower rim of the telescope and darting his eyes around the room. I realized he was waiting for my verdict.

It was tempting to toy with him a little, but somehow it wouldn't have felt right. Not there.

I nodded. "Very cool. So what now?"

"First"—he fumbled around in his backpack and pulled out a paper grocery bag—"essentials." He tossed me two bags: a Ziploc filled with the remaining bar mitzvah Kisses, and a package of Mini Reese's Peanut Butter Cups.

"My favorites!" I ripped into the Reese's. "How'd you know?"

"You keep forgetting, I know—"

"Everything," I finished with him. "Right. So tell me this, how exactly are we supposed to look up at the stars"—I looked up at the metal dome—"through the roof?"

"That's step two." He headed toward the wall and flicked a switch, plunging us into darkness. Then, a low-pitched whine and the squeal of metal on metal.

"Look up," he said, his voice floating across the black.

I did—and, as the roof slid open like the hatch of a spaceship, I saw stars.

The ladder groaned with every step, but it wasn't very high. And I knew I wouldn't fall, not with Eric standing a step below me, his arms bracing me, his chin resting on my shoulder. "It should be in focus now," he said. "Just look through the eyepiece, and—"

"I see it!"

It was just a tiny gray circle with reddish stripes, surrounded by black. But it was a planet. I'd never seen anything like it.

"Can you see the two tiny white dots on either side?"

I squinted, and the image went fuzzy for a moment, then cleared again. "I don't think so, I . . . no, wait, there they are."

"Those are Jupiter's moons," he said. "Some of them, at least."

"This is incredible."

I felt his hand graze my arm, so gently that I thought I might have imagined it. "Yeah. It is."

"You'll laugh."

"Probably," I admitted.

We were sitting on the edge of the roof, the open dome beneath us and the lights of Boston and Cambridge spread out in every direction.

Eric sighed. "You really want to know?"

"Well, *now* I do," I said, giving him a light shove. "You've built it up too much."

"Fine." There was a long pause. "Batman."

I laughed.

"Shut up!" He tried to shove me back, but I grabbed his arms and wrestled them back down. His hands were icy. Our eyes met, and I let go. He was blushing. "I told you you'd laugh."

"You just told me you wanted to be Batman when you grow up," I pointed out. "What was I supposed to do?"

"I tried to give you the normal answer," he complained. "You said to think outside the box. You said my *dream* job."

"And then *you* said Batman." I started laughing again, letting myself slide backward until I was lying flat on the thin picnic blanket he'd brought along. Even with all the city lights, we could still see the stars.

"Well, not really, not with the costume or anything. And I don't want to live in a cave. But look, he's a millionaire, he's got all these amazing gadgets, he goes out every night and battles the forces of evil, he always gets the hottest—" He stopped abruptly.

"What?"

"Uh, cars," he said quickly. "Very cool cars. You telling me you wouldn't want a ride in the Batmobile?" He started ticking the advantages off on his fingers. "Cool car, cool toys, cool mission. That's my answer, and I'm sticking. Laugh all you want."

I had to admit, it was more interesting than his "normal" answer, something long, complicated, and impressive-sounding about designing affordable computers for the third world by using microprocessors that . . . well, that's where I'd tuned out.

Batman I could at least understand.

"I just want to . . . I know it sounds stupid, but I want to change the world," he said. "Somehow. Do *something*. You know?"

I knew.

"Okay," he said. "Your turn."

I took a deep breath, watching the dots of light over my head, remembering that when I was a kid, I'd thought every airplane was a falling star.

"When I grow up? My deepest, darkest, most laugh-worthy desire?" I shrugged. "I don't know. Ballerina? Vampire slayer? Top secret international spy?"

"Come on. Really. I told you mine."

What was I supposed to do? Admit that I didn't have a plan, laughable or otherwise? That the future seemed flat and finite, like if I tried to sail past the horizon of high school graduation, I might fall off the edge of the world? "Big Dipper," I said instead, pointing out to the west, or at least, the direction I thought was west. "It's the only one I ever learned to recognize."

"Okay, so we can cross astronomer off the career list. That's Orion."

"Oh." And now I was laughing at myself. "As far as I'm concerned, it's just a bunch of random white dots on a black screen. I can never tell where I'm supposed to connect all the stupid imaginary lines. Obviously."

"It's not so hard," he said. "I'll show you."

He lay down next to me, and we stared at the sky. The moon was only a sliver, but I could see his arm, reaching out toward the chains of stars. The night had a reddish glow.

Eric pointed out Cassiopeia, Andromeda, Pisces, the low-hanging bright star that was actually a planet, and, eventually, the Big Dipper. Half of me was paying attention, while the other half was noticing how close our cheeks were to each other, and the fact that if I rolled a little to the left, and he rolled a little to the right, we would collide, face to face.

The half-empty bag of Reese's lay between us.

"I don't know why no one comes up here," he said, propping his hands behind his head. "It's such a waste."

Someone came up there. But I decided not to tell him about the condom wrappers I'd seen in the trash. He was right. It was a waste.

I didn't know what I was doing. I'd forgotten all my plans for the night, and instead, I just lay there, totally relaxed, like all the crap that had been weighing me down was back on the ground, and as long as we stayed up there, in the dark, nothing mattered.

"What are you scared of?" he asked suddenly.

"What?"

"Before. On the bridge. You said you were scared of something, but . . ."

I didn't have to answer. I definitely didn't have to answer honestly. I was good at lying.

But I was also tired of it.

So I didn't say anything.

"You're scared of not getting in, aren't you?" he asked quietly.

"What makes you—"

"I can just see it. You look around, like you're trying to picture yourself here but you don't want to let yourself do it. Like you don't want to count on it, right?"

He said it, I didn't. Just remember that for later. *He's* the one who brought the whole thing up. All I could do then was tell the truth.

"Yes. That's what I'm scared of." Among other things. "It's like, what if, whatever I do, it's not enough? Everyone's expecting—and even if they say they're not, I know they are, my parents at least, and my teachers, and—what the hell am I supposed to do if something goes wrong? What happens then?"

"Alicia Morgenthal," he said quietly.

I didn't say anything.

"I was in that class, you know," he said. "I saw her. When she—when it happened. I was there."

I hadn't known that.

"You're not like her," he said. "You'd never . . . you're just not."

"You barely know me."

"I know you're different."

I squeezed my eyes shut for a moment, blotting out the stars. When I opened them again, the world seemed too bright. "I bet that's what her friends would have said, too. Before. You think anyone who knew her saw it coming?"

"I didn't," he said softly.

"What?"

"I was her friend. Sort of. I mean, I knew her. And I saw her that night—you know, that last night."

I propped myself up on my elbows and gaped at him, hoping I didn't look too nakedly curious. No one knew where Alicia had disappeared to in the hours between the inbox stuffed with rejections and the calculus class meltdown the next morning. "Saw her where?" I asked, trying to sound casual.

"She came over, and she—" He shook his head. "She didn't tell me about, you know. The rejections. She didn't really talk at all. She just . . . I should have known. I should have known something was up."

"How could you, if she didn't say anything?"

"Because she—" Eric broke off abruptly then contorted his face into a fake smile. "It doesn't matter."

I wanted to know more; I *needed* to know more. But I didn't want to push. So I lay back down and stared at the sky, waiting.

"It's got nothing to do with you," Eric finally said. "*You'll* get in somewhere great."

"Unless I don't." He couldn't understand. He'd been working for some professor at MIT for the past four years. They were probably begging him to go there. The first day of freshman year they'd probably send a limo and roll out a red carpet. And if he changed his mind about Harvard? It was his for the taking. As if the whole genius thing wasn't enough, his father was some big professor there—not only would they let him in, for all I knew they'd probably let him go for free. It wasn't his fault, but it was true. Me, on the other hand?

"There's nothing I can do about it, one way or another. I have no control."

"And you hate that most of all."

So he got me. So what? It didn't mean anything. I wasn't too hard to figure out. "I guess."

He didn't try to argue me into admitting that it didn't matter where I got in. And he didn't lie and say it would all work out the way I wanted it to. He didn't even look at me. When I glanced over, he was still staring up at the stars. But he moved his hand, just a little, to the right, until it was resting on top of mine. He wasn't holding it—he wasn't even pressing down. He was just touching it, as lightly as he'd touched my arm by the telescope.

"I'm sorry," he said.

"It's not like you did anything."

"Lex, there's something I should . . ." But his voice faded out.

I turned onto my side, and so did he. Our faces were almost touching. I'd only ever been this close to one other guy. Jeff had been taller than Eric, and better built; his eyes hadn't been as close together, he hadn't worn glasses, he hadn't had that crooked front tooth or a dimple when he smiled, his lips hadn't been so thin.

And I had never wanted to kiss him this much.

I hadn't stared at Jeff's lips wondering how they would feel and what they would taste like. Jeff always tasted like spearmint.

Why was I thinking about Jeff when I was staring at Eric?

Gazing. I was *gazing* at Eric, there was no other word for it—moonlight, whispered secrets, and *gazing*. It wasn't the kind of moment I'd expected someone like me to have. Especially not with someone like him.

"Eric . . ." I could see the broad contours of his face, but no more than that. It was too dark to read his expression. I wondered if he could see mine.

Kiss me, I thought, trying to force the words out of my head and into his. Someone was going to have to make a move. And it wasn't going to be me.

He brushed a piece of hair out of my face. He smiled, then opened his lips a little, as if he was about to say something, but was pausing, holding the words back. This was it. Sometimes life really

is like the movies, and even without a script to follow, you just know.
I knew.

He closed his eyes, leaned in.

And I rolled away. Sat up. Jumped to my feet. "I have a curfew," I lied. "We should really start heading back."

Okay, I hurt his feelings, I get that.

He didn't talk the whole ride back. I assumed he was embarrassed. But maybe he just couldn't get a word in, because I couldn't shut up: Did you see this movie, did you read that book, how'd you like that class, what did you think of that album, and on and on until I was on my doorstep and he was walking away as fast as he could without actually breaking into a run.

I could have explained to him that I was just trying to do the right thing. But he wouldn't have understood. Not unless I explained the whole thing. And I couldn't do that; he could never know about the mistake I'd made.

At least, not until I'd fixed it.

PHASE THREE

November 17
THE GAME
Objective: Observation of drunken admissions officer and sycophantic legacies

November–December
THE APPLICATION
Extracurricular, Personal, and Volunteer Activities
Educational Data
Supplementary Material
Personal Statement
Objective: Construction of irresistible on-paper persona

December 31
APPLICATION DEADLINE/NEW YEAR'S EVE
Objective: Completion, Submission, Celebration, Inebriation

13

During the next few days the thoughts of most of us will center on little besides football. . . . Harvard men, both graduates and undergraduates, feel an all-absorbing interest in their team which finds an expression at this season on every occasion that any number of us come together. . . . Such occasions, when entirely spontaneous, are not merely demonstrations over one team: they express in a wider sense the devotion of us all to the University.

—editorial attributed to Franklin Delano Roosevelt '04,
"The Devotion of Us All," *The Harvard Crimson*,
November 18, 1903

"*Ten thousand men of Harvard, want victory today!*"

Maxwell Sr. slung a meaty arm around his son's shoulders, his morning breath already sour with whiskey. A blond, beefy man on Max's other side joined the human chain.

"Sing along, Junior!" the guy on the left whispered hoarsely. "All together now."

They were swaying back and forth as they boomed out the fight song, matching idiot grins beaming from their faces like Girl Scouts in the throes of "kumbaya."

An endless flood of "buddies" was streaming by the Kim tailgate, dropping in for a drink ("the Crimson Tide"—a whiskey sour with red food dye), homemade rice balls, pork ribs, fried dumplings, French toast sticks, and a mano a mano chat with the boy of the hour.

"He's a spitting image!" Maxwell Sr.'s buddy from *The Crimson* said once the men ran out of lyrics. He grasped Max's hand and scattered flecks of saliva across his nose. "The spitting image of your dad. You're gonna love it here!"

"Got that application in yet?" asked Maxwell Sr.'s buddy from the Owl finals club—one of Harvard's over-privileged, over-inebriated, over-rated versions of a frat. He clapped Max on the back and took another swig of whiskey straight from the bottle. "Not that you need it, from your family. By now they should just let you Kims in automatically!"

"Where ya been, Junior?" Maxwell Sr.'s buddy from the golf team complained, tugging his knit Harvard cap down on his forehead, careful not to smudge the crimson H's painted on each cheek. "Haven't seen you here in years. You been on the *Yale* side?"

The men—a podiatrist, a corporate attorney, and a well-known journalist whose monthly column prophesized the imminent cultural collapse of the Western world—burst into a barrage of cursing and booing, shaking their fists in the general direction of the Yale tailgate zone, two fields and a parking lot away.

"We'll run them off the field, gentlemen!" one boomed.

"Send them crawling back to New Haven—"

"In tears!"

"Like the little babies they are!" Max's father concluded triumphantly.

"Yeah, *you'll* kick their asses," Max muttered, eyeing their spindly legs and beer bellies.

"What's that?" Maxwell Sr. wanted to know.

"We'll kick their asses!" Max shouted with feigned enthusiasm. "Ten thousand men of Harvard, right?"

It did the trick.

"Ten thousand men of Harvard, want victory today . . ."

Max faded back from the group as they got swept up in another chorus of the fight song. But his mother caught him before he could escape.

"Your father really appreciates you coming today," she said, putting a hand on his shoulder.

Max forced a smile. "Yeah. Well, I figured if it would make him happy . . ." He hadn't attended a Harvard-Yale game since he was nine: old enough to be humiliated by the family tradition and still young enough to throw a temper tantrum to get out of it.

"Does this mean you've changed your mind about next year?"

"It's done, Mom." Max grabbed a few French toast sticks, wrapped them in a napkin, and stuffed them in his coat pocket. "I know you guys don't like it, but I'm not changing my mind."

"We'll talk about it later," she said, patting his shoulder and then turning back to the pot of coffee she'd been stirring. It was untouched. The pitcher of Crimson Tide, on the other hand, was nearly empty. "Today is your father's day. So thank you for giving him the gift of your presence."

Parents. How was it they always knew exactly the wrong thing to say?

Max tried to fan the flames of his anger and disgust. *Look at him.* His father, a grown man, a research chemist, dressed like an over-grown frat boy with war paint smeared across his face. He was squeezed into a fake football jersey ten years too old and two sizes too small, stomping his feet and waving his arms like he'd been infected with the dancing plague. And no one was even giving him a second glance.

Welcome to the Game, the annual opportunity for Harvard undergraduates to experience what everyday life might have been like at a beer-drenched, football-crazed, Big 10 school, complete with bloody burgers and keg stands. And, more important, the annual opportunity for wealthy alumni to regenerate their school spirit—and lubricate their wallets—by wallowing in the muddy fields of their youth. The order of priority was less than subtle: The undergraduates roamed like livestock in a penned-in, mud-splattered field, guzzling thermoses of Gatorade-vodka, eating, dancing, hooking up, freezing, and, as the day wore on, pissing behind parked cars and throwing up in the porta-potties.

The alumni tailgates were more refined, at least at first. Recent alumni hovered by the undergraduate madness, huddling under banners—'03!, '04–'05!, '07!—and taking private joy in being iden-tified by a number once again. They pretended to remember their old friends and like their old enemies; they wandered through the undergraduate hordes, feigning surprise when someone noticed they were no longer twenty-one. By eleven a.m., once the cheap beer had done its work, the surprise was real.

Further from the center of things lounged the yuppies, alumni in their thirties who'd driven up from Westchester and Park Slope and Greenwich, bringing the shiny new car and shiny new spouse to show off to old friends, along with the standard 2.5 kids, always decked out in Harvard regalia, H bibs and crimson booties, waving tiny Harvard banners and zipped into fuzzy hoodies that read CLASS OF 2028! Max had a box of such crap in the back of his bedroom closet.

The final set of alumni, the middle-aged, balding, bearded men and Burberry-clad women, hung back on the fringes, where their elegant tailgates would be safe from the masses. There were battery-powered espresso machines, elaborate cocktails in thin-stemmed glasses, fading memories pulled out and polished to a shine, cashmere scarves, embarrassed offspring, camel-hair coats, and Harvard officials wandering through and glad-handing all the alums they could find, as if expecting that next multimillion-dollar donation to be handed off like a tip to the valet. It would begin as sedate as a museum fund-raiser, but by halftime—although watching the game was only a minor component of the Game experience—the only thing distinguishing them from the undergraduates was a better quality of beer.

It was Maxwell Sr.'s favorite day of the year. And as Max watched his father revel, he reminded himself that he felt nothing but disdain for this kind of thing; for Maxwell Sr., Harvard was a cult, and Max wouldn't be a true man—a true son—until he'd drunk the Kool-Aid.

Max's father caught his eye, waved, and his smile. . . . It looked like pride and unadulterated joy, though more likely, Max reminded himself, it was liquor. That didn't stop him from grinning back, flush with an instinctual pleasure that he'd made his father proud with such a small expenditure of effort. Then he remembered why he was really there, and all he felt was guilt.

Max joined Schwarz and Eric in the empty lobby of the Harvard Athletics front office, which was close enough to be in range but was locked up for the day. As usual, locks weren't a problem.

"Congratulate me, boys," Max said, sweeping into the lobby. "I—" He froze, staring down at Schwarz. "What the hell are you wearing?"

Schwarz was kneeling by the wall, a small receiver by his feet.

Feet that were clad in garish gold and silver sneakers, peering out from beneath a pair of ragged, oversize jeans whose legs were so wide, each would have fit Schwarz's whole head, Jewfro and all. Instead of his usual collared polo shirt, his scrawny arms jutted out from a gray tee emblazoned with a giant green pot leaf.

"Like it?" Schwarz asked, grinning.

Max gaped. "Are you on *drugs?*"

"Clay took me shopping. He is helping me be my own man," Schwarz said proudly.

Max turned to Eric, who held up his hands in protest. "Don't look at me. He's a big boy, he can pick out his own clothes."

"You, of all people, are defending *Clay Porter?*"

"Clay did not make me do anything!" Schwarz protested. "I am my own man."

"Want to explain to me how looking like Weird Al doing a bad Jay-Z impression counts as being your own man?" Max asked.

"*Clay* likes it," Schwarz said.

"Great idea, do whatever Clay tells you," Max said. "Excellent start on the whole standing-up-for-yourself thing."

"Clay says I have to stop doing everything you say," Schwarz said.

"Schwarz?" Max said, his tone dangerously sweet.

"Yes?"

"Can you do just one more thing I say?"

"What?"

"When you go home today, I want you to take off that dumbass T-shirt, roll it up into a tight little ball, and stick it up Clay's—"

"Can we get back to business?" Eric cut in. "Did you get it done?"

"Did I get it done? Who do you think you're talking to?" Max knelt down and flicked on the receiver at Schwarz's blinged-out feet. "Listen for yourself."

A scratchy voice burst through the small speaker, static-y but audible. "So nice to meet you, Mr. Atherton. And this is my son, of course. Jeremy. You've already heard so much about him."

"Mission accomplished," Max said, taking a deep bow. That was Mr. Atherton, as in Samuel Atherton III, veteran admissions officer and, more important for the day, Harvard College class of '82. Atherton was renowned for his Harvard-Yale game antics; bugging him would not only give them the final, unguarded insight into their prime admissions officer's character, but would offer them another shot to observe the competition. Not that there was much to be gleaned from legacy kids, who were in a completely different admissions category, separate from the hoi polloi. But listening to Atherton react to his petitioners, especially after they'd left and he was alone with his cronies and his gin, could give them just the leg up they needed.

Besides, it was easy and—for all but Max—painless. Maxwell Sr. had been only too happy to march Max over to the Atherton tent for a hearty introduction. After that, all it took was a stiff handshake, a pat on the back, a six-centimeter bug weighing less than three ounces slipped smoothly into a coat pocket, and they were in business.

"*So* nice to meet you, sir." A new voice blared out of the speaker, and this one was familiar. "I brought you something I thought you'd like—single-malt Glenmorangie."

Eric gaped at the receiver. "Is that *Salazar*?"

"My favorite!" Atherton's voice was already slurred.

"Of course it's his favorite," Max muttered. "We don't supply inaccurate intel."

"What a coincidence!" Bernard smarmed. "You have incredible taste, sir."

There was a shuffling sound, and then a distinct spattering of liquid. Two glasses clinked. "To Harvard!" Atherton shouted.

"To Harvard! The school of kings."

"Let's have another, young man," Atherton said. "'S great to meet someone with the proper respect for the institution."

"Oh, I couldn't agree more. So many young people today . . ." Bernard paused to clear his throat. "I don't want to speak ill of my peers, sir, but they just don't embrace proper values, wouldn't you say?"

"What did you say your name was?"

"Bernard, sir. Bernard Salazar. Here, take my card."

"This excrement is sickening," Schwarz complained. "Do we really have to listen to this?"

"Every disgusting minute of it," Eric said. "And you can thank Max."

"It's not my fault!" Max said. "I had to tell him we were coming today—he demanded to see where his cash is going. What was I supposed to do?"

"As a wise man once said, tell him to take his cash, roll it up into a tight little ball, and stick it up his—"

Max twisted the receiver volume up as far as it would go, so that each of Bernard's carefully prepared compliments came through loud and clear. "Look, he's getting the guy drunker, faster, which can only help things along," Max argued. "More to the point: The more time he spends with Atherton, the less he spends with us."

"This spy shit sucks shit," Bernard complained, leaning back against the wall. He'd ditched his usual style, or lack thereof, for a pair of tapered corduroys, a Harvard polo shirt, and a tweed jacket. "I'm bored."

The various forms of toadyism and sycophancy were finite, even for a seasoned pro like Bernard, so after a half hour or so of sucking up to the high and mighty, he'd abandoned the cause and, like a pestilent rat with a homing device, sought out his new friends to offer his assistance with their latest subterfuge. Though for Bernard, who was unaccustomed to working on anything but his tan, "assistance" translated loosely to "unwelcome suggestions, nosy questions, and an unending stream of complaints."

"Feel free to leave at any time," Eric said.

"Not that you're not needed here," Max added quickly.

"Right. Of course." Eric rubbed his eyes and began pacing back and forth across the empty lobby. They'd been in there for an hour listening to Atherton drinking, boasting, bashing Yale, and drinking some more. So far they'd learned that his first car was a Pontiac, his first wife a "Xanax zombie," and his first sexual experience at age nineteen, with a Wellesley field hockey halfback. It was all potentially useful information, but listening to a bunch of middle-aged assholes reliving their glory days made for a long morning.

And Bernard's presence made it even longer.

"Uh, guys?" Schwarz was still huddled by the receiver; it was his turn to take notes. "I think you will want to hear this."

"Sorry I'm late, hon, I couldn't get away." It was Atherton's voice. But the soft, breathy woman that spoke next was—according to Schwarz, expert on all things Atherton—definitely not his wife.

"I've been waiting for an hour," she—whoever she was—complained. "I was about to leave."

"Uh-oh, am I in trouble?" Atherton's voice took on a childish tone. "Have I been bad?"

"You know it." There was a long silence punctuated by some disgusting squishing noises.

"And that's my punishment?" Atherton asked. "I should be late more often."

"Shut up and—" This time, the silence was punctuated by some more squishy smacking, a couple gasps, and a long moan.

Eric leaned in. Bernard and Max smirked. Schwarz looked like he was about to throw up.

"What are they doing?" he squeaked.

Max clapped him on the back. "You see, Schwarz, when a man and a woman love each other very much—"

"Ohhh," the woman moaned. "I've been waiting all week for this."

"I tried to get away," Atherton gasped, his words tumbling out all in one breath. "These high school kids are like vultures, they won't let go."

"Poor baby," she murmured, and then there was silence again.

"Did you have any trouble convincing Paul not to come?"

"Nada. He's stuck at home with the kids. Ashley has the flu—vomit everywhere."

"But he let you get away?"

She put on an artificially sweet wifely voice. *"Oh, I'm so sorry, honey, but as a dean, I really have to be there to support my charges.* It was almost too easy. I've been feeling guilty all morning, but now here you are . . ."

"And here you are. . . ." The conversation ended, and once again, the porn noises kicked in.

Max, Eric, Schwarz, and Bernard stared at each other, frozen.

"A dean?" Max finally whispered, like it was too good to spoil by saying out loud.

Bernard had no such compunctions. "A fucking dean!" he shouted, jumping to his feet. "He's fucking a dean. Sweet." He flicked the receiver off. "So we're all done, right? We're gold."

Eric switched it back on, with a *don't touch my stuff* glare. "Meaning what?"

"Aren't you supposed to be some kind of genius?" Bernard asked. "He's cheating on his wife. With a *dean*. And we've got it on tape. The guy will do anything we want now. We're in. Which means *I'm* in."

"You want to blackmail him?" Eric asked incredulously.

Schwarz was nibbling at a thumbnail; Max's face was unreadable.

"*Hello?* Am I missing something?" Bernard threw up his hands in disgust. "You losers bugged the guy, and now he's handing you the bullets. Shoot the damn gun."

Max, still on the floor, tilted his head up toward Eric. "He's not completely wrong. . . . One could make the argument that it's too good not to use, don't you think?"

"No, I don't think! First rule of hacking: Be ethical. Remember?"

"The first rule of hacking is to get the *job* done," Max said.

"Not by any means possible," Eric countered.

"If you guys are gonna pussy out on me, I'll handle this myself." Bernard made a lunge for the receiver, but Max snatched it away. "Give us a minute, *Bernard*"—and from the expression on his face, it was clear that he would have liked to substitute another term— "my *colleague* and I here need to confer."

"I want out," Eric said, once they were outside.

"*What?*"

"Out. This is fucked up, and you know it. I'm not blackmailing anyone."

"Just calm down." Max put a hand on Eric's shoulder. Eric shrugged him off. "No one said anything about blackmail."

"You just—"

"I was only trying to soothe the savage beast," Max said, and Eric could tell he was doing everything to turn on the charm. The problem was that when you'd known someone for ten years, covered for them, nearly got arrested with them (twice), cleaned up their messes and their puke, charm lost its effectiveness.

"You want to do it," Eric said. "I can tell. You're thinking about it."

"Well . . ." Max kicked at the wall. "Of course I'm thinking about it! I'd be crazy not to. What we've got riding on this . . ."

"It's *blackmail*, Max! That's not just illegal—"

"Like we've never done illegal before. It doesn't violate the terms of the bet, and that's what counts. Anything else is just drawing an arbitrary line. Yes to cheating on the SATs, no to a little harmless—"

"It's not harmless!" Eric lowered his voice as a group of drunken lacrosse players stumbled by. "How do you not get that? It doesn't matter what the terms of your stupid bet say. This is different. We could ruin this guy's life."

"*Our* stupid bet. And you're being a little melodramatic, don't you think? What about the ends justifying the means? What about the cause?"

"Like you give a shit about 'the cause,'" Eric shot back. "All you care about is winning. So enjoy. But I'm out."

"Oh, give it up!" Max shouted. "If you're going to ruin everything, at least be honest about it. Don't give me this moralistic crap."

"It's not—"

"This isn't about blackmail and it isn't about Salazar," Max said. "It's about *her*."

"Her who?"

"You think I don't know what's going on here? You feel guilty, I get that. So what? She'll get in, she won't get in, whatever. It's not your problem."

"You're talking out of your ass," Eric said.

"The whole thing won't come down for months, and she seems

like a girl who goes after what she wants, so I'm sure even you can hit third base by then, maybe even slide into—"

"Shut up about her!"

Max leaned against the wall and tipped his head back. "So I take it we're done playing clueless?"

"This isn't about Lex," Eric said firmly. "But fine. You're right. I feel guilty. Happy now? This hack doesn't feel right—we're screwing people over, and now you've got Salazar involved, and everything's messed up."

"Giving you the perfect excuse to back out. To betray your best friend, just so you can get some."

"I'm not—" Eric took a deep breath, resisting the urge to punch the snarl off of Max's face. "I'm not betraying anyone."

"You can tell yourself that, if it makes you feel better, but you know we can't do this without you." Max dug his nails into the brick. "I can't do this without you."

"So don't do it at all. Just back out. What's stopping you?"

Max pursed his lips. "Nothing."

"Fine. Then do it without me, or don't. But I can't be a part of it anymore." He gave Max an apologetic smile, unsure of what he was apologizing for. Max could believe what he wanted, but Eric wasn't betraying him for a girl. No matter how it felt. He was just trying to do the right thing. And that meant walking away.

"Eric—wait!"

Eric stopped and turned. Max closed his eyes, drawing in a deep breath. "I can't back out," he said quietly.

"Why?"

"The bet. It's not twenty-five hundred dollars." His voice was now so quiet that Eric could barely hear him.

He took a step closer, feeling sick. "How much, Max?"

"There's some stuff you don't know," Max said. "Extenuating circumstances."

"Max?"

"The thing is . . ." Max thudded his head against the brick, then rubbed his hands through his spiky black hair like if he pressed hard enough, he could squeeze out the answer. "You'll think it was stupid, but when you hear the details, you'll see it was really genius."

Eric waited. He could feel his half-digested burger bubbling and churning.

"And it's not a problem. It sounds bad, I know it sounds bad, that's why I didn't tell you, but we're good. I've got it handled. I'm handling it. We're good."

"How much?"

Max shook his head.

"Max! *How much?*"

"Twenty-five thousand."

Eric pressed his lips together, trying to swallow down the bile. It burned his throat.

He spun away, unable to look at Max. Tried to process. Tried to breathe.

No yelling, he told himself. There had to be an out. Every problem had its solution, even something as unbelievable, as ridiculous, as offensive, as outrageous—*Calm down,* he thought. *Breathe. Figure this out. Think.*

He turned slowly, expecting Max to show some sign of shame or remorse. Or even fear. But, now that the truth was out, Max stood firm, meeting Eric's gaze without flinching.

"Twenty-five thousand dollars," Eric said.

Max nodded.

"How is that possible?" He kept his voice cool and measured. He shoved his hands in his pockets, where they could do no harm. "Where would the Bums even get that kind of money?"

Max sighed. "Remember a few months ago, when I bought up all that StasiTech stock?"

"And they lost their patent and it crashed?" Eric remembered. He'd invested a hundred dollars from his bar mitzvah savings account in Max's can't-lose endeavor. He'd lost. "You dropped a couple thousand, right?"

"Yeah . . . if a couple can be construed as ten. I lost everything. My whole savings."

Eric's eyes bulged. "How could you be so stupid?"

"You and Schwarz are the prodigies." Max shrugged, sounding far more listless than he looked. "I'm just . . . the idea guy. And sometimes my ideas are . . ."

"Moronic?"

"I was going to say, in need of some fine-tuning. But whatever. Semantics, right?" He gave Eric a wry smile. "The Bums, on the other hand . . . that whole buy low, sell high thing seems to have worked out a bit better for them."

"The Bongo Bums are *day traders*?"

"Yeah, and the best." Max linked his hands behind his neck. "I don't know how much they've got, but . . . it's enough to cover the bet. It was all their idea."

"But why?" It came out as half-question, half-growl. Eric's calm and rational side had put up a brave fight, but it was losing ground. "Why would you go along with it?"

Now Max did, finally, look away. "My parents are cutting me off. If I don't play their little game, do the Harvard thing, then I'm off the Kim meal ticket. And XemonCo . . ."

"They're paying you in stock options," Eric said, beginning to understand. "Which are worth nothing."

"*Yet.* But they will be. In the future—"

"In the now, you're broke."

"Broke and screwed. All thanks to Maxwell Sr." He looked up again, his face eager and hopeful. "But he hasn't won yet. I just need some starter cash, something to get me on my way. And this will be good for all of us—tell me you don't want a cut of twenty-five thousand dollars!"

"Tell *me* what you're planning to do if we lose."

"We can't lose. We *won't* lose," Max said defiantly. "And I'm not backing out. I need this too much." The fight went out of his voice, along with the huckster charm. It was just Max, naked and desperate. "I need you."

"I can't believe you did something so stupid."

"Believe it."

Eric sighed. "I can't keep lying to her," he said, almost to himself. "And if Clay gets in and she gets rejected . . ."

"Maybe you can just tell her the truth," Max suggested. "We could feed her info, like Salazar. She might be so grateful, she would—" Seeing Eric's expression, he shut his mouth.

Eric couldn't do it. He couldn't tell her anything. She'd never understand—and she'd probably never forgive him.

"You're my best friend," Max said. "Ten years. And how many times have I asked for your help?"

"Plenty."

"I don't mean like asking you to contribute to the term paper file or stash some evidence. I mean, how many times have I asked you for something big, something that I really needed?"

Never. Not like this.

"How long have you known this girl?" Max asked. "How well could you know her? It's not like she knows anything about you—half of everything you've told her is a lie."

Eric still believed in the cause. In some ways, Lex just made him believe in it more. But he didn't want to be the one who hurt her. On the other hand, Eric thought, what were the odds that Clay's application would have any impact on Lex's? Harvard got twenty thousand applicants a year; statistically, nothing Eric chose to do could have any effect. But that didn't mean she would see it that way.

He didn't want to lie to her anymore. He didn't want to screw everything up. But maybe it didn't matter what Eric wanted. Not today.

Max watched him closely. *Ten years,* Eric thought. It was a long time.

"No blackmail," he said finally. "Tell Bernard whatever you have to, but we're not playing by his rules."

Max sagged with relief. "Done."

"And we don't tell Schwarz. He'll freak out and go into Playboy Bunny panic land, and that won't help any of us."

"My lips are sealed."

"And if you lie to me again . . ."

Max shook his head, and held his hands out to his sides, magician-like. *Nothing up my sleeve.*

"If I find out there's more you're not telling me, I'm out."

"Which means?"

Eric sighed, pulled off his glove, and whacked Max's shoulder. "Which means, for the moment . . . I'm in. Let's get this thing done."

14

Immoral and cutthroat schemes have become so much a standard mode of academic survival—experts say it now begins in elementary school, and I've heard of kindergartners cheating on Field Day—that many students accept it as an unavoidable part of working the system.

—Alexandra Robbins, *The Overachievers: The Secret Lives of Driven Kids*

"I'm out."

I felt like I was in a high school production of *The Godfather*. Which, I suspect, was exactly what they were going for. I was sitting in a high-backed wood chair in front of a burnished red mahogany desk wider than my mom's Buick. They sat on the other side in identical leather armchairs, facing me down like I'd come to ask for a favor from the geek mafia.

"Meaning what, exactly, Alexandra?" In his sharp-edged voice, my name sounded like a threat.

"Meaning I don't want to do this anymore," I said. There were no windows in the basement, and the only light came from a small, Tiffany-style lamp on the desk between them. It cast both Bongo Bums in an ominous, reddish light.

Again, probably their intention.

"*You* were supposed to guilt-trip *him*," said the one on the left— I'd only met them in person the one time, and couldn't remember which was which. "Not vice versa."

"It's not a guilt trip. I just—I'm out." In the movies, it was usually that simple. Unless they killed you, and, cheesy *Godfather* trappings or not, these guys didn't really seem the type to whack me with a shovel and bury me in the backyard next to a dead pet hamster.

"We had a deal," the one on the right said. "You promised certain things. We promised certain things. We all agreed."

"And now I'm unagreeing." I wondered how many times I would need to repeat the point before it sunk in and I could return to the world of the normal, or at least the aboveground. "I'm out."

Imagine there was something you really wanted. Not something petty, like knee-high leather boots or a new boyfriend, but something major. Something so significant that it would change your life forever. And imagine that you wanted that thing the way a child wants, without perspective, without restraint, a whole-hearted longing that consumed your entire being with the certainty that life would not, *could not* continue without it. Imagine that, like a child, you had no control over getting your heart's desire. You couldn't do anything other than lie awake at night and wish, furiously, desperately, hopelessly—because, not actually *being* a child, you would know that wishing was useless. You would know that there are no magic wishes, no fairy godmothers descending with a wink and a wand. Still, useless or not, you would dutifully squeeze your eyes shut every night, curl your hands into fists, listen to your heart thud, and, like a child, let yourself believe that someone was listening when you whispered: *I wish.*

Now imagine that your wish was granted.

Imagine someone showed up on your doorstep uninvited and unannounced, and made you an offer. Everything you'd ever wanted on a silver platter, in return for a few small favors. It wouldn't cost you anything.

It would be wrong, sure. It would break all the rules.

But say that this person, this guy who looked less like a fairy god-mother than like the lead singer of a Belle and Sebastian tribute band, who'd singled you out for some reason he wouldn't explain, could guarantee you'd never be caught. Never get in trouble.

You would just get what you wanted.

Would you take him up on the offer? Or shut the door in his face, despite knowing that the universe doesn't give out medals for honesty? Good deeds go unrewarded all the time, and despite what the song says, that dream that you dare to dream almost never comes true.

Maybe there's no such thing as an offer you can't refuse; maybe you would have had the strength to turn him away.

I didn't.

The one on the right—he was taller, I noticed, and his lower lip curled down slightly, making his mouth look permanently puckered—leaned forward, his hands clasped together on the desk. "I don't think you get what we're saying." I could tell he was trying for low and threatening, but the natural tenor of his voice was too high. If I had closed my eyes, I might have mistaken him for a girl—and it occurred to me to ask whether the telemarketers ever confused him with his mother.

I cut off the impulse just in time.

The one on the left was trying to grow a mustache. Either that, or he hadn't noticed the wispy blond hairs sprouting out above his upper lip, which was possible, since they were nearly invisible, at least until you noticed them, and then it was hard not to stare. They looked like baby hairs, soft and super-fine, and though they were long enough to indicate they'd been growing for a while, there were still only about twenty of them. I realized he also had a couple growing out of his chin, like an albino billy goat.

"What's done can be undone," mustache boy said ominously.

"And what's built can be destroyed," added the one with the puckered smile.

"Before you ask what that means," mustache boy continued, "it means you."

Show, don't tell.

That's what they always say, right? So that's what I try to do, because I always follow the rules. But I didn't show it all, because nobody's perfect, even though some of us like to act the part.

Or maybe because I'm a coward.

So I *told* you I was ruthless, like a bulldozer, service and backstabbing with a smile; but I didn't back it up with details. I told you I wasn't a very nice person, then I acted like it wasn't really true.

I told you I didn't trade a blow job for the valedictorian spot.

Truth.

But I didn't show you what I traded instead.

So let's start over. A little show and tell. Emphasis on the show.

Picture me as a sixth grader, hair a little blonder and chest a bit (and *only* a bit) flatter, taping up a big poster board: ALEXANDRA FOR 6TH-GRADE PRES: X MARKS THE SPOT! The X was in a check box that looked like a ballot. I thought I was pretty clever.

But not as clever as I was the next day, when I sent an anonymous e-mail to Farrin Phelps suggesting she sneak a peek inside Katie Gibson's locker. That's where she found a love poem from Brett Lieberman to Katie:

You are the prettiest girl in school.
I think you're really cool.
If you think I'm a cool dude,
Will you let me touch your boob?

I happened to know that the answer was yes, and that Katie had let him touch it not once, but three times, up in the music room while they were supposed to be practicing their solos for the winter concert. I knew this because Katie Gibson was, at the time, technically my best friend.

Farrin Phelps was both the most popular girl in school and, until she discovered the note, Brett Lieberman's girlfriend. She also had a big mouth and a grudge-holding ability well beyond her years.

Katie Gibson was the only other candidate for sixth-grade class council president.

She didn't win.

Afterward, I didn't even feel guilty. Katie was the one messing with Farrin's boyfriend. And Farrin would have found out eventually. (Brett was barely smart enough to spell "boob"; no way could he have juggled four at once for very long.) Besides, winning felt pretty good—good enough to let me ignore a lot.

Lest you think that was a one-time thing, fast-forward to ninth grade. That's when things got bad. Teachers had been talking about our permanent records since nursery school, but everyone knows that nothing's *really* permanent until ninth grade. Colleges don't count anything before that.

If a tree falls in the forest and it's not noted in your application, does it really make a sound?

So there I was, determined to make my permanent, ninth-grade mark, and as far as I was concerned, that meant joining the newspaper staff. There was one spot left and it was going to either me or Ella Stryker. Ella may have been the better writer, but I wanted it more. Which I proved when Ella dropped out of the running to protest the fact that the newspaper wasn't printed on recycled paper.

Yes, I talked her into it. Or maybe it would be more accurate to say I guilted her into it. And it's possible that, in my zeal, I may have exaggerated some of the facts and figures of exactly how much devastation the *Wadsworth Courier* was wreaking on the environment. But once I was on the staff, I wrote a profile about her new pro-recycling campaign, so that's got to count for something.

Everyone was happy.

I think I've already mentioned that Evan Stein, student life editor of the yearbook, wanted my job. But I might have forgotten to explain that it was because he had been in line for editor-in-chief—

and deserving of it, whether you went by seniority or majority rule—until the principal explained to the yearbook sponsor that someone who'd been caught smoking pot in the parking lot, *twice*, wouldn't make the best role model for other students and should, if at all possible, be kept out of any prominent leadership positions.

Don't look at me. I didn't force that joint into his mouth. I didn't light it up.

I only called the principal pretending to be a reporter—technically true, since I still had my press pass from my two years at the *Courier*—and asked for his take on the administration's tolerant attitude toward stoners. And okay, I may have implied that a feature was in the works, with Evan and his imminent coronation for my prime example. It would have made a great article—so eventually, I'm sure someone would have written it. If you look at it that way, I was saving the principal—and Evan, and the yearbook, and the whole school, really—from public humiliation.

Fact: I didn't lie, cheat, steal, or bribe. I just used the information that was at my disposal, and I used it to my own advantage. I wasn't like that Florida cheerleader who tried to kill off all her rivals so she could make the team, or those kids in Virginia who were cheating their way through college.

I wasn't Bernard Salazar, groveling for cheat sheets and lunging for blackmail material.

I wasn't Max Kim, raking in the cash with forged term papers and last-minute homework answers.

I was Alexandra Talese, weasel, tattletale, mole, suck-up with a can-do attitude, willing to do what I needed to get what I wanted. And I guess I must have had a reputation, because they came to me.

◆ ◆ ◆

"We've already given you a show of good faith," the one with the micro-mustache complained.

"If you got into the system once, you can get in again," I told them. "Just change it back."

"Do you really want us to do that?"

I pictured graduation day. I pictured sitting up on the stage next to the principal, everyone staring at me, my extra tassel hanging from my cap and my speech neatly folded up on my lap. And then I pictured Katie Gibson sitting next to me, standing up and sauntering over to the podium, knowing that she was number one and I was number two.

It's not really winning if you're in second place.

Of course I didn't want them to do it.

"Yes," I said, leaning back in the chair, trying to look casual, as if I couldn't care less about such petty things. "She—" But I couldn't choke out the word *deserves*.

I deserved. Katie just *got*. But that's life, right?

"She can be the valedictorian. I don't care."

The clean-shaven one—who could have used some deodorant—frowned. "Do you know how much trouble it's going to be for us to bring someone else in at this stage?"

"I don't care about that, either."

They didn't literally show up on my doorstep, of course.

First they e-mailed me, some cryptic message that was just intriguing enough for me to meet them in Starbucks and hear them out. That was the end of September. They told me about the bet. And then they made me the offer.

"We want you to keep track of what they're doing." Back then, he hadn't grown the mustache yet, but he was still ugly, his blond hair already thinning enough that I could easily picture his future comb-over. "And when the time is right, we'll want you to interfere."

"You'll get close to Roth, he's their weak link," the other said. "Throw him off his game."

"Why would I get involved?"

They leaned forward, and that's when they made it: the offer I literally couldn't refuse.

"You want to get into Harvard, right?" the shorter one asked—they hadn't yet told me their names. "These guys are trying to screw you out of your spot. We can keep that from happening."

"There's a backdoor into the computer system," the taller one said. "You want to guarantee an A for Admit next to your name? All you have to do is say the word."

It sounded immoral, unethical, and, I was pretty sure, illegal. It also sounded too good to be true.

"If you can get into the computer system and change the decisions, why do you even need me? Why don't you just hack in and make sure this guy gets rejected?"

They looked at each other, eyes wide, then gaped at me in indignation. "That would be cheating!"

I laid my equipment on the mahogany desk, piece by piece.

The bugs.

The dossiers.

The RF jammer—disguised as a pencil—that I'd switched on during the SATs to interrupt Eric's transmission signal.

"You think you can get in on your own?" mustache man asked, arching an eyebrow. "Someone like *you*?"

I shrugged. The truth was, no. I didn't.

Typical Northeast overachiever, high SAT scores (and I was still hoping for those perfect eight hundreds, since the Oscar-worthy performance I'd put on for Eric had been purely for show), plenty of leadership positions, four summers of prestigious internships, some community services thrown in for good measure, and . . . that was it.

No national prizes. No prodigy-level skills. No Carnegie Hall performances or published memoirs or pending patent applications for new molecular constructs.

Nothing to set me apart. Nothing to make me special.

"I'll take my chances," I told them.

"Don't bother," the mustache warned me. I wanted to reach across the desk and pluck it out, hair by hair. "We can still get into the admissions system. You back out on us now, and we will."

There were beads of perspiration forming on his upper lip. I wondered if he could taste the sweat.

"You back out, you can forget about getting into Harvard. It's just as easy to type in *deny* as it is to type *admit*."

"You wouldn't do that," I said, calling what I hoped was their bluff. "You don't need me. Just find someone else."

"We could," the mustache said, "and if necessary, we will. But we don't like people who back out on their promises. We don't back out on ours."

"Do this one last thing for us, or we will make sure you don't get in," the other one said firmly. "We promise."

15

Occasionally candidates for admission make inaccurate or incomplete statements or submit false materials in connection with their applications. In most cases, these misrepresentations or omissions are discovered during the admissions process and the application is rejected.

—*Harvard University Handbook for Students*

Extracurricular, Personal, and Volunteer Activities
Objective: A dynamic, engaged, well-rounded applicant with interpersonal skills and leadership potential

"Please don't come back again," the receptionist at the Sunset Pines Retirement Home told Clay. "You frighten the residents."

At first, reading to the blind seemed like it would be a better choice—from the sound of his voice, no one would know that Clay looked like an ex-con—but the reading part posed a problem. Not that he was illiterate.

Not quite.

The dog that bit him at the humane society wasn't rabid; nor was the squirrel with the broken paw. But when the angry red scratches on his arm got infected, they decided to call that quits as well.

The engineering club staged a mutiny when Eric requested permission to induct Clay—until, as president, Eric amended the bylaws and added Clay as a member at large, no attendance required. And the captains of the chess club and the academic decathlon team were only too happy to tell anyone who asked that Clay was a full and valued member—at least once Clay offered his guarantee that no one would flush their heads in a toilet anymore.

All was well, then, for Wadsworth High's chess wizards and burgeoning bridge builders; Eric, on the other hand, had vowed to infuse some element of legitimacy into each of the extracurricular endeavors. Which meant: late nights in a mildewed basement soldering stereo wires while Clay retooled an amp (engineering). Afternoons watching old game show tapes—including Max's tenth-grade championship run on *Teen Jeopardy*, a string of victories that ended with a spectacular meltdown when Max bankrupted himself in the final Final Jeopardy, thanks to an ill-timed inability to remember a name that had haunted his nightmares ever since: Alger Hiss (academic decathlon). A painfully long Sunday trying to explain the rules of chess, a day that, pathetically, culminated in Eric losing three checkers games in a row.

They had more luck with the invented organizations. Clay was soon president of the Art Appreciation Society, which, according to its mission statement, "toured local galleries and museums to perform a critical analysis on current trends in modern art within the context of the classical establishment and, in order to foster the creative spirit within the community, conducted weekend and after-school art classes for children deprived of a curriculum-based outlet for their artistic efforts."

Mostly true: For the sake of Clay's faux-art portfolio, they had indeed visited nearly every gallery in town. And, as for deprived children, the two hours Max had spent airbrushing Lissa Roth's yearbook photo while Lissa batted her eyes at Clay easily counted as a weekend graphic arts tutorial.

As president of the Skeptics Society, Clay—hypothetically—moderated discussions on philosophical attempts to comprehend the universe, from Sextus Empiricus, Montaigne, and Descartes through Kant, Kierkegaard, and Hume, focusing on the transition from Enlightenment to Romantic efforts to establish a fundamental order and rationale in the natural world. There was no need for the admissions committee to know that the in-depth roundtable debates largely raged around the competing world views presented in *Star Trek*, the collected works of Vonnegut, *Battlestar Galactica*, *Star Wars*, *The Hitchhiker's Guide to the Galaxy*, *The Matrix*, and—Clay's chosen font of philosophy and only contribution to the discussion beyond a glazed and confused stare—*Sin City*.

"Life is shit and then you die," he said. "That's like, a philosophy or whatever, right?"

And so it was.

The real coup required neither fraud nor forgery—and even Max had to admit that a little full-fledged legitimacy would make their victory that much sweeter.

"Marvelous!" the owner of the Bishop Gallery had exclaimed, gazing at the miniature canvas covered in white paint with a nearly invisible black dot at the center. "How many more are there?"

The show hung for a week. The "gallery" was, by day, a meeting room in the back of a Somerville bowling alley that still stunk of beer and sweatsocks, but Clay's work was enough of a hit to score a mention in the *Cambridge Firebird*, an indie arts zine published every few months by a pair of militant vegans who dreamed of some-day printing on recycled paper laced with LSD.

No matter. A show was a show; a news clipping was a news clipping.

And Clay Porter was officially a star.

Educational Data
Objective: 4.0

"We did the extracurricular crap your way," Max said. "This, we do mine."

Eric was pacing back and forth across his den. "We could use the weak transcript to make him look deep. You know, position him as the brooding intellectual who's *beyond* high school."

Max shook his head. "Cs say deep. Fs say community college. They'll never overlook that, and you know it."

Eric did. And he also knew it was ridiculous to even hesitate. There was no room for error, not with twenty-five thousand dollars at stake. Forging a transcript was no worse—no better, maybe, but no worse—than scamming the SATs. It wasn't necessarily the most stylish way to win, but it was clearly permitted by the terms of the bet. It would hurt no one. And, he told himself, it was in service of a greater cause—a cause that, despite everything, he still believed in. *The ends justify the means.*

Right?

◆ ◆ ◆

Ms. Winters didn't like Eric. He didn't need her.

Not that she liked the students who *really* needed her, the deadbeat delinquents who either skipped meetings or, when they showed up, inevitably broke something. No, she preferred to stick with the timid, terrified honors students, the desperate ones willing to take advice from anyone, even a middle-aged, overmedicated burnout whose own internal guidance system had steered her directly toward a twenty-year career in the Wadsworth High School guidance department. They nodded eagerly upon receiving her flimsy advice. They pretended to believe that she cared—or maybe they were clueless enough to buy the act. Eric Roth, on the other hand, was not.

But she accepted his request for a meeting, listening as he laid out his plans for the future. The all-purpose placid smile masked her true opinion: *What a geek.*

She would have liked nothing more than to shut him up with a detention, a suspension, anything that would blemish his disgustingly perfect record and force him to realize that he wasn't so superior after all. But of course, the kids like Eric would never get into that kind of trouble.

They were too weak, too cowardly, too dull.

Eric was still talking, something about MIT and extension courses and since she couldn't have cared less, she was relieved when the call came in, alerting her that she'd left her headlights on. "I'll be back in a moment," she said apologetically, and then strolled out to the parking lot, hoping he would be gone by the time she got back.

She was so grateful for the temporary reprieve that it didn't occur to her to wonder how she could have left her headlights on when she hadn't turned them on in the first place.

And it certainly never occurred to her that while she was gone, perfectly boring Eric Roth was digging through her cabinet of Permanent Files, slipping out the manilla folder marked CLAY PORTER, making a series of speedy photocopies, and then slipping everything back into place exactly as it was (just as Max had done when he'd let himself into her car).

If she had known, maybe she would have liked him better.

Suman Agarwal had one, and only one, job in the Harvard University admissions office. He was to pull the transcript and secondary school evaluations from the application file. Scan them into the computer system. File the hard copies in the metal filing cabinets along the wall. Then he would move on to the next application, and the next, ad infinitum, ad nauseum.

It was simple. Especially for someone who'd developed a new method for synthesizing organic molecules when he was only seventeen. Someone like Suman. Even simpler was the one rule he had to follow: Let no one else touch the applications. The admissions officers would read them online, from the comfort of their own home. A trusted secretary opened the packages, sorted the materials, and passed the transcripts along to Suman; no one else in the office was to have contact with the raw materials.

Even Schwarz, the most diligent employee that the admissions office had ever seen, was never allowed across the sacred threshold. When he brought Suman coffee, or Doritos, or gossip, or whatever else he thought might brighten Suman's day, he was always stopped just outside the filing room.

Until the day that Suman let him in.

"Are you sure, man?" Suman asked, one eye on his watch and one foot out the door. It was his one-month anniversary with his pissy girlfriend, who had gotten even pissier upon learning that Suman was too busy scanning in applications to treat her to a surprise anniversary picnic at Walden Pond.

Enter Schwarz.

"No one will ever know," Schwarz assured him. "It is just for one afternoon. They will never realize you were gone."

"I owe you one. If I had to spend another day down here . . ."

"I am sure it is not so bad," Schwarz said. "At least there is no one looking over your shoulder. It sounds peaceful."

"Yeah, peaceful like a crypt." Suman handed over the keys to the filing cabinets, the code for the scanner, and the security password for the digitized files. "Remember, you can't tell anyone."

Schwarz grinned. "You can trust me."

Fifteen minutes later, Clay Porter's permanent file—the one submitted by the Wadsworth High guidance department—was stuffed into Schwarz's monogrammed L.L. Bean backpack. A lovingly made fake had been inserted into the file and scanned into the system, detailing Clay's A-plus performance in every AP class Wadsworth High had to offer. The forged recommendation from guidance confirmed that Clay Porter was "enthusiastic and engaged, ravenous for knowledge and intellectual challenge—a joy."

Schwarz spent the next four hours scanning in files, but when you could calculate cube roots in your head while simultaneously playing out a game of mental chess, time passed quickly. And in the end, a few hours and more than a few paper cuts were a small price to pay.

Supplementary Material

Objective: Demonstration of exceptional artistic talent

The portfolio of slides included:

Distance: The white space on this canvas represents the emotional space between man and woman, while the narrow blue border indicates the tie of humanity that binds us together, disguising the empty space as a material presence. Note the smooth brushstrokes giving way to a rough patchiness, to evoke the active tension between turbulence and peace.

Lost and Found: An experiment in mixed media juxtaposing two found objects—the crumpled newspaper clipping and plastic bottlecap—with a patchwork of earth tones rendered in oil. The artificial and the natural, tied to the canvas, and to each other, with a homemade tar of honey and liquid polymer, exist in a symbiotic relationship, the balance maintained by the empty strip along three edges symbolizing boundless—but not unbounded—possibility.

Blue 6: The sixth in a series of color studies investigating the emotional qualities of light, the two-dimensional quality of the blue sphere, with its flat color and sharply defined edges, exposes the fragility at the core of the human experience while reveling in the strength of purpose to be found in the embrace of that fragility. The black outline and the white background offer a geometrical explication of human companionship, while the salt particles glued across the canvas reflect both the bitterness of interconnectivity and the ascetic purity of an ocean devoid of life.

While Max had supplied the necessary interpretive support, Clay himself had created the "art." One afternoon, six pots of paint, ten canvases, three brushes, one half-full kitchen trash can . . . and an artist was born.

Also included in the thick portfolio were photographs and clippings from the Bishop Gallery show, as well as an authentic and glowing recommendation from Arik Stella, the Wadsworth High art teacher, an embittered Rhode Island School of Design drop-out who found Clay's work to be: "A welcome respite from the normal high school dreck, dominated as it is by the assumptions and strictures of the Western art hegemony. Demonstrating a remarkable openness to Eastern ideas and a welcome willingness to attack the status quo with his subversive message of alienation and connectivity in the modern Western world, while eschewing the mundane representational efforts more typically seen among the brainwashed high school masses, Clay Porter demonstrates a talent and vision well beyond his years."

Days later, on the forceful recommendation of Maxwell Kim (Clay's "artistic manager"), the owner of the Bishop Gallery paid Arik Stella a surprise visit. Stella just so happened to have his work assembled for display. He was—again on the recommendation of Maxwell Kim and the unsolicited opinion of two anonymous "collectors"— offered a weeklong showcase of his mural-size works, each featuring a variety of leaves and feathers glued to the canvas with a glue made from birdshit.

But surely that was just a coincidence.

Personal Statement
Objective: Heartwarming, tear-jerking, awe-inspiring, chees-erific chronicle of a "significant life experience"

"So what now?" Clay asked as he finished with his life story and Eric turned off the digital recorder.

Eric shrugged, trying not to meet his eyes. "I'll write it up, pretty much like you said. Except, you know, smooth it out a little, make it more inspirational, and, um . . . tack on a happy ending."

"Like I saw the error of my ways and cleaned up my act and all that shit?" Clay rolled his eyes, stretching out on the Roths' new sofa and kicking his legs up on the glass coffee table. "And now my life is all rainbows and ponies?"

"Pretty much." Eric didn't know where to aim his eyes. He didn't want to look at Clay, but everywhere else he turned, he was staring at some overpriced electronic gadget, whether it was the flat-screen TV, his father's BlackBerry, or the five-hundred-dollar electrostatic germicidal air purifier his mother had just ordered from The Sharper Image. Nor did he want to look toward the kitchen, where his mother was heating up some left-over takeout while Lissa complained that they never got a home-cooked meal.

Instead he stared down at his hands. "Sorry about . . . all this. Schwarz checked through the archives, and statistically, this kind of essay's going to give us the best shot. We just figured, you know, when in doubt, honesty's the best policy and all."

"Honesty?" Clay snorted. "Sounds like you're gonna turn it into some happily ever after bullshit." He pulled out a lighter;

Eric didn't say anything. There was some air freshener stashed under the couch that would take care of the smell. "Whatever. You do what you gotta do. But you're not gonna make it sound like I'm whining, right? Because that's not what I'm about."

Eric shook his head. "No whining."

They sat in silence for a moment, both of them watching the floor.

"So . . . maybe we should try rehearsing for the interview again?" Eric suggested.

The Binder of Power contained a series of scripted answers. The plan was for Clay to memorize three of them each week, in the hopes he'd be ready by February. But Clay had already fallen behind.

"Clay, can you tell me why you'd like to attend Harvard?" Eric asked, dropping his voice a register in imitation of Samuel Atherton.

"I, uh, yeah. The thing is—"

"Make sure you look up when you talk," Eric said. "Eye contact, remember?"

"Yeah. Right. Forgot. Okay, so I want to go to Harvard because . . . the educational opportunity that it offers would be . . . uh . . ."

"Superior to . . . ," Eric prompted him.

Clay gripped the edges of his chair. "Superior to, uh, anything else. I want a, uh, athletic challenge—"

"Academic challenge."

"Academic challenge, and also a, you know . . . those people in the, uh, community that I can, uh, commune with. Artistically. And immerse, also. With the people."

The line was: *As an aspiring painter, I'm eager to immerse myself in such an artistic community.*

Eric smiled tightly.

"We'll just do a Cyrano, wire him for sound and feed him the answers," Max had said, but once again, Eric had insisted on doing things the hard way.

"Shit!" Clay smacked the end table, hard. "I got this, man. I know I can."

"There's still time," Eric said. "Take a break for the rest of the day. We'll get it."

"I'm not an idiot," Clay growled.

"Yeah. I mean, no. Of course not."

"I can get this. I can do it."

And Eric suddenly realized Clay wasn't angry at him. "I know you can," he said, hoping it was true—and not just because he wanted to prove something to Max. He stood up and pocketed the digital recorder. "But not today. I've got to type up the essay. There's plenty of time to get ready for the interview. The important thing this week is the application."

Clay stood up, too, and followed him to the stairway, his fists still clenched.

"You want to see it?" Eric asked, hoping he would say no. "The essay? When we're done writing?"

"What? See the way my life could've turned out, if this was some kind of fairy tale?" Clay shook his head. "All I want to see is the cash. You just do what you got to do to get it."

Personal Statement
By
Clay Porter

*In 1,000 words or less, describe an experience in your
life that has shaped the way you view yourself or the
world around you.*

I never knew my father. According to my mother, I'm
probably better off that way. Mom and I were on our
own, and that's the way we liked it.

It wasn't quite a trailer park we were living in, but it
was close. I slept in the "master" bedroom, which was
about the size of an SUV. I complained about that once,
after I slept over a friend's house, but my mother just
told me I was lucky we weren't living in her car. After
that, I didn't complain anymore. I also stopped going to
sleepovers. Mom slept on a fold-out couch in the living
room, her feet pressed up against the tiny stove and
mini-fridge that served as our kitchen.

She wasn't an alcoholic, like the woman who lived
next door, and she didn't have a boyfriend in prison,
like the woman two doors down. I wasn't afraid to come
home, like the two kids across the street who always
hung out on our front steps until their stepfather passed
out for the night. And even though I didn't see her that
much—she never held a job for more than a few months,
but she always *had* a job, and she always worked the
graveyard shift—I got along with her. I knew she was
doing everything she could to give us a life. I knew
I was lucky.

I just didn't feel lucky.

I couldn't invite friends over. It was too embarrassing. I couldn't tell anyone at school where I lived, or why my clothes were always the wrong size. I couldn't tell my teacher that my mother hadn't paid the electricity bill that month, and I couldn't do my homework because it was too dark. I couldn't stand up for myself with my mouth . . . so I did it with my fists.

I was seven when I got suspended for the first time, and the second. It happened again when I was eight. Fourth grade I got sent home for fighting six times. In fifth grade, they told me if it happened again, I wouldn't be allowed back.

I said I didn't care, and I meant it. That's when the principal closed the door to his office. And then, instead of sitting back down behind his desk, he came over to me and knelt down on the ground in front of my chair.

I laughed in his face.

"No one's watching," he said. "You don't have to act tough for them. And you don't have to act for me, either—because I can see through it."

I would have laughed again if I hadn't been so close to crying.

"You think you don't have a choice," he said. "But you do." Then he told me about where he'd come from and what he had accomplished, and where I would end up if I didn't start to change. He told me about the value of education and what I was throwing away. I wasn't listening to any of it. But then he said it again.

"You have a choice, son. Things can go on the way they are now, *forever*—or you can choose to give yourself a future."

No one had ever called me *son* before.

And no one had ever told me that I had a choice.

He didn't think I was too stupid to learn, and he didn't think I was too undisciplined to teach. He didn't think I was lazy or violent or hopeless. He just thought that no one had ever explained to me what I was passing up—and he was right.

My mother never went to college and, according to her, my father didn't either. But *I* will. That fight in fifth grade was the last one I ever had, just like that was the last year I got an F, the last year I skipped a class, the last year I got sent to the principal's office. I never even spoke to him again, since the next year I went off to middle school. So I never got to thank him for showing me the truth: I didn't have a father. I didn't have any money, or nice clothes, or a big house.

But I had a brain, and I had a choice. I chose the future—and I never looked back.

16

> ## December 31
> ## APPLICATION DEADLINE/NEW YEAR'S EVE
> *Objective: Completion, Submission,*
> *Celebration, Inebriation*

Take a deep breath and celebrate! . . . It's been a long haul, but you're almost there.

—Sally P. Springer and Marion R. Franck, *Admissions Matters*

D ecember 31, one p.m., and the packet was in the mail.

The four of them lay on the floor of Eric's den, the shag rug tickling their necks.

"I'm too tired to move," Max complained.

"You've done nothing but sleep since Christmas," Eric reminded him.

"Too much sleep makes you sleepier—it is a scientific fact," said Schwarz, who had given up on his new "tough" wardrobe after getting scabies from a thrift store leather jacket. He was back in polo shirts.

"This shit is pure," Clay drawled, taking another deep pull off his joint. "You sure you don't want some?"

"*You* sure you'll be able to get the stink out before my parents come home?" Eric asked, even though the last time his parents had ventured down to the den, it had been to make sure a six-year-old Eric hadn't changed the channel from *Barney* to *Crossfire*. Again.

"I'll try some of that." Max raised himself up on his elbows. He reached out, but Eric gave him a swift whack in the ribs before he got very far.

"My sneakers still smell like puke from your last trip to the dark side," Eric said. "You want to experiment, take it to your house."

"You want me to beat him up for you?" Clay said.

"Him or me?" Eric and Max asked at the same time, then burst into laughter.

Clay shrugged, as much as it was possible to shrug when you were lying on your back, stoned out of your mind. "Whichever."

"Just turn it off," Max complained, when Schwarz's phone began ringing for the third time.

"It could be important." Schwarz picked it up.

"Schwarz! Thank God, where have you been?" It was Stephanie, sounding desperate.

"Um, hello. I am kind of in the middle of—"

"I need you!" she screeched. He held the phone away from his ear.

Eric rolled his eyes. "Is that her?"

"Just remember, dude, be tough," Clay advised him. "The bad boy with a little hurt inside."

"Or you could just hang up on her," Max suggested. "That's tough."

"What is it, Stephanie?" Glaring at his friends, Schwarz got up and huddled in the far corner.

"Well, you know I came back to town for the big New Year's black-tie thing at the Pudding?"

Schwarz hadn't known—hadn't been invited, and couldn't keep Harvard's million and one black-tie events straight. It was only December, and there had already been four tuxedo-required freshman events . . . although Schwarz, dateless as always, had attended none of them.

"And Tyler *promised* he'd take me, but he totally flaked, just like always, and now I'm totally screwed, Schwarz, and I can't go to this kind of thing without a date—"

Be tough, he told himself. *You are* not *her backup plan.*

"Come on, there's going to be all this ballroom dancing, and you can help me practice my salsa, you know I can never get the footwork right—"

Schwarz winced, glancing over at his friends and hoping they hadn't overheard. The last thing he needed was for Max to find out that he'd been accompanying Stephanie to her weekly ballroom dancing lessons, after her original partner had backed out. It was humiliating, but it was also an hour each week that he got to spend with Stephanie's arm around his waist and her hand lodged in his. Plus, she had begged.

"So will you?"

"Will I . . . ?"

"Be my date tonight? Come on, Schwarz, it's New Year's Eve, I have this awesome new dress, you have to come."

"I do not have a tux."

"Not a problem. I already checked, and there's a rental place that's open till eight."

"I kind of have plans. . . ."

There was a long sigh. "Yeah. Of course you do. It's New Year's Eve. It's just . . ." She sniffled. Stephanie was an amazing crier. Most of the time she was loud and confident and sure of herself—some might say too sure of herself—and then, without warning, tears would explode out of her and she would crumble. "It's New Year's Eve," she got out, in between whimpers and gasps. "Who am I going to kiss at midnight?"

"What time should I pick you up?"

"It's ten to midnight," Eric said. "You want to shut this off and catch the ball drop?"

Max paused *Empire Strikes Back* and switched to NBC.

"You could've gone with Clay on that pub-crawl thing, you know," Eric said, stuffing a handful of popcorn in his mouth. "I wouldn't have minded."

"What, and miss all the excitement?"

"It's a *Star Wars* marathon in my parents' basement," Eric pointed out. "Not exactly an explosive way to ring in the New Year."

Max tipped the popcorn bowl to his mouth and guzzled down the remaining kernels. "Doesn't matter. It's tradition."

The clock ticked down. A series of lame one-hit-wonder bands played to the Times Square crowds, their hands too frozen to hit the right notes and the crowd screaming too loudly to notice. The announcers made annoying small talk, and everyone stared at the sparkling ball, waiting for the drop.

At five minutes to midnight, there was a knock on the door.

Schwarz was shivering, his tuxedo jacket dusted with snow, his shoulders slumped.

"Don't tell me," Max said. "The boyfriend showed up at the last minute. And she waved bye-bye to her backup date."

"Max." Eric quieted him with a glance. "Come on in, Professor. It wouldn't be the same without you."

"How far did you get this year?" Schwarz asked.

"Halfway through *Empire*," Max said, handing him a fizzing glass of cheap champagne. "But we fast-forwarded through most of Episodes One and Two. Of course. How far did *you* get? Under her shirt? Into her—"

"*Max.*" Eric shook his head. "It's okay, Schwarzie. Who needs women when you've got Jabba the Hut? Maybe it's time to accept that this is it for us. New Year's Eve 2058, we may still be sitting here, with our walkers and our colostomy bags, watching *Star Wars*, Episode 107."

"Speak for yourself," Max said. "I plan on spending my golden years with a harem of lovely ladies. And said golden years begin the day after graduation."

"How much are you budgeting to pay these lovely ladies for the honor?" Eric asked, smirking.

"Just because you already have a girl—"

"Shut it, Max. I haven't even talked to her in weeks." *And you know why,* he wanted to add, but didn't. Not when they were celebrating. It was New Year's Eve, maybe the last one he would celebrate with his two best friends, clinging to old traditions in his parents' basement. Next year they would still be in Boston together, but high school would be over, everything would be different—and even the strongest of traditions didn't always last.

He didn't want to think about it, but he also didn't want to fight. Not with them—not tonight.

"You should call her," Max said. He reached for the phone. "Or maybe *I* should—"

Eric smacked his hand away. "It's not going to work, okay? We don't fit."

"Give me one good reason," Max demanded.

I lied to her, Eric thought. *I'm still lying.*

"She's obsessed with rules," he said aloud. "She's a total control freak. Everything has to be exactly the way she wants it to be. Everything has to be safe. And I—"

"Yeah, you're danger boy," Max said sarcastically.

"I happen to believe that disorder is good for the soul."

Schwarz lurched forward so abruptly, he nearly spilled his champagne. "It is like the two laws of thermodynamics!" he blurted. "She is conservation of energy, orderly systems, productivity. And you are entropy. Disorder. Chaos. Two opposing forces that seem contradictory—but fit together perfectly to govern the universe as we know it."

"Geeky but freakishly brilliant, Professor," Max said approvingly. "Just like you. That's it, Eric. Order and chaos. It's not destiny, it's science: You two are meant to be."

But Eric wasn't listening. He was in another place, another time, shivering on a street corner in Kendall Square, babbling about the laws of thermodynamics while steeling himself to ask the almost-pretty control freak on a date.

And he was reminding himself of all the reasons that he couldn't—shouldn't—ask her on another one.

"You still with us, Eric?" Max asked. "Are you . . . it's not possible . . . *blushing*?" He slapped hands with Schwarz. "We have definitely achieved blushing!"

"Drop it!" Eric said, trying to shake himself out of the memory. He raised a glass of Champagne, trying to ignore the fact that his cheeks were warm. "One minute to midnight. Resolutions, boys?"

Max shook his head. "Screw resolutions. We've got everything we need right here. Why change anything? Instead, a toast." He raised his glass. "To winning."

"To winning." Eric clinked his plastic glass against theirs and downed the cheap Champagne in a single gulp. He had to stop thinking about the past, about all the ifs and maybes and might-have-beens. He still had his best friends; he still had the hack. Soon, if all went well, he would have one third of twenty-five thousand dollars. He would have his principles; he would have his victory.

Maybe, once he had all that, he would no longer need to have the girl.

PHASE FOUR

February 3
THE INTERVIEW
Objective: Complete personality overhaul

March 10
ADMISSIONS COMMITTEE DELIBERATIONS
Objective: Surveillance,
precautionary measures

17

Don't do anything during an interview that you wouldn't do at a dinner party. Or in front of your grandmother.

—former admissions officer Lloyd Peterson,
The New Rules of College Admissions

E ric held out for as long as he could.

Clay couldn't get through five lines of the script without stuttering, cursing, or stringing together a chain of nonsense syllables in the dim hope of stumbling upon an actual word. Still, rehearsals continued, while Max badgered Eric daily to go to plan B, wire Clay for sound, and talk him through the interview minute-by-minute. Eric wasn't sure why he was hesitating, or why it seemed so important that they let Clay fend for himself.

"This is psychotic," Max complained, the day before the interview. "We can't take this kind of risk." He shot a glance at Schwarz, who was across the room, immersed in some kind of algebraic morass. Max lowered his voice. "You know what's at stake."

"You don't have to remind me," Eric said. "But you agreed: This one's my call."

"Then make the call, Eric. If you really believe you're right, if you believe Clay's up to this, then great. Let's do it. But you're the one who's been drilling him. And you're the one who's been calling him a moron all year. So you know if he can handle it—and if he can't. You make the call you have to make."

According to Eric's calculations, in the history of his life, he had almost never been wrong. He had a complete faith in his ability to make the right choices. But having faith in other people—especially certain other people who'd never lived up to any expectation except the expectation of failure? That was something else.

"If you really believe you're right," Max had said. "If you believe Clay's up to this . . ."

But those were two separate questions. They were opposing teams, facing off on a mental battlefield.

Believing I'm right—that's the easy part, Eric thought. *But how am I supposed to believe in* him?

Thirty-two percent of successful applicants since 2002 listed their favorite color as green.

Twenty-three percent claimed their favorite book was *The Catcher in the Rye,* while 17 percent preferred *The Great Gatsby.* According to their confidential roommate surveys, 41 percent were "morning people," 33 percent were "very neat," while 15 percent were "slobs," 63 percent listened to top-40 music, 31 percent to hip-hop, 7 percent to jazz, 29 percent to classical, and 11 percent to Broadway showtunes.

The list went on, some of the qualities relevant, some not, with no way of telling the difference . . . not unless you had access to several years' worth of surveys and a computer program able to sift through the data and spit out a graphic interpretation of relevant patterns along with a magic formula for success in less than twenty seconds of number-crunching.

Like Max did.

Then, of course, there were the personal factors. Under normal circumstances, applicants were randomly assigned to their interviewers. But there was nothing random about *Schwarz's* carefully engineered circumstances. As the admissions office's most trusted employee, Schwarz needed only a couple of minutes to gain access to the system that matched up interviewer and interviewee—after that, it was only a matter of a few keystrokes and Clay was guaranteed an interview with one Samuel Atherton III. Of course, most applicants would have no way of knowing that Atherton preferred blue ties to red, sports coats to blazers, and kayaks to canoes. The average applicant wouldn't know anything about Samuel Atherton III's passion for fly-fishing, his secret love of Dilbert comics and *Big Brother*, or the fact that six nights a month, he rendezvoused with a freshman dean in the empty administrative building, locked the door, and emerged two hours later, his hair and suit rumpled, a wide smile on his face. Not that details like that need come up in the interview.

But it would certainly be useful to know that Atherton's favorite poem was Eliot's "The Love Song of J. Alfred Prufrock"—that, in fact, he was prone to quoting lines for interviewees ("I grow old . . . I grow old . . . I shall wear the bottoms of my trousers rolled . . ."). He would wait for the dazed applicant to realize that he was quoting a poem and not just having a premature senior moment, and then challenge him or her to identify the poet. It wasn't the answer he cared about; it was the reaction. He loved to see how his interviewees stood up under pressure, how they acted when confronting a situation they didn't expect. Atherton loved surprises. Most applicants didn't.

Most applicants, on the other hand, hadn't spent two months watching Samuel Atherton in his home and office, pawing through his garbage and listening in on his phone calls until they were able to construct a detailed plan of what to wear, what to say, and what to do, from start to finish, from hairstyle to brand of shoelaces, each detail carefully chosen to suit Samuel Atherton's hidden whims. They would even satisfy his desire for the unexpected, allowing Clay to act caught off-guard for a moment by the out-of-left-field stress questions. But it would all be for show.

Surprise wasn't part of the plan.

"Looking good," Max said into the mic. From where he was sitting, just beneath Atherton's living room window, he had a perfect view of Clay in the doorway, decked out in impeccable "arty-intellectual" gear: tweed blazer, khaki pants, perfectly scuffed loafers, orange socks, funky thick-rimmed glasses, hair neatly trimmed and just slightly spiky on top, and, beneath the jacket, a black T-shirt with a bright blue lightning bolt slicing across the front. They'd argued about the shirt, Max claiming it was the perfect idiosyncratic artist's touch, Schwarz, the self-proclaimed Atherton expert, concerned that it was too risqué for the conservative admissions officer. Eric, uncharacteristically, had offered no opinion.

In the end, Clay himself cast the deciding vote, warning them that, six hundred dollars or not, if they forced him to wear a button-down shirt and tie, he couldn't be held responsible for his actions.

They went with the T-shirt.

"Shake his hand firmly, but not too firmly," Max advised. "Don't forget to look him in the eye and smile."

"He can handle the handshake," Eric said. "I spent a week training him."

"We're not leaving anything to chance," Max whispered, pressing his hand over the mic. "This is too important."

Eric let it go. The interview wasn't his operation anymore. He'd given up—given in—and let Max take over. Eric, as usual, had supplied the equipment. But Max was running the show.

"Okay, follow him into the living room," Max said into the mic. "No, don't sit on the couch, it's a trick! He wants you to sit on the chair—good. Okay, good. Legs crossed at the ankles, right. Good. No—no, you don't want anything to drink! Trick question. Thanks but no thanks, then cue the charming smile. Look relaxed. Good. Very good."

"So, Clay, tell me a little about yourself," Atherton said, his voice clearly audible to the three aspiring Cyranos huddled in the bushes.

Clay—smoothly parroting the words Max whispered in his ear—described his passion for his studies and his art.

"And how about for fun?" Atherton asked. "Any hobbies?"

"I'm a runner and an amateur chef. But what I really love is fly fishing."

"Really!" Atherton exclaimed. "How remarkable. That's quite a passion of mine—but you don't find too many students around here who know anything about it."

"Oh, I've been doing it since I was a kid," Max said, looking down at his notes. Clay repeated it word for word. "Do you use a split-cane bamboo rod or synthetic?"

Atherton leaned forward eagerly. "I usually prefer the natural wood—carbon-graphite performs better, but there's just something about the natural wood. . . ."

"I know what you mean," Clay said, nodding. "It makes the whole endeavor into less of a sport, more of an—"

"Art!" Atherton finished with him. "That's just how I've always felt. Tell me, how do you feel about the manually operated fly reels?"

Max let the fly-fishing talk continue for ten minutes—he was waiting for the perfect opening. It finally arrived.

"There's just something so calming about the water," Atherton said, staring off into the distance. "I can lose myself in it for hours."

"I know what you mean," Clay said, and Max instructed him to furrow his brow. "It always makes me feel like J. Alfred Prufrock, contemplating my life—you know, 'I shall wear white flannel trousers, and walk upon the beach. I have heard the mermaids singing, each to each.'"

Atherton looked at him in surprise, almost shock, and for a moment, Max, Eric, and Schwarz held their collective breath, wondering if they'd gone a step too far.

Then Atherton shook his head. "That's it exactly. I've just never heard it put so well before by someone your age. Remarkable."

The foreplay having gone better than expected, they settled in for the main event.

"Tell me, Clay, why do you want to go to Harvard?"

They'd battled over the answer for days, distilling an ideal response from hours of subpar interviews, searching for the magic words that would unlock the ivy gates. Max took a deep breath and began.

"I really believe that beneath the hype, Harvard has—" He

stopped abruptly, realizing that Clay wasn't following his lead. Wasn't, in fact, speaking at all, but was just staring dumbly at Atherton, like an actor waiting for his cue. *"I really believe that beneath the hype,"* Max said louder, and still, Clay didn't respond. "Scratch your nose if you can hear me." Nothing. "Clay? Clay!"

Max turned away from the window to meet Eric's panicked expression. "What the hell is going on?" he asked, fury bubbling beneath his words. "Tell me this isn't happening again."

"This *can't* be happening again," Eric said, checking all the equipment, tightening connections, spinning dials, and refused to look Max in the eye. "But . . ."

"The feed is down?" Schwarz asked. *"Again?"*

"This isn't us," Eric said frantically. "There's got to be some kind of interference—everything's working fine."

"Except for the fact that he can't hear us, and we can't hear him, and we're totally fucking screwed!" Max yelled.

"Shhhh!" Schwarz hissed.

"What's the difference?" Max rubbed his hands across his face. "It's over."

"Maybe not," Schwarz said hopefully. "You rehearsed all month, right? Maybe Clay knows what he's supposed to say. Maybe he does not need us."

Max snorted in disgust.

Eric sighed. "Yeah. Maybe."

They watched in horror as Clay stared blankly at Atherton, then, after a moment, looked to the window, once, twice, then back at Atherton. They watched him open his mouth, then close it, then open it again. They didn't need lip-reading ability to know that, so far, the response had been something like, "Uh . . . uh."

"I can't watch this," Max said. "I'm going to—" But he slipped away before finishing the thought.

"What now?" Schwarz asked.

"He exposes himself as a fraud, breaks down under pressure, tells Atherton about us, and we're all screwed?" Eric said.

"I could go ring the doorbell."

"And say what?"

"Something—maybe I am Clay's brother, and there is a family emergency?"

Eric nodded. "It could work. We could just call him—but shit, his cell phone's off."

"We could call *Atherton*," Schwarz said. He pulled out his phone. "We know the number, and—"

Eric grabbed his arm. "What's he doing?"

Schwarz leaned closer to the window. His mouth dropped open. "That cannot be—"

But it was.

Clay had dug something out of his pocket and was leaning forward to hand it to Atherton. It was thin, white, vaguely tube-shaped, and Clay had one of his own.

"It's a cigarette," Eric moaned, trying to persuade himself. "Just a cigarette." But he couldn't quite force himself to believe it.

Their frantic plans forgotten, they just sat and stared. Max had the right idea running away, Eric thought. At least he wouldn't have to watch his dreams literally turning to ashes.

Atherton held the slim white—*cigarette,* Eric thought furiously, *just a cigarette*—beneath his nose, closed his eyes, and inhaled deeply.

Clay held his up for display, the tip dancing as he waved his hand around, illustrating whatever disastrous point his was making.

And then, without, warning, the audio kicked back in.

"I let it, like, burn down all the way, right?" Clay was saying, holding the blunt between his thumb and index finger. "And then I glue it to the canvas with this paste stuff, and you can, like, still smell the pot, right? And the whole rest of the canvas is white—like, pure white. So with the joint in the middle, it's like, it's this statement on drugs and sh—stuff like that. Like the joint burned away everything else, and all you've got is blankness. And there was a spark, but now it's burned out, and the whole thing is dead—except that the canvas is white, not black, right? So maybe it's not a death kind of blankness, maybe it's birth. The blank slate, you know? Everything starting, everything open. Because it all starts with fire. But it could go both ways. So there's not just this one statement, there's like, all these levels of statements, just like there's all these levels when you look at the painting, you know? Because you can see it, but you can also smell it, and it's like, telling you all different things at the same time. So, uh. Yeah. That's what I'm working on now."

"What is he talking about?" Schwarz whispered. "Did you write that? Is he back on the script?"

Eric shook his head, confused. "No, that was Clay. That was all Clay."

"See, it's not just that's it's a good school and you've got all those good classes and sh—other things," Clay continued. He slid the . . . things back into his pocket, unlit. Unsmoked. Just props in the Clay Porter show—for which Clay was writing his own script. "It's like, I've got all this stuff to say, right? And that's what I'm trying to do with my, uh, art. Say what I want to say. And that's hard, because, it never comes out right. And high school, it's like, all about what other people want to say, and what they want you to say. They just tell you what to think, and you've got to, like spit it back at them or they kick you out. But I think, maybe, college is different—like, if I go to Harvard, it won't be about what other people want me to say. It'll be about what I want to say. Maybe that's what they're there for. To, like, help people get it out—the shit they need to say. Or paint. Or whatever. You know?"

Schwarz gaped at Eric, his mouth open. "He came up with all that? Himself? Did you know he could do that?"

I knew he couldn't *do it,* Eric thought. *I was so sure.*

Instead of answering, he hunched back over the equipment, searching for a loose wire. "I don't get it. Why's it suddenly working again?"

"Does it matter? It seems Clay does not need us." Schwarz poked his head out from under the bush, scanning the lawn. "Where do you think Max went?"

"It didn't just break and then unbreak," Eric muttered. "There's got to be a reason."

"My computer breaks and unbreaks all the time. That is the way machines are."

Eric shook his head. "Not my machines."

"It didn't break. At least, not by itself." Max had snuck up behind them.

And he wasn't alone.

18

Advancement is partly a game, I learned in college, and while games are not always fair, they're still worth playing. So say the victors, anyway.

—Walter Kirn, "The Ivy League's X Factor,"
Time magazine, August 21, 2006

"I'm sorry." I blurted it out before Max could say anything.

There was no point in denial. He'd found me sitting on the other side of the house, my back against the wall, my knees in the dirt, a blue RF jammer in my hand.

Caught blue-handed, so to speak.

Max had gripped my elbow firmly and marched me back to the others, but once we got there, I wrenched away. He let go. As I knew he would. These guys were determined, but they weren't fighters. Of course, neither was I. But I was, at least, a girl. And guys like this wouldn't hit a girl. So I had that going for me. Just not much else.

Eric froze. "Lex, what are you—what's she—"

"Jamming our signal, that's what," Max said, flinging the jammer to the ground. "You're working for the Bums, aren't you?"

I didn't say anything.

"Aren't you?"

I waited for Eric to stick up for me, to tell Max to calm down, chill out, look at things rationally for a moment. But he didn't.

"Lex? Is he right? You're working for . . . ?"

I still didn't say anything. I couldn't. But I nodded.

"The whole time?"

I nodded again.

It was like he couldn't decide whether to yell or cry or break something. Or break me. "I guess this explains why someone like you would—with me. Stupid." He closed his eyes, shook his head violently. "I'm so stupid."

Max gripped his shoulder. "Deal with it later," he said quietly. "We've got audio back. We can finish the interview. And then . . ." He glared at me, as if daring me to run away. "We'll deal with her."

I didn't run. What was there to be afraid of?

More to the point, what could be worse than getting caught?

Atherton lived in a small Cape Codder about ten blocks from campus. After the interview, Clay headed off to hang with his friends in the Pit, while Eric stormed away in what seemed like a random direction, Max and Schwarz following closely behind for moral support.

And traipsing after them like a disobedient child waiting for her punishment: me.

We ended up in the empty parking lot behind a liquor store. It was Sunday morning, and even though after two hundred years of Puritan blue laws it was finally legal in Massachusetts to sell beer on the Lord's day, Lloyd's Liquor Mart didn't open until noon.

Eric glared at me. He paced. Stopped, and glared some more. Opened his mouth and held up his arms like he was going to start preaching, then shut up tight and dropped them. He started pacing again. I waited. Schwarz leaned against the side of the liquor store; Max perched on a fire hydrant. I waited some more.

Finally. "You've been *spying* on us?" Eric asked, his voice husky. "*Sabotaging* us? For *them*?"

I nodded, reluctant to speak until I absolutely had to. I wasn't sure I could get my voice to work.

"You've known what was going on the whole time, and you put on this little show like—this whole thing has been a lie? Everything?" His voice jumped up to a nasty falsetto. "Oh, Eric, I'm so scared I won't get in. What if I get rejected? What if I screwed up my SATs and—wait." His face, which was already a fiery crimson, turned an even deeper shade of red. "That was you, too, wasn't it? At the SATs. *You* jammed the feed?"

Yes, I mouthed silently.

"So the whole thing was bullshit. You were just playing me."

"You were playing me, too," I said, and it turned out my voice worked just fine. "Pretending like you just wanted to get to know me. Like you were just this nice guy. You were lying too."

"That's different," he said.

"How?"

He pressed his lips together. And, for a long moment, I thought maybe I had him.

"Because I trusted you," he said, finally meeting my eyes. "Because I was going to walk away from it, for you."

"But you didn't."

"Neither did you."

"Eric—"

"What a fucking waste!" He took a step toward me. "I actually felt *guilty*, you know that? I actually wasted time, worrying about you, about what would happen if—" He blew out his breath in a short, loud burst. "And it was all a lie."

"It *wasn't*." I glanced over at Max and Schwarz, wishing they would disappear. I may have known everything about them from their dossiers; I may have spent the last couple months watching, but I didn't *know* them. And I didn't want them to hear this.

But I wasn't really in a position to choose.

I drew closer to him. He turned his back, but he didn't walk away. "It wasn't all a lie," I whispered. "Not the important parts. Everything I said . . . I *am* scared. That's why—"

"It must have been torture," he cut in bitterly, jerking away from me. "Hanging around the *nerd*, pretending to be into all his geeky astronomy stuff, pretending to care what I had to say. Did you just go home to your friends and laugh about me all night?"

"Did *you*?" I asked, feeling an unexpected stab of anger. "You're the one who was spying on me first. You're the one trying to get some deadbeat into Harvard—even though getting him in may mean knocking me out. Did you ever stop to think about that?"

"You don't get the moral high ground," he snapped. "Not anymore."

"Neither do you."

"It is *not* the same. What you did—it's not the same."

"I lied. You lied. We both—"

"You know what? I don't have to stand here and justify myself to *you*," he snapped. "Screw this. I'm out of here."

And now he did walk away, with Schwarz scurrying after him.

"Just let me explain!" I called after him. "Can't you just listen to my side of the story?"

He glanced back without slowing down. "I've heard enough."

I guess I could have followed him. But instead, I stood frozen in the middle of the parking lot, watching Eric disappear down the block. "If you'd just listen to me," I said softly. "I could tell you why. . . ."

"I'll listen." Max hopped off his fire hydrant and sidled up beside me. "So why don't you tell me exactly what's been going on these past couple months."

"Why should I tell you anything?"

Max smiled, but his eyes stayed cold. "Because you need to tell someone—and I need to hear it."

I didn't tell Max everything. I didn't tell him about the night with Eric on the roof of the observatory, because that belonged to the two of us. Even if Eric didn't want it anymore.

I didn't tell him when things had shifted, when Eric stopped being a target and the game stopped being any fun. Mostly because I didn't know myself.

I did tell him that I'd wanted to walk away—and that I hadn't been strong enough to do it. I didn't expect it to matter. Because in the end, I'd gone along with the Bums. I'd done everything they'd asked, all so I could get my reward.

I told him that the Bums had promised to make me the valedictorian, had promised to get me into Harvard. I told him everything they'd made me do, and everything I knew about their plans and their operation which, even after all these months, wasn't much. Max guided me through every detail, making sure not to miss anything that mattered. I talked for two hours, rehashing conversations, comparing strategies, examining equipment, treading and retreading the same worn ground. I talked about everything.

Everything except Eric.

One month before, I had sent off applications to sixteen schools.

There was the dream: Harvard.

Then my other reaches: Yale, Princeton, Stanford (even though my parents had already forbidden me to go to college on the West Coast).

Schools I thought I could probably get into and wouldn't absolutely hate: Penn, Columbia, Dartmouth, Brown, Cornell (because Ivy League is Ivy League, even when it's stuck in cow country), Duke, Northwestern, University of Chicago, Emory, and Berkeley.

Safeties: BU and UMass.

Even though Harvard was mine if I wanted it—at least assuming the Bums came through—I had written my personal statements, filled in all the personal data, secured extra teacher recommendations, aced my interviews . . . I was finally, after weeks of work, months of preparation, years of stress and anticipation, finished. The decision was out of my hands. And if the Bongo Bums delivered on their promise, I didn't have anything to worry about.

But that night, I couldn't fall asleep.

Guilt sucks.

You won, I told myself, staring at the row of junior high plaques and trophies that still lined the top of my bookshelves. Even if they'd caught me, they hadn't done it in time—I'd managed to screw up the interview, at least for a few minutes, just as the Bums had commanded. I would get what I'd been promised.

I would get what I deserved.

But something felt off. I was, as my father always told me, a natural winner. Born to be number one. So I knew precisely what winning felt like.

It didn't feel like this.

19

The enemy's spies who have come to spy on us must be sought out, tempted with bribes, led away and comfortably housed. Thus they will become converted spies and available for our service. It is through the information brought by the converted spy that we are able to acquire and employ local and inward spies. It is owing to his information, again, that we can cause the doomed spy to carry false tidings to the enemy.

—Sun Tzu, *The Art of War*

There were one too many people in the room.

Eric's first thought was that Schwarz's roommate had returned, girlfriend in hand. It was a reasonable guess, as it had already happened once before. Toward the beginning of January, the girlfriend's proctor had discovered she was hoarding an illicit boy in her room and, citing chapter and verse of the Harvard housing code, outlawed the cohabitation. So the inseparable pair had returned to Schwarz's room and taken over.

Schwarz wasn't used to living with another person, much less two other people, much less two other people who didn't seem to mind having sex while a third person cowered under the covers six feet away. Or so he had discovered, trying to sleep while mattress springs creaked, sheets rustled, a voice of indiscriminate gender moaned, and, one memorable pre-dawn morning, the girlfriend shrieked, "I told you, *never* do that again!" before conceding, "Okay, but just one more time."

Schwarz spent the month of January living back in his old bedroom at home, until the Canaday Hall proctor got a girlfriend of his own and stopped monitoring his students' sex lives. The roommate and his appendage moved out; Schwarz moved back in.

Now, there was a girl in the roommate's bed all right, lying face down with her head buried in a pillow, but she wasn't a brunette, and she wasn't attached to the roommate, a tall, muscular prep school jock who exemplified the kind of words Eric had read but never before seen in the flesh: Hale. Strapping. Robust.

Nor was it Schwarz's beloved Stephanie, whom Eric had met only once but whose mere presence, Eric knew, would have been enough to turn Schwarz—who was calmly flipping through a notebook at his desk—into a quavering, stammering, Bunny-mumbling mass of goo. No. This girl was someone else, someone more familiar and more devious, someone, as he'd very clearly informed both of his friends, he intended never to speak to again.

Eric turned toward the other side of the room to glare at Schwarz, who looked up from his notebook only long enough to give him a defensive *Don't look at me* wave, and then at Max, who remained infuriatingly serene.

"What's *she* doing here?" Eric growled.

I sat up in bed and glared right back at him. "*She* is about to save your ass."

I had tried apologizing. Twice in person. Then by phone, e-mail, instant message, text message, snail mail—if there were still a Pony Express, I would have turned his house into a stable. He wouldn't listen. He wouldn't answer his phone. He wouldn't return my e-mails. His IM status was permanently stuck on "Away from computer. Try again never."

I tried again anyway. I tried harder. Even knowing I was veering into pathetic *Fatal Attraction*-stalker territory, I kept trying.

And then one day, I stopped.

Enough. If he wanted to be pigheaded, let him.

So I wasn't in that dorm room for Eric. I wasn't there for Max, who'd listened to my side of the story and, after taking a few days to digest it, called to congratulate me on the subterfuge. And then to ask a favor.

I was there because I hadn't been able to sleep all week, and I was tired. Tired of it all.

"We have a crisis here, guys." Max paused and shot a glance at me. "Guys and girl. Two crises, actually, but"—he checked his watch—"we've still got time before the second one arrives. So let's deal with what we've got."

"You should've told me she was coming," Eric muttered, looking everywhere but at me. I kept my eyes on him, but molded my face into a mask of casual, couldn't-care-less detachment, like staring at him was only slightly preferable to staring at a pile of Schwarz's dirty underwear. Like he just happened to be in my line of sight.

"Then you wouldn't have come," Max pointed out.

"Of course I would have," Eric said. "I just would have made sure that she didn't."

"*She* is the one who brought crisis number one to my attention," Max said. "Aside from the fact that I think you should take the stick out of your ass and give her a break. She's my kind of woman."

"Thanks, Max," I said, beaming.

That only made Eric scowl more. "You mean cold, calculating, duplicitous, and completely untrustworthy?"

Max grinned. "Exactly."

"Excuse me, but maybe you should just tell us what the crisis is," Schwarz said.

"Gladly." Max updated them on my encounters with the Bongo Bums. When he got to the part where they promised to get me into Harvard, Eric's eyes darted toward me for a second; when he got to the part where I tried to back out, Eric looked again, and I wondered if he was trying to figure out the timeline, and whether he would guess exactly when I had lost my nerve.

Or, depending on how you looked at things, found it. And then lost it again.

"Why would they bother?" Schwarz asked. "Why not hack into the admissions system themselves and change Clay's status?"

"Exactly," Max said. "Why not?"

"They said that would be cheating," I reminded him.

"And this isn't?" Eric asked, being very careful to direct his question to the room, *not* to me.

Max grabbed a yo-yo off of Schwarz's bookshelf and began flicking it idly up and down. "Maybe not in their minds," he said, staring down at the yo-yo like it could offer up some answers. "They probably told themselves that sabotage was just part of the game."

"Well, it's not," Eric said. "It's cheating."

"Yeah, which is why I'm sure they weren't planning to get caught. I'm just saying that if we confront them, they'll try to weasel their way out of a forfeit. And if we *don't* confront them, I assume they'll keep right on cheating. Which means no cash for us, either way."

Eric scowled. "If they think sabotage is fair play, then they're just as free to hack into the computer system as they are to hire a spy."

"Exactly. And when they realize that their spy here—deliciously sneaky though she may be—didn't get the job done, what do you think their next step's going to be? Especially since—"

"Especially since they're planning to hack the system anyway," Eric realized. "To reward *her* for a job well done."

I was distracted, wondering if Eric had gotten a haircut since I last saw him. Had his hair always flopped over his forehead like that? And hadn't it been a little longer around the ears, a little shaggier? I felt like I could remember running my hands through it and rubbing the soft fuzzy hair behind his earlobes, but that was silly, since I had never touched his hair or his ears, or that spot at the nape of his neck where his T-shirt met his skin. I was just imagining it.

Still, his hair looked softer than I remembered.

"They're going to cheat," Max said firmly. "No question. They're just waiting for the right time. The application's in, the interview's over, we've done everything we can do—and now they're going to try to steal our win."

"*If* we have a win to steal," Eric pointed out.

"Oh, we won. Clay killed the interview." Max pounded his hand against the mattress with a soft thwack, looking disappointed that it hadn't made a more satisfying sound. He slapped the yo-yo down on the bookshelf with a sharp crack. Much better. "We're *going* to win. And Lex here has volunteered to help seal it. As long as she's still willing to make the sacrifice."

"Sacrifice?" Schwarz asked. "Is someone getting thrown into a volcano?"

"Why, Schwarzie? Scared that when they come a-calling for sacrificial virgins, you'll be the most obvious candidate?"

Schwarz made a noise like someone had punched him in the stomach. He turned his face toward the wall. It might have made him feel better if I'd pointed out that the volcano gods would be equally happy to have me. But I kept my mouth shut.

"If we lock the Bums out of the admissions system, we can keep them from changing Clay's file," Max said. "But that means they won't be able to change Lex's file, either."

Eric laughed, a nasty noise that sounded like scraping metal. "After all this, you're going to give it up, just like that?" he asked, finally acknowledging me. "Don't do me any favors."

Had I actually been attracted to such an egomaniac? "You think this is about *you*? We've been out on what, one date?"

"That wasn't a date—as you were oh so quick to remind me."

"Exactly. So you really think I'd be willing to throw away my whole future for you? Forget Harvard just to make *you* feel better?"

"If not that, then why?"

I finally looked away from him. "I think you've given up the right to ask that kind of question."

"Fine." Eric shrugged. "It's not like I care."

"You've made that obvious enough."

"Ladies, please." Max gave us both a time-out signal. "Save the mud-wrestling for later. We've got plans to make, not to mention—"

"Crisis number two?" Schwarz asked.

There was a knock on the door. Max checked his watch and nodded. "Speak of the devil—he's right on time."

"I told him, and now I'm telling you, I won't be treated this way," Bernard Salazar raged from the doorway. He'd refused to come inside. I was hiding in Schwarz's closet, peering through a crack in the door and trying not to breathe in the fumes of his dirty laundry. Bernard, of all people, couldn't be trusted to know I was involved. "I gave you losers a shitload of cash, and what did you give me? Nothing."

"We gave you information," Max said impatiently. It was obvious he'd said it before, probably more than once. "You got a full description of your admissions officer, everything he was looking for in a candidate, statistical likelihoods of success with every possible answer to every possible question, a full run-down of everything you needed to do to be accepted. It was practically paint-by-numbers. Throw in the fact that you're claiming to be, what is it today? One eighth Latino and one eighth Native American? If you don't get in, I guarantee you it's not our fault."

"I *am* one-eighth Latino—my ancestors fought at the Alamo!"

"Yeah? Which side?" Max asked.

"Huh?"

"Do you even know which sides there are to choose from?"

Bernard punched a fist into the door frame. He sucked his knuckles, then thrust his chin up and his shoulders back. The black ballpoint tattoo on his left bicep twitched, and I wondered if he was trying to flex his nonexistent muscles. "Quit changing the subject. You think you can pull this on me? This is fraud."

"Daddy taught you a lot about that, did he?" Max asked.

"Shut up."

"Fraud. Noun. The crime of obtaining money or some other benefit by deliberate deception. Look it up." He turned toward Eric and lowered his voice to a stage whisper. "I guess we know why he tanked the SATs."

"Stop poking the hungry lion," Eric whispered back.

Max ignored him. "This isn't fraud, Bernie. You've known all along what we were willing to do for you and what we weren't."

"And *I've* known all along what I was willing to do *to* you," Bernard snickered.

"Are you planning to spell this out for us? Or are there too many letters?"

"You're going to hack into the computer system and get me in. I know you can do it."

Max snorted. "Of course we can do it. But why would we do it for you?"

Instead of answering, Bernard unzipped his shoulder bag, the opulence of its creamy leather clashing loudly with his ripped T-shirt and baggy jeans. Silk screened across the front of his T-shirt was a fist with the middle finger extended. The blue binder that he pulled out of his bag, on the other hand, had a *Star Trek* sticker pasted across the front of it and a small pink *Playboy* logo on the spine.

Schwarz jumped off his bed. "The Binder of Power!" His voice squeaked.

Bernard's grin said *Game over*. "I told your buddy Clay that you needed it. And, like the mental defective he is, he just handed it over."

"You can't prove anything in there is connected to us," Eric said. "For all anyone knows, you came up with it yourself. Your word against ours."

"My word—and your fingerprints," Bernard pointed out. "And ink that I'll bet came out of that printer." He pointed at the Canon laser beneath Schwarz's desk. "And I'm sure that's just the beginning."

"Someone's been watching a little too much *CSI*," Max said.

"Someone hasn't been watching enough," Bernard sneered. "You broke into the admissions office—under false pretenses—and altered a transcript file. I looked it up: That's a felony. Some kid in Philly got ten years for the same thing. So if you think the cops won't be interested in what I've got here"—he tapped out a jaunty rhythm on the blue binder—"or if you are sure you didn't leave any identifying evidence behind, then go ahead. Risk it. Let the admissions committee take a nice *close* look at Clay's application. Lose your little bet, get kicked out of school and tossed in jail. See if I care. Or you can do this one simple thing for me, and you get your precious binder back."

"You're such an asshole," Eric snapped, and I was waiting for him—for any of them—to get up and *take* the binder. Bernard was bigger than Max, bigger than Eric, and probably twice as big as Schwarz. But it was still three against one—and the math on that was remedial.

No one moved.

"I sure am. Stick with what you're good at, right?" Bernard said. "You could've made this a whole lot easier on yourselves if you'd just let me blackmail Atherton."

"You still can," Max pointed out. "You want the tape?"

"We're not giving him that tape!" Eric protested.

"Doesn't matter." Bernard shook his head. "You said it yourself—too risky. Too much chance of getting caught."

"So you came up with this brilliant idea instead?" Eric asked. "You realize how much worse it'll be if we get caught doing this?"

"That's what makes this so sweet. *You'll* get caught. Not me. So what do I care?"

Silence.

"It's your call. According to the timetable in here"—Bernard waved the binder again, then tucked it safely into his bag—"admissions decisions are being made as we speak. So you're running out of time. Let me know what you decide."

"Fornicate you," Schwarz muttered. But he waited until the door had closed.

"You said you could *handle* him," Eric said accusingly. "You said we could trust him."

"I never said that," Max protested. "I just said he could pay. Which, lest we forget, he did."

"Yeah, you were right about everything. You've got everything under control. So tell us, oh master of strategy and tactical planning—what the hell do we do now?"

"I'm glad you asked." Max stood up and wandered over to the window. He spread his arms across the frame and stared out at the Yard. "Fear not, brave fellows. In the immortal words of every great general, every criminal mastermind, every empty-headed politician in the course of human history, *I have a plan.*"

20

March 3 · **EMERGENCY COMPUTER HACK**
Objective: *Damage control*

If at all possible, dispense justice.

—Neil Steinberg, *If At All Possible, Involve a Cow:
The Book of College Pranks*

Smile, I instructed myself. *Not too wide* or they'll know you're bluffing. *Not too eager* or they'll think you're scared. I rang the doorbell, and composed myself on the porch, leaning oh-so-casually against the white railing. I would be the Goldilocks of facial expressions. I would talk my way inside that house.

It turned out, I didn't have to.

"Come in, come in, dear." The slim, perfectly polished woman behind the door reached out to me and, in one smooth, elegant motion, shook my hand and maneuvered me inside. Before I knew what was happening, she had slipped off my coat and floated it toward a nearby hook. It was as if I'd stepped into a TV screen and this twenty-something, DKNY-clad, capped teeth, blond-highlighted starlet had hastily wrapped an apron around her waist in preparation for playing the role of The Mother.

"I'm Alexandra," I said, wondering if I'd come to the wrong house. She pulled a plate from behind her back and suddenly I had a fresh-baked chocolate chip cookie in my hand. "You must be, uh, Gerald's . . ."

"Stepmother," she said, with an airy giggle. "The boys are downstairs, like always." She shook her head in bemusement. Her hair didn't move at all. Last I heard, hairspray had gone out in the eighties, along with acid-wash denim and shoulder pads. But obviously one of us had missed a memo. "Would you like me to call them up here for you?"

"I'd rather surprise them."

But if I'd been expecting gasps and gaping jaws, I was disappointed. When I made my appearance at the bottom of the stairs, Gerald and Ash—or, as I still thought of them, mustache man and BO boy—barely looked up. Gerald had shaved his mustache but sprouted a spot of hair on his chin that was probably supposed to be a soul patch and looked more like a dribbling of applesauce. He was sprawled on a leather couch playing Xbox, while Ash, still deodorant-free, sat at the mahogany desk, doing something on the computer. It wasn't plugged in to anything, which meant, as we'd suspected, a wireless modem. But the router had to be somewhere—and judging from all the equipment down here, it was probably somewhere nearby. I started my search for telltale cables or phone jacks, pretending to be admiring the fake wood panels and shag carpeting.

"What're you doing here?" Gerald mumbled, too intent on his game to turn his head away from the TV. "I told you, we don't need you anymore. There's nothing more for you to do."

"Unfinished business." I tried to sound tough. "You promised that if I did what you wanted me to do, you'd get me into Harvard."

"We will," Ash said. "But that doesn't explain why you're ruining our afternoon."

"How do I know I can trust you?" This was delicate. I needed them to hack the system on my timetable—soon, but not yet, not until I'd found the router and installed the device. I dug my hand into the pocket of my hoodie and curled my fingers over it again; there was something comforting about pressing the prongs into the flesh of my palm and running my fingertips across the bumps and dips on its flat surface, like I was trying to read a message in Braille. I'd run through the steps in my mind so many times that I thought I could probably install it in the dark—that is, if I could find the router. If there was an open USB port. If the device worked the way it was supposed to.

And if I could do it all without them noticing.

"What's the difference if you can trust us or not?" Gerald drawled. Then he cursed as, on the screen, his character's head got blown off with a hand grenade. He let loose a stream of shouted obscenities, then threw his head back, his words billowing a howl. As I stared—while assiduously pretending I was somewhere else—he bashed the controller against the wall, once, twice, and then once more for good measure. Then he sat up straight, crossed one leg over the other, and started a new game. "Either we'll do it, or we won't," he said calmly, as if the last few seconds hadn't happened.

Okay, now I was a little freaked out.

Geeky, computer-hacking, power-tripping, wannabe men of mystery cheaters were one thing.

Crazy, geeky, computer-hacking, power-tripping, wannabe men of mystery cheaters who might at any time go off in a violent rage were something else altogether.

"That's why I'm here," I said, striving for the perfect mix of devil-may-care and don't-tread-on-me. "I want you to do it. Now. While I'm watching."

That made Ash look up from his computer. "Or what?"

I knew my part. And this was the point where I was supposed to come up with some kind of threat. I needed to demonstrate my leverage.

I chewed on my lip, my eyes ping-ponging back and forth between their faces, which wore identical ferret-like expressions. And then, midway between them, snaking along the baseboard on the opposite side of the wall, I saw it: the cable line. It was covered over with wood-colored tape, but I could trace its path along the molding until it disappeared under the couch. It didn't come out on the other side and, looking closer, I realized there was a wedge of space between the couch and the wall, just wide enough for a cable modem and router.

I brandished my cell phone. "Or I call Eric Roth right now and tell him how you're trying to cheat him out of twenty-five thousand dollars."

"That's our cue," Eric whispered. "She must have spotted the router."

Max gave him a mock salute and reached for his walkie talkie. "You're up," he told their agent in the field. Two hundred yards away, a small figure emerged from the shadows and signaled his readiness, then darted across the street, crossed Gerald's wide lawn, and climbed onto the front porch. From Max and Eric's hiding spot two lawns away, they could see him pause for a moment to get himself into character, then ring the doorbell.

This part of the plan, at least, would go smoothly. A consummate professional, Seth Filch lived six houses down from the Roths, and had been a reliable go-to guy for Eric and co nearly all his life. He was cool and collected under pressure, an award-caliber Method actor, and willing to do anything for ten dollars and an ice-cream sandwich.

Most seven-year-olds are.

From where they hid, they couldn't hear the conversation, but they could picture the scene playing out well enough—after all, they'd written the script. Seth would be bawling, tears streaming down his face, his irresistibly cute button nose red and stuffy, his lips wobbling; no adult would be able to resist. Just as he'd been instructed, he would introduce himself as a new neighbor and tell Gerald's stepmother about his lost soccer ball—about its sentimental value and how it belonged to his father and he wasn't supposed to be playing with it and he was going to get into trouble and he was sure it was in someone's yard and he just needed find it and please please please . . . Max had advised at this point he just give up on words all together in favor of a miserable wail.

He would cry uncontrollably for a moment, letting the stepmother attempt some brand of comfort—preferably in the form of baked goods. And *then*, in a quiet, wavering voice, he would ask if her son could help find the ball.

The whole transaction took about five minutes, and right on cue, Gerald and Ash, their body language screaming put-upon reluctance, burst through the front door and led sad little Seth into the backyard.

Eric gave Max a high-five and began whispering into the mic.

I'd been left alone in the basement with strict instructions not to touch anything.

The instructions were disregarded.

I installed the device in the router, then hurried over to the laptop, where, following Max's instructions to the letter, I got past the password encryption, established our connection, and reset the network so that every piece of data, every mouse click, every kilobyte would run through Max's computer before it hit the outside world. Then, my fingers stumbling over the keys, I erased all traces of my presence.

"Done," I said. It felt strange to be talking to myself in the empty room, even knowing that the microphone sewn into the lining of the hoodie would pick up everything. But at the same time, there was something weirdly comforting about knowing that someone was listening in—that they would have to listen, even if they didn't want to hear what I had to say.

"Eric, I—"

"Wolverine," he snapped.

Right. The stupid code names. Eric was Wolverine. Max was Magneto. Schwarz, even in absentia, stuck in midterms, was Professor X.

I was Leech.

It didn't seem like a coincidence.

"*Wolverine*, I just wanted . . ." But I had promised myself I wasn't going to apologize anymore. Not when he didn't want to hear it, and not when he wasn't willing to consider the possibility that I wasn't the only one in the wrong.

Wolverine? More like Pighead.

"Just wanted to say good luck," I said finally. "I hope this works."

There was a pause. Then Max's voice came on the line. "We're sending them back in now. One last time, you sure you're willing to do this for us?"

I didn't let myself stop to think about what I was giving up. I'd done too much thinking already.

"One last time," I said, watching the stairway and steeling myself for the next phase of the plan, "I'm not doing this for you."

As Seth trotted away, soccer ball in hand, Gerald and Ash retreated to their basement. Max and Eric moved into position. For the plan to work, they needed to be within fifty yards of the basement, and there was an old shed in the backyard with their name on it.

"Don't you think you should give her a break?" Max said, as they eased the rusty broken padlock off the door and let themselves in. "When's the next time you're going to have a chance with a girl that hot?"

"Since when do you think she's hot?" Eric set the wireless receiver in place as Max logged into the network. The bug was working perfectly—they could see everything Ash was doing on his laptop.

"Hotter than you, at least. And she said she was sorry. She's making the grand sacrificial gesture—what more do you want?"

"I don't want anything." Eric nodded toward the computer screen. "Can we just focus?"

"We can't do anything until she convinces them to start the hack."

"*If* she convinces them."

"She will."

"Since when do *you* know her so well?"

"Jealous?" Max asked.

"Yeah, right."

"Then why are you whining?" Max dodged the handful of dirt Eric tossed in his direction. "I know she's good—she had you fooled, didn't she?"

Eric shrugged. "Whatever."

Max narrowed his eyes. "That's it, isn't it? You're not pissed because she played you—you're pissed she *out*played you."

"No, I'm pissed because she's a lying—" Eric gasped and jerked his head toward the screen. "They're actually going for it."

Someone inside the house was attempting to access the Harvard admissions system. Max was on it instantly. His hands flew across the keyboard, and then, with only the merest flicker of the screen, he'd made the switch.

Gerald and Ash were now hacking their way into a simulated admissions system, housed on Max's computer and designed to look identical to the Harvard network. After a few minutes, Max keyed in the command that would give the Bums backdoor access to the fake system; Eric could hear the hoots of victory coming through his earpiece.

The Bongo Bums thought they were in.

Max allowed them access to the fake *Decisions* directory and steered them toward the file he'd labeled "Alexandra Talese." It took only a few seconds for them to change the status from "Deny" to "Admit."

Then, for several long moments, nothing else happened.

"They're weighing their options," Max guessed. "It's safer to do it all now, in one shot—but riskier to do it while Lex watches. But they must know she's not going to tell anyone. They have the ultimate leverage. They'll go for it."

"Maybe. Or maybe they're not going to do it at all," Eric said. "Maybe we were wrong, and they're not planning to cheat."

"And maybe fairies will come down to earth and sprinkle you with fairy dust and you'll turn into George Clooney." Max rolled his eyes. "We're talking about twenty-five thousand dollars here. Anyone would cheat for that."

"*We're* not."

Max muttered something too soft for Eric to hear. But before he could ask, the Bums snapped into motion again.

"Here they go," Max said triumphantly, as the would-be hackers ran a search for Clay Porter's file.

Max let them find it. He let them change the status to "Deny." Then he let them log out, thinking they had won. He knew exactly how they felt.

Two days before the main event, Schwarz had successfully navigated their trial run with a mission of his own. "Are you sure we have to do this here?" Schwarz had asked, as Bernard watched the screen, his nails clawing into Schwarz's shoulder.

"You're the genius," Bernard jeered. "Think about it for a second. If something goes wrong, they could trace it back to us. You think I'm going to risk using *my* computer?"

"I was not suggesting your house. But any anonymous network, an Internet café, or—"

"Nice try, but if you know how easy they can track you down, you'll have extra incentive not to get caught. You do this right, and we all win."

Schwarz suppressed a grin. "I guess you thought of everything."

"You bet I did."

Let Salazar think it's his idea. That had been Max's advice, and Schwarz had followed it to the letter. Now they were in his dorm room, on his computer, a perfectly controlled environment—Bernard had no cause to think that this was to his disadvantage.

Schwarz logged into the fake network, a mirror site to the one through which Max and Eric would guide the Bums. He pretended to wander down a number of blind alleys and be driven to the very edge of his capabilities before he finally broke in. The only capabilities pushed to the limit were his acting skills, but so far, so good.

"Schwarz! Schwarz, I need you!" The door burst open, just as Bernard's admissions file popped up on the screen. Schwarz slammed the laptop shut.

"Um, hi, Stephanie, I really cannot—"

"This is serious," she moaned, tipping her head forward so that her hair cascaded over her face, then pushing the golden strands back into a ponytail with an exaggerated sigh.

Schwarz was transfixed.

"I need you—there's this party tonight that I totally forgot, and I have to go because Jake's going to be there, you know, Ned's hot cousin, the one on the football team? And I told him I was going, but I've got a chem problem set due tomorrow, and I'll never get through it in time, unless you—"

"I am sorry," Schwarz said, finally shaking off his paralysis. "But I am busy."

"But—"

"I wish I could help, but . . ."

Her eyes were watering.

"Sure," she said, her voice a little higher than a whisper. "Okay. I shouldn't have asked, I guess. I'll figure it out. Or maybe I'll . . . it's fine."

Schwarz sighed. "Can you wait half an hour?"

"Of course!" The pout disappeared, and her eyes dried—so quickly that Schwarz had to wonder how real the tears had been in the first place.

"Just come up as soon as you can," she said. "Oh, and maybe on your way, you could grab some Ben & Jerry's from 7-Eleven?"

7-Eleven was definitely not on the way from the ground floor to the second. But Schwarz nodded.

"You're the best!" The door slammed shut behind her.

Bernard whistled, then mimed cracking a whip at Schwarz. "Dude, she's got you tamed like a dog."

Schwarz scowled at him. "Shut your mouth, please."

"Play nice, tough guy."

"No need," Schwarz said. "I am in." He opened the laptop, and Bernard's fake records flickered onto the screen. The decision status indicated "WL." He shook his head. "I am sorry. Wait list."

"Good thing I've got additional resources. Go on," Bernard said, thumping his palms against the desk. "Do it. Do it."

Schwarz replaced the "WL" with an "A" for admit. His hand hovered over the "enter" key. "Where is the binder?"

Bernard pulled it out of his bag and almost handed it to Schwarz, then snatched it away at the last second.

"The longer we are in the system, the more likely we are to get caught," Schwarz warned him.

"Not we. You. *You* get caught."

"And, um, *you* get waitlisted."

Bernard put the binder down on the corner of the desk. There was a tear in the lower right edge of the *Star Trek* sticker, but Schwarz elected not to say anything. Never taking his eyes off Bernard—who was definitely impatient and probably dumb enough to start playing on the network himself—he tossed the Binder of Power safely into the back of his closet, then sat down again in front of the computer.

"Are you sure about this?"

"Do it!" Bernard shouted.

Schwarz hit "enter."

It was the first real smile he'd ever seen on Bernard's face. "Pleasure doing business with you," Bernard said, reaching out his hand.

Schwarz declined to shake.

"Crisis averted," Max said, shutting down the program. "Now we just sit back and wait for the money to come rolling in."

"If we win," Eric pointed out. He started stuffing the equipment back in his bag; the sooner they got out of the shed and away from the Bongo Bums, the better.

"Actually, I've been meaning to talk to you about that," Max said hesitantly—at least, as hesitantly as Max ever said anything, which wasn't much.

"The money?"

"The *if*."

Eric clenched his jaw.

"We can do it," Max said, his voice a millimeter away from a whine. "If the Bums can do it, you know we can do it."

"The Bums *didn't* do it, remember?" Eric slipped the laptop into his bag, slung it over his shoulder, and stood up. "The Bums did exactly what we let them do. No more."

"Only because they're incompetent. If we wanted to get into the network, we could. It would take ten minutes, and we could guarantee a win."

"Guarantee jail time, too," Eric said. "If we got caught. Or at least guarantee that no college would ever have us. And some of us are still hoping for a diploma."

"Don't be such a wuss. What makes you so sure we'd get caught?"

Eric resisted the urge to slam the door of the shed on the way out. But they were still too close to the house, still in the danger zone. He slipped it shut gently and forced himself not to yell. "It doesn't matter whether we get caught," he hissed. "It's wrong, and I'm not doing it. And you're not doing it."

"Says *you*?" Max raised his eyebrows. "I don't need you, not for this."

"Do you need me at all?" Eric asked. "Because if you're the kind of person who would do that . . ."

"Then what? We're not friends anymore? Are you kidding me?"

"You said it. I didn't."

"We could get Lex in, too," Max said. "She would never even have to know we did it for her. Or she *could* know you did it for her—I bet she'd do whatever you wanted after that. I'm talking *any-thing* you wanted."

"You're disgusting."

"And you're tempted. Admit it."

"Not all of us are like you, Max."

"And there he goes again!" Max said loudly. Too loudly. Eric tugged him down the sidewalk, away from Gerald's house and the scene of their crime. "You just can't resist, can you? You have to throw it in my face. You're Gallant and I'm Goofus. You're Lisa and I'm Bart. You're Austin Powers and I'm Dr. Evil. You're Luke Skywalker, and I'm Darth—no, not even that, in your mind, I'm probably Jar Jar Binks. You're Pikachu and I'm—"

"I get the picture, thanks."

"You *drew* the picture," Max retorted. "And it's black and white, just like everything else in your life."

"Do you have to be so melodramatic?"

"Do *you*? You've got these unreasonable standards and we're all sup-posed to dance around living up to them. Or we end up like Lex—out of your life. End of story. It's blackmail." They finally reached the car.

Eric opened the door, but didn't climb inside. "There's nothing wrong with having high standards."

"Yeah, you're right." Max slapped his palm against the car roof. "We should all be like you. Incorruptible. Lucky we've got someone like you to judge us and point out everything we're doing wrong."

"I don't judge," Eric said indignantly.

"Give me a break. You're *still* judging Clay for crap he pulled ten years ago. You won't talk to Lex, and I don't even get why you're mad in the first place."

"You wouldn't."

"Oh, right, because I'm defective. I almost forget. Why do you even stick around? Do you just like standing next to someone who makes you look good?"

Eric's fingers tightened around the door handle. "What am I supposed to say to that?"

"Nothing." Max opened the driver's side door and slid behind the wheel. "You should just know, you make it really hard for someone to be your friend."

"I didn't realize I was so much work. Maybe I should just make it easy for you." The passenger side door slammed shut with a dramatic bang.

Of course, it would have been a bit more dramatic if Eric had been on the outside.

Max looked over at him and raised an eyebrow. "Wasn't that supposed to be an exit line?"

Still fuming, Eric strapped on his seat belt. "Pretend it was. I'm not walking home just because you suck."

"So I'm supposed to pretend you're not here?"

Eric didn't say anything.

"Just act like you're standing on the curb in a snit and I drove away without you?"

Eric crossed his arms and stared straight out the windshield.

Max turned on the radio, choosing a hip-hop station he knew Eric detested.

Eric began humming a Beatles song under his breath.

Max turned up the volume.

Silence for ten minutes, until Max drove right by Eric's house.

"You want me to jump out while the car's still moving?" Eric asked sullenly.

Max gave an exaggerated jerk of surprise. "Oh, I'm sorry, are you still here? I thought I left my best friend back there on the curb, sulking."

"Just stop the car and let me out."

Max slammed on the breaks. He turned to Eric, then sighed. It's challenging to cram exasperation, frustration, amusement, dismay, regret, defeat, concern, and boredom into a single exhalation of breath.

But Max was a champion sigher.

"Give me a break. Are you really threatening to ditch me for good if I decide to cheat?"

Eric closed his eyes and responded with a more amateur sigh, resignation tinged with a hint of exhaustion. "Of course not. Are you really going to cheat?"

Max glanced at the stuffed crimson H dangling from the rearview mirror—and back at the Harvard sticker emblazoned on the rear windshield. Then he shook his head. "Of course not."

And, unlike most of the things that came out of Max's mouth, it was true.

21

April need not be the cruelest month.

—Bill Mayher, *The College Admissions Mystique*

"I'm here because Max invited me," I said before Eric had a chance to ask. But he just shrugged and stepped into the dorm room, pulling up another chair in front of the computer screen. The shrug's message was obvious: *I don't care.*

But what did that mean?

Was that, *I don't care because I'm glad you're here?* Or *I don't care what you do? I don't care because I'll hate you forever?* Or maybe, *I don't care because I've already forgotten that we ever knew each other and I have a new girlfriend, an MIT freshman named Aimee who designs circuitry and wears a size two?*

I shrugged back.

"Ladies and gentleman!" Max exclaimed, pausing for the non-existent drumroll and trumpet blare. "Welcome to the festivities. I'd just like to take this time to thank you all for contributing to what I think we can safely call our greatest hack, one step closer to the attainment of the unattainable, the brass ring that—"

"Just turn it on," Eric said.

"It's a momentous occasion," Max protested, "we should—"

With a nervous glance at Max, Schwarz leaned over his shoulder and double-clicked the mouse. We fell silent as a dark grayish conference room popped up on the screen. Schwarz had hidden a camera inside the smoke detector lodged in a corner of the ceiling, giving us a fly on the wall view. Thanks to the high resolution, we could not only see which admissions officers suffered from male-pattern baldness, we could tell which was wearing a toupee.

There were twelve of them assembled around the conference table, each with a stack of folders piled in front of them and their faces fixed in a solemn expression, as if they were composing themselves for the hidden camera—but maybe that's just how you look when you've got the fate of twenty thousand desperate teenagers in your hands. The woman at the head of the table had her rust-colored hair pulled back into a bun and wore glasses that were almost as thick as Schwarz's. She was the only one without a stack of papers in front of her; all she had was a list. It was the day's docket—and Schwarz's snooping indicated that Clay's name was about forty names down. If our calculations were correct, and if they didn't take too many bathroom breaks, this was judgment day.

Clay had been invited along for the fun; he'd opted to stay home and rotate his tires. Max didn't get it, but I did. After all, I could have had Schwarz find out when *I* was going to be on the docket. I could have watched them debate my merits, weigh my SAT scores against my grades against my essay against the hundred other applicants who all said and did exactly the same thing (or worse, the hundred applicants who did it all, but better). I could have ignored Eric ignoring me and sat there trembling as the admissions officers picked me over like a giant tomato at a country fair, trying to decide whether I was big enough, round enough, supple enough, red enough, and firm enough to get the blue ribbon.

Not that I'd ever been to a county fair.

And not that I ate tomatoes.

But you get the point.

So I decided against watching my own fate be decided. But I had to see *something*. I had to know what went on in that locked room and who these people were who would be stamping me with the "approved" or "defective" label I'd be wearing across my forehead for the rest of my life.

Schwarz passed around a bowl of popcorn, and we gazed at the screen, waiting to be blown away.

But it turned out spying on an admissions session was a lot like watching baseball. That is, if you're like me, and find baseball about as interesting as picking gum out of your hair. For those of you out there who get all fired up at the thought of watching a bunch of lumpy, overweight guys standing in the middle of a field spitting and scratching themselves—and you're entitled to your opinion—feel free to substitute bowling. Or backgammon. Because I think we can all agree that some things just aren't meant to be a spectator sport.

Most decisions had already been made before anyone hit the table—the admissions officers had pored over the files, ranked the applicants, and convened in small groups to decide on a recommendation. So at the full committee meeting, they had only to sum up each case, concluding with a recommendation of either "admit," "wait list," or—and this was usually issued with a dismissive head shake and a toss of the folder onto a towering pile in the corner—"deny."

We did our best to pay attention, but it was a losing battle. And when the popcorn was finished, so were we.

"So, what are you guys going to do with your cut of the money?" I asked. "If you win, that is." I was lying on the floor, my feet propped up against the wall and my head on Schwarz's roommate's pillow. It smelled faintly of old cheese and cheap cologne, but I was trying to ignore that, since it was softer than the hardwood. Max was looking out the window and playing idly with a yo-yo, Schwarz was at the computer still half-monitoring the proceedings, and Eric was sitting on Schwarz's bed, pretending to read.

At least, I told myself he was pretending. He wasn't turning the pages very often, or with any regularity, and every once in a while, I thought I caught him looking at me, although I couldn't be sure. It occurred to me that when I was lying on my back, my chest looked even flatter than usual, so if he *was* looking, he wasn't exactly getting the most flattering view.

But then, he probably wasn't looking at all.

"If we win, I am buying an iPhone," Schwarz said dreamily. "And also, a vintage print of—" He glanced at me and flushed pink. "Uh, there is an old magazine photo I would like to have the original of."

I laughed, and not just because I already knew what magazine he was referring to. "A phone and a picture? Schwarz, you've got to think bigger. We're talking about—"

"I've been saving up for this new Alienware desktop, the Aurora

ALX," Eric said quickly. "An AMD Athlon 64 FX-62 dual-core processor, AM2 DDR2 memory technology . . . it's the ultimate gaming machine. And with the installment plan, I only have to pay a hundred bucks a month."

"*When* we win," Max said, "I'm going to find myself a sweet apartment in Somerville, sign a lease, and get the hell out of the Kim house of crimson horrors once and for all." He tucked the yo-yo—a mint-condition 1984 Papa Smurf spindle with the original silver-blue lettering along the edge, estimated worth on eBay: $27—into his backpack. "The other half goes into the market. I make back everything I lost and more, enough to get in on the ground floor before the XemonCo IPO, I get rich, buy a mansion, retire early—and I'll even leave Maxwell Sr. with something nice to hang up on his damn wall." He raised a fist in the air, and his middle finger popped to attention. "A nice, hi-res, eight-by-ten photo of *this*."

"Excuse me, but you are planning to do all that with six hundred and thirty three dollars?" Schwarz asked.

"You break your calculator?" I asked. "Try *eight thousand* dollars."

There was a long silence. And not like the cozy, peaceful one we'd been enjoying a few minutes before, the kind where no one feels the need to talk because there's nothing much that needs to be said, and the quiet gives you space to think about how, for once, everything feels just right and you know—even though they're not saying anything, or maybe because they're not saying anything—that the people you're with feel the same way. This silence was heavy, and filled with a series of meaningful looks that lacked any meaning for me. Schwarz's wide eyes stared at Eric, then turned to Max, who gave Eric a helpless half-smile, which Eric greeted with a glare. It couldn't have lasted for more than thirty seconds, which—if you've ever sat in a room while everyone but you is engaged in a complicated game of silent assassin—is a really long time.

"You'd better tell him," Eric finally said.

"Tell him what?" Schwarz's voice carried the churlish note of someone who's been referred to in the third person once too often.

"You tell him," Max said.

"Let *her* tell him," Eric said, "since she practically already did."

"Tell him what?" Now I sounded churlish.

"How much the bet is for," Max mumbled.

"Twenty-five thousand dollars," I said. Then, "What?"

There was another silence, an expectant one, as everyone stared at Schwarz.

He held himself perfectly still, with his mouth twisted, his forehead wrinkled, and his eyes scrunched so closely together they nearly melded into one giant, owlish field of green. He looked like a cautionary statue erected in testament to the "Don't make that face, it could freeze that way" credo.

"Why?" It came out as a croak. Schwarz cleared his throat and tried again. This time, his voice cracked. "Why didn't you tell me?"

"I didn't know either," Eric said. "Well . . . not at first."

"We didn't want you to freak out," Max said. He rolled his eyes. "Don't know *what* we were thinking."

Schwarz was a statue again, his pupils darting back and forth between his two best friends while the rest of him stayed immobilized. A bead of sweat had broken out along his hairline.

"You were better off not knowing," Eric said. "Trust me."

"No. I get it." The color was starting to leech back into his face and, with surprising speed, his shade shifted from paper white to pale pink, right on through to tomato red. "Why bother tell me what was really going on? Why would I need to know? It does not matter what I think, right? Poor little Schwarzie, he will do whatever anyone wants him to do. He will believe anything, he'll do anything, so why bother to tell him anything? Better to just give him a pile of excrement and call it the truth, right? Better protect him from finding out the facts, he's so *sensitive*, he's so *fragile*, he might *break*."

Eric shook his head. "That's not—"

"That *is*! That is what you all think, isn't it? *Is it not?*" Schwarz's voice, high to begin with, was climbing the octaves with acrobatic speed and skill.

"Schwarz?" the door pushed open slowly, and a tall, slim girl with a Harvard hoodie, wavy brown hair, grey sweats, and incredibly bad timing peeked her head in. Max had said she was average looking, but that's not the word I would have used. She was *polished*—even in sweats, even with her hair pulled up into a sloppy ponytail and her face pale and wind-chapped, she looked ready for a photo shoot. She was straight out of a New England girls' prep school catalog. And even though she was only a year older than me, she was a college woman, and she made me feel like an eighth grader. "Oh, sorry, you've got people here, but Schwarz, I really need your help—"

"And *you*!" Schwarz whirled on her, all five feet two inches of him ready to pounce. "You may be beautiful, you may look like a goddess, you may be brilliant and funny and have Miss December's smile, but you are also selfish! And arrogant! And you treat me like excrement!"

Eric winced and took a few steps toward him, but, as if afraid to enter the danger zone, didn't come any closer than that. "Uh, Schwarz, maybe you—"

"*No!* No. She has to know—you have to know. You do not think about anyone but yourself. And you manipulate people into doing whatever you want. And you're needy and whiny and melodramatic. And you only date losers, and you rub my face in it, even though you must know . . ." He took three deep breaths, closed his eyes, then muttered a list of his favorite Bunnies. It seemed to have a magic calming effect—until he opened his eyes, and his face turned pink again. "A picture would be easier," he said, almost to himself. "A picture would make sense." He glared at Stephanie. "But *you* don't make sense, because all those things are true about you and you're still—whenever I look at you I—" He shook his head. "But you have to stop. You *all* have to stop! I'm not a little kid. I'm not your servant. I'm not here to do whatever you say. I am a *man*, and—"

She kissed him.

She took two steps toward him, grabbed his shoulders, pulled him toward her, slammed her lips against his while his arms flailed wildly, searching for purchase, and then found it, found her, digging into her waist and staying there, holding tight, like he knew that as soon as he moved, even an inch, whatever fantasy he'd created for himself would disappear in a puff of air.

But I knew better. I was watching. She was real, and she was *still* kissing him.

I couldn't help but glance at Eric. He was staring at me. Probably twelve steps between us, I calculated. Two would have been easier. With two, there was less time for second thoughts.

Stephanie finally let go, and Schwarz took a deep, wheezing

breath, as if he'd been holding it all this time. Which he probably had. His face was even redder than before, his eyes half-closed, his mouth trembling.

"I—I—um—" His voice was a whisper. He tipped his head back and sighed. It was the sound of someone who'd been waiting a very long time. "Shiiiiiit," he moaned. Schwarz, who never cursed. Who hated cursing the way my vegan cousin hated pork rinds. "That was . . . *fuck*."

And then he passed out.

Two hours later. Schwarz was up in Stephanie's room, making up for lost time. When he'd woken up to see her face looming over him, he'd promptly passed out again. But five minutes later, upright and blissed out, Stephanie's arm around his waist, he'd floated out the door to the staircase, mumbling something that sounded like, "Clay is smarter than he looks," though afterward the rest of us agreed we must have misheard.

Max, Eric, and I stayed in the dorm room and watched the minutes tick by. We played cards, struggled to remember old cartoon theme songs, and argued about whether Will Ferrell was "inspired" (Max), "overrated and dangerously dumbing down American humor, tranquilizing his audience rather than puncturing the assumptions of his society as all good comedy should do" (Eric), or "that doofy-looking guy who used to be on *Saturday Night Live*, right?" (me). An hour passed.

By hour two, Schwarz was still up in Stephanie's room, either passed out again or . . . I preferred not to know, or at least, certainly not to imagine. Eric and Max were poring over some kind of programming manual—that's what I'd decided it was, since the parts of their conversation I could overhear didn't appear to be in a human language—while I kept an eye on the screen. According to the admissions docket, Clay's file was coming up any minute.

I zoned out, letting the *denys, wait-lists,* and *admits* wash over me. So I almost didn't notice it.

A change in the pattern. Something new. An assistant standing in the doorway. Interrupting. The flicker of motion caught my attention, and I turned up the volume.

"He said it was for you, Samuel." She handed Atherton a square package, about the size of a textbook. "He said it was an emergency and that you would want to see its contents as soon as possible."

Atherton rolled his eyes. "He didn't leave his name?"

The assistant shook her head. "Just some kid. He said he was 'a concerned citizen trying to help.'"

"Probably another lame stunt," he said. "Yesterday I got a sneaker with a note that said 'Just trying to get my foot in the door.'" The committee cackled. "I'll check it out at our next break." Atherton turned back to his stack. "Sorry, folks. Anyway, as I was saying about . . ." He snuck a glance at the open file in front of him. "Sarah Stratton. A mundane record, nothing to really set her apart, and if you ask me . . ."

I stopped listening, and zoomed in on the package sitting at his elbow.

Because, I realized, it wasn't a package at all.

"Uh, guys, that binder with all the incriminating stuff in it," I called over my shoulder. "Remind me—did the sticker have a big picture of that spaceship on it?"

"The Enterprise. Yeah." Max laughed. "Schwarz is such a dork."

Eric punched him on the arm. "And that would make you—"

"The preferred term is *geek*," Max said with dignity. "If you don't mind."

"Guys, the binder . . ." I gulped. "I think Bernard held on to it. And I think he just delivered it to the admissions office."

"And what makes you think that?" Eric asked.

"Because I'm staring at it right now. And Samuel Atherton's about to look inside."

The jig, as they say, was up.

22

There's nothing casual about this. It is serious business—it's someone's life. The stakes are very high.

—Harvard University Dean of Undergraduate
Admissions and Financial Aid William Fitzsimmons,
quoted in *The Harvard Crimson*, July 7, 2006

We tore the room apart looking for the binder. Max finally found it, lodged in the back of the closet behind a stack of *Playboy*s and under a pile of unwashed polo shirts. It was the binder all right—or at least, *a* binder, bright blue with a *Star Trek* sticker on the front and bunny ears on the side.

And it was filled with a ream of scrap paper.

Surprise.

"How could Schwarz not look inside the damn thing?" Max raged.

"Not our current problem," Eric pointed out.

The clock was ticking, the boys were panicking, and I couldn't help but wonder what Atherton would find when he finally opened the binder and looked inside.

My name?

I wish I could say I was mostly worried about the guys, who were more likely to get in trouble—not to mention lose twenty-five thousand dollars they didn't have—but I'm not that person. A small, weak, easily distracted part of my mind worried about them. The rest worried about me, and whether I was about to be totally screwed.

By which I mean, rejected.

Same difference.

"Come on," Max said suddenly. "We can deal with this." He glanced at Eric. "Same deal we pulled at the bakery last year, right? When they almost caught us with the thing—"

"And then we did the—"

"Right, with the—"

Eric nodded. "Could work. Let's go." They made it to the hallway before they realized I wasn't behind them. "Well? Come on!"

"I don't—come where?"

"It's a three-man job," Max said impatiently. "And since Schwarz is otherwise occupied . . ."

I didn't do capers. I didn't do break-ins or pranks or hacks or whatever immature, illegal activity they were about to drag me into. I'd tried, yes—a little surveillance, a dash of sabotage—and look where it had gotten me.

"No. Not me. I can't."

Max massaged his temples. "Can't what?"

Couldn't help.

Couldn't play along.

Couldn't run or climb or sneak or spy or save the day.

Couldn't anything.

"Go without me," I said.

"Lex." That was Eric, meeting my eyes for the first time since he'd found out the truth. It was also the first time he'd said my name. "Please. We need you."

It turned out, I could.

Max pulled the fire alarm. He just waltzed in the front door, a T-shirt over his face to disguise his identity for assistants and security cameras, and pulled the red lever.

After that, it was simple.

Or, at least, that's how it was explained to me.

The siren shrieked, the building emptied out, and Eric and I snuck around to the back, where a ramp led down to a locked door into the basement. It took him twenty seconds to pick the lock.

We crept inside, running as fast as you can when you're trying not to make any noise, my heart thudding about three times faster than my feet. I stumbled once, but Eric's hand shot out, his fingers wrapped tightly around my wrist, and he kept me from slamming into the ground. I pulled away, and we kept running.

Up the stairs to the ground floor, now empty, but the fire engines were screaming in the distance and soon the place would be crawling with firemen. I dimly remembered hearing that setting off a false fire alarm was a felony. If I spent graduation in jail, would I still get my diploma?

"Okay, you know what you need to do?" Eric whispered.

I nodded. "You sure we have to split up?"

He gave me an awkward pat on the shoulder. "You'll be fine." And then he was gone. I was on my own.

I was breaking into the Harvard University Admissions Office.

I was *stealing* from the Harvard University Admissions Office.

And if I got caught—when I got caught—I would be on my own.

Don't think, I told myself, knowing that if I paused even for a second, I would never get going again. So I followed instructions, sneaking through the empty offices, trying to remember the floor-plan they'd sketched out for me, dreading the consequences of a wrong turn, a dead end.

Down the hall, two rights and a left, and there it was: the conference room. I glanced up at the security camera, hoping that Eric had followed through on his promise to switch off the system.

The binder was still on the table. All I had to do was run across the room, grab it, and run out again. Easy as that.

My legs were shaking.

One second passed, then another.

In a dream, my feet would have stuck to the floor.

But I was awake, and I jolted myself into motion, rushing across the room, wobbly but fast. I grabbed the binder and stuffed it into my backpack, slung it over my shoulder, raced to the door—and froze.

A door slammed in the distance. And then the shouting began—too muffled for me to hear what they were saying, but loud enough that I got the idea. The fire department was in the building. And they were closing in.

"Down!" Eric hissed, blowing through the doorway and dragging me back into the room, down to the floor, under the conference table. I hugged the leg and, trembling, waited to be caught.

Some hero, right? That's me. Nerves of steel.

"Close your eyes," Eric whispered, fumbling with something in his bag.

"What?"

"*Now!*"

I squeezed my eyes shut just in time; the bright flash blazed through my eyelids. "Go!" Eric shouted, pulling me up and out of the room before I could figure out what was going on. We wove through the firemen, who were frozen in place, their hands pressed to their eyes. Back down the hall, through the office, out of the building—out the front entrance, pushing through the crowd, then running, racing across the Yard, dimly aware that someone was following us, maybe a horde, but the running pushed away all the fear, narrowed the world down to my feet slamming against the pavement, my lungs screaming, the air slicing against my cheeks, the green smear of grass blurring by, Eric's hand on my arm pulling me this way, then that, around a corner, through an alley, down the stairs and into a dark passageway behind the library where there was nothing but huge, empty boxes, a bush whose leaves had all withered away, a low concrete wall, a rusted door to the building that looked like it hadn't been used in years, and us.

We sat on the ground, our backs pressed against the concrete, our chests heaving. We sat silent and still, savoring the sensation of being at rest, of breathing.

"They won't find us here," Eric said, still wheezing. "We'll wait a while, just to make sure, then we can go back to Schwarz's."

It was another minute before I had enough air to speak.

"What the hell was that back there?"

"What?"

"The light."

"I call it a flasher," Eric said. "It lets off a single burst of light, bright enough to blind you for twenty seconds, with absolutely no lasting effects. I designed it myself. Schwarz keeps a couple in his room for emergencies."

"Sounds dangerous."

"It's totally harmless."

"You could have warned me."

"I told you to close your eyes."

I wanted to yell at him; I wanted to thank him. My heart was still pounding, and I couldn't stop smiling. It was like stepping off a roller coaster for the first time, half-exhilarated, half-terrified, still trying to convince myself that the world had stopped spinning and I wasn't going to plummet to my death. A little nauseous. Almost ready to go again.

"What if they recognized us?" I asked.

"Who would recognize us?"

"Are you sure you shut down the cameras?"

"Every last one of them. When I take on a mission, I get it done."

"What's that supposed to mean?" I asked bitterly. "That I screwed up? That I should have gotten the binder faster? I told you this wasn't my thing, and you—"

"Hey." He put his hand on my back, lightly. "You did fine. You did great."

I jerked away from him. "So great we almost got caught."

"The firemen showed up faster than we calculated," Eric said. "It wasn't your fault."

"No, it was *your* fault for dragging me into this in the first place."

"It all worked out okay, didn't it?"

"You call this okay?" I kicked at one of the empty cardboard boxes. "We're hiding in a trash alley and we almost got arrested back there—which, by the way, you swore was *not* a possibility."

"It wasn't," he said obstinately. He held up his wrists. "Do you see any cuffs?"

"Easy as pie," I said sarcastically, quoting what he'd told me. "Couldn't be simpler."

"Who asked you to come along?" he snapped.

"Uh, *you*."

"Not in the first place. I'm not the one who invited you over today."

"Trust me, that was made perfectly clear," I said. "I'm well aware you don't want me anywhere near you."

"And you know exactly why."

"Because you're a baby?" I suggested.

"Because you're a liar."

"Because I'm a better liar than *you* are, you mean. Because you can't handle the competition?"

"Yeah, competition," he snorted. "If it weren't for me, you'd still be back under that conference table, hugging the leg and crying for your mother."

I gave him the fish eye. "There were no tears involved, and you know it."

"Only because I got us out of there."

"You wouldn't even have been there if it weren't for me," I said. "You'd still be back in the dorm room and Atherton would be poring over your precious binder, and—"

"What?"

"Nothing." It didn't seem like the time to admit that I'd just noticed the freckles on his right cheek looked a little like the Big Dipper.

"Lex . . ." But now he was the one who couldn't get his sentence out.

The sun was starting to set, which gave everything a reddish tinge. It was also freezing, but I only noticed because I saw him shivering. I put my hand against his cheek, just to see if it was cold.

And then I realized what I'd done. Before I could move, Eric put his hand over mine. He smiled.

"It wasn't all a lie," I said quietly.

I couldn't hear his reply, but I could read his lips: *I know*.

And then he leaned in, and for a moment, I felt like running away again. But I stayed where I was.

His lips were soft. The kiss was firm.

For the two months I'd dated my one and only boyfriend—the two months before he'd ditched me for ABP girl—I'd strived to kiss him as infrequently as possible. There was his tongue, which had always seemed short and stubby to me, and too red. And then there was everything else. Too much drool, or not enough drool and thus too much scraping. His nose would loom in my face like a fleshy tumor, but I would keep my eyes open because when I closed them, it was too easy to hear all the slurping and sucking noises, and all the little grunts he breathed out every few seconds, just as he squeezed my shoulders or dug his hips into me. I'd told myself that it wasn't *kissing* I hated, it was just that he was doing something wrong. Or, more likely, I was.

This kiss was different.

There was no tongue. And no drooling, no saliva, no messy sticky sounds or slurping or anything else that I'd come to identify with kissing. There was just this perfect moment, a soft pressure, warmth, a hand against my neck, a tingling in my lips, and then, too soon, it was over.

We stared at each other, our faces about an inch apart, his eyes and nose huge in my field of vision, my gaze straying down to his lips, trying to make it seem real that, just a second ago, they'd been attached to mine. He smiled. I laughed.

"What?" he whispered.

"I don't know."

Then he laughed, too. But only for a moment.

"You're not about to run away, are you?" he asked.

I traced a finger across his cheek. "Why would I?"

"And you're not . . . you're not in the middle of some kind of psychotic break?"

"I don't think so." I smiled. "I'm beginning to think *you* might be. What's wrong?" Our faces were still so close, I could feel his breath.

"I just . . ." He chewed on the edge of his lower lip. I brushed a swath of hair away from his face, and he grabbed my hand, wrapping his fingers around mine, tight. "I just want to make sure I know what this is. I want this to be real."

"It's real," I said. "I swear."

And then he kissed me again.

This time, there was tongue.

But not in a bad way.

ALL'S WELL

THAT ENDS.

March 15
D(ECISION)-DAY

Objective: Admission

23

As an admissions officer . . . I travel around the country whipping
kids (and their parents) into a frenzy so that they will apply. . . .
Then . . . we reject most of them.

—Rachel Toor, *Admissions Confidential: An Insider's
Account of the Elite College Selection Process*

You know how in the movies, they always try to ratchet up the
tension by pretending that the whole "thick-versus-thin" envelope thing is just a myth? The stressed-out—though always well-
coiffed—heroine quivers in front of her mailbox and pulls out a thin
envelope, her expression crying, *Oh no, thin! My life is over!* And then
she opens it up, only to pull out, in an oh-so-shocking twist, the
congratulatory letter: "Fictional University is pleased to welcome
you to the class of when Hell freezes over."

My point?

It's a plot device.

In real life, some things are exactly the way they appear to be.

A big, fat envelope that barely fits in the mailbox and appears to contain forms and brochures and stickers and a crimson "Admissions Certificate Suitable for Framing" isn't going to tell you "Sorry, try again next year." And trust me when I say this. Much as you may tell yourself it's possible that the razor thin envelope—the one that obviously contains only one piece of paper, one typed page with very little text—might still be good news, it's not.

Size does matter.

Bernard Salazar knew about size.

He had the biggest stack in town. A thick stack of skinny, skinny envelopes.

Princeton. Brown. Yale. Stanford. Berkeley.

Wait-list.

Wait-list.

Rejection.

Wait-list.

Wait-list.

Soon he'd have enough for a bonfire.

Of course, he hadn't had to wait for the mailman. Not thanks to the technological wonders of the modern era. Life and death decrees were all available online. Key in a name, a password, and there it was, black and white, instantaneous and inescapable: a dead end.

He had saved Harvard for last, knowing it was a sure thing.

He hadn't been angry or upset about any of the others. They were all second-raters, beneath him. He was destined for Harvard, just as he and his father had always planned. There was a sizable check and a new car waiting for him as soon as he had the acceptance letter to wave in his father's face. It was only a matter of time.

He paused at the computer, feeling almost sorry for everyone else, the suckers who'd played things straight. He even felt a little sorry for Eric, Max, and Schwarz, the dweebs he'd screwed over without a second thought. Which, after the way they'd treated him—the way they looked down on him—was one thought more than they'd deserved.

He hit return, and his file flashed up on the screen.

`Applicant: Bernard Salazar`

`Status: Wait-list`

Bernard got very angry, and very drunk.

He was still drunk three days later when the official letter arrived. And he was even drunker when he built his fire.

The house didn't burn down. Not quite. But the pool table, leather couch, and Bernard's wall-to-wall collection of hip-hop CDs were all burned beyond recognition.

It was Clay's name on the application, so Clay got to sit in the official Harvard chair. The rest of us hovered behind him, holding our breath. Eric's arm was around my waist, my head on his shoulder. It still didn't feel quite real—but it felt right.

Clay keyed in his name and password. Then he stopped, turning around to face us.

"I want to go," he said.

Blank looks all around.

"If I get in, I want to go."

"What do you mean?" Max asked. "Since when?"

Clay didn't explain or elaborate. But he looked sure. "You can keep the money. I just want to go."

It seemed like he was asking for permission, which I didn't get—

until suddenly, I did. Clay was a fraud. And when the guys made their hack public, he'd be out before he had a chance to be in.

Schwarz grinned. Nothing new there. His life had been bisected into two eras: Before Stephanie, and After Stephanie. Now, in A.S., Schwarz was a new man—emphasis where he liked it: on *man*. A happy man. A joyous, devil-may-care, whatever-you-want, perpetually grinning idiot of a man. "Fine with me," he said in a dreamy voice. In A.S., everything was fine with him.

Max shrugged. "As long as I get my money, I don't care what you do. It's not about the bragging rights for me, or the principle. But Eric . . ."

Eric was only in this to make a statement.

And you couldn't make much of a statement with your mouth shut.

You certainly couldn't stand up for principle and take down the admissions system—or at least give it a good jolt—without revealing some crucial details and offering some proof. You couldn't do it without Clay.

Eric stepped away from the group, away from me. Toward Clay. "You really don't remember me from elementary school?"

Clay shook his head. "Dude, why do you keep asking me that? It was, like, ten years ago. A lot of shit went down."

Max pressed his lips together. "Eric, why don't you just—"

"Yeah. I know all about the shit," Eric said.

"So were we friends or something?" Clay asked. "Is that the deal?"

"No, not quite—"

"Seems like we would've been."

"What?"

"Friends," Clay said. "Right?"

Schwarz stifled a laugh. Max shoved him.

Eric just smiled, if you can call it that. The corners of his mouth twisted up, but the rest of his face stayed frozen in place. "We weren't," he said flatly.

"Yeah, well . . ." Clay paused, and in that pause, there was something—some flicker of expression across his face, something about the way his mouth was still half-open, like there was more he wanted to say. Something that made me wonder if he remembered more than he wanted to admit.

Eric looked thoughtful, and I wondered if he had seen it, too. "You hate school. Why would you want more of it? Why would you want Harvard?"

Clay shrugged. "It'd be . . . better. You know?"

I waited for Eric to ask, *Better than what?*

He didn't.

"Okay." Eric nodded once, slowly. "I won't say anything. None of us will. If you get in, you go."

They shook on it.

I waited for the hug, or the tears, or the emotional outburst, or anything to indicate that something big had just happened. But they were guys. They shook. And then they were done.

Clay clicked the mouse, and his results popped up on the screen.

Applicant: Clay Porter

Status: Admit

Max fell to the floor, spread-eagled on his back, like he was trying to make a snow-angel on the hardwood. *"Twenty-five thousand dollars!"* he screamed.

Clay looked bewildered.

Schwarz, as per usual, looked delirious with joy.

And Eric looked at me.

"You did it," I said.

He laughed. "No thanks to you."

"You're welcome."

And this time, *I* kissed *him.*

There would be no feeble mouse click for me. I wanted the whole experience: the long walk to the mailbox, the gaping hole at the pit of my stomach as I held my breath and, with equal parts terror and excitement, pulled it open and peered inside. . . .

I'd been visualizing the moment for years, walking myself through every step, right up to the triumphant end, as if somehow watching the scene play out in my head enough times would somehow make it all real. Now that the time had come, I wasn't going to cheat myself out of my moment of victory. Even if the wait was killing me.

Every day, I walked down to the mailbox, opened it up, flipped through a pile of bills, held my breath, and prayed I wouldn't see that familiar crimson seal—because I knew that if the envelope was small enough to get lost between the credit card mailers and the cell phone bill, it wasn't the envelope I was hoping for.

And every day, before I opened the mailbox, I tested out my new mantra: *It doesn't matter.*

Acceptance, rejection, whatever. I'd go to college somewhere— probably somewhere good. It didn't have to be Harvard.

It was just one decision out of a lifetime of decisions. I'd let it rule my life for far too long. More than that—I'd pretty much given up having a life, all for a single goal, a goal I couldn't even come up with a good reason for pursuing. I wasn't going to live like that anymore. No more blinders. No more ignoring everything else, every*one* else, no more pretending that nothing mattered except where I was going, even at the expense of where I was now.

If I got in, so be it.

If not? I'd survive.

And on the day I opened the mailbox and discovered my envelope, I finally believed it. Thick or thin, yes or no, admit or deny—even wait-list—it didn't matter.

Not to this story.

And, in the end, not to my life.

24

I see no harm in telling young people to prepare for failure rather than success, since failure is the main thing that is going to happen to them.

—Kurt Vonnegut, *Hocus Pocus*

B ullshit.

You didn't actually buy that, did you?

Of course it matters.

When you're a high school senior, two months away from The Rest of Your Life, it's pretty much all that matters.

People—especially adults, especially adults who don't remember what it was like and wonder why half the high school population is zonked out on mood-regulating medication—like to tell you that it doesn't matter where you go to college. Let me say it again, just to be clear.

Bullshit.

College is the start of real life. High school is practice. (Middle school is torture.) College is the beginning. Chapter one. College is where you become the person you're going to be.

As for the person I was going to be?

She wouldn't be a Harvard student.

The envelope was thin.

I held out hope to the bitter end. Even though I knew better. I closed my eyes, I came up with a host of possible explanations for a thin letter, and I told myself that the brochures and the forms and the certificate, the *packet*, could all be arriving later. This was Harvard, I told myself. They didn't need fanfare.

And they didn't supply it:

Dear Ms. Talese,

It is with sincere regret that we inform you we cannot offer you a place in our incoming freshman class. We received an unprecedented number of applications this year and were forced to turn away many candidates with exceptional personal and intellectual qualities. Please understand that this decision is not necessarily a true indicator of your potential. We wish you the best in your future endeavors.

Note the "not necessarily."

As in, *maybe* you'll manage to be successful at something, someday.

But not necessarily.

I wish I had saved it. But I tore it into tiny pieces and let them sprinkle down onto the ground, where they mixed in with the snow. It was the last snowfall of the season.

And the first time in my life I'd ever littered.

I'd like to say I took it well.

Of course, I'd also like to say I got in.

I can at least say that I had no regrets.

And that the mourning period only lasted a week. There was a fair amount of crying. Several long days when I refused to get out of bed. Infrequent showering.

There didn't seem to be much point.

There didn't seem to be much point in doing anything except lying in bed, the soggy pillow littered with snot-encrusted tissues, my hair knotted, my eyes red, my blinds closed, and my iPod playing "Everybody Hurts" on an endless loop.

On day eight, I got up. Got out of bed. Shut off the music, opened the blinds, and piled all my getting-into-college books into a giant cardboard box. I sealed it up and left it in the hallway with a big sign taped to the top: TRASH.

On day nine, I dug up the postcard from Brown with the hand-written "Hope to see you next year!" scrawled across the top. I checked off "Yes."

Things don't always go the way you expect them to.

I know, huge shock, right?

I didn't expect to spend prom night rappelling down the side of a roof while my boyfriend fiddled with sprinkler pipes, Max laid down an indoor river of detergent across the dance floor, and Schwarz kept the car warm so we could escape the wrath of the soapy, sopping prom king and his princely henchmen.

I didn't expect to fall in love.

I didn't expect to like Katie Gibson's valedictory speech . . . and, okay, I didn't. Who would? It was pretentious, rambling, self-congratulatory and, in the end, boiled down to the stunning revelation that "This isn't the end, it's the beginning!" But I also didn't expect to clap just as loudly as everyone else, and to discover that I wasn't jealous anymore. I wasn't bitter, I wasn't even a little sorry that I'd persuaded the guys to fix her file and set things right. Because none of it mattered anymore; things were over. High school was over.

And, most of all, I didn't expect that.

High school had always felt like a life sentence—and deep down, who ever expects parole?

Max made his fortune at XemonCo. His cut of the bet paid his rent for six months—then came the IPO, and payday. Six months later, the stock crashed and he'd lost everything all over again. But he hopped to another company, then another, racking up debts and the occasional windfall along the way, always breaking even and never giving up. Some weeks, he slept on Eric's couch and scarfed ramen noodles; others, he splurged for a room at the Ritz-Carlton and treated everyone to champagne. And somewhere in there, he found time to attend night classes at BU. When he finally earned his degree, his father—without warning or explanation—framed the certificate and hung it on the wall of achievement, right next to the letter from Bill Gates proposing acquisition of Max's latest creation.

Schwarz graduated from Harvard a few days after his eighteenth birthday and turned down a promising academic career to become the first-ever in-house mathematician at Playboy Enterprises, using his prodigious skills and encyclopedic knowledge of the *Playboy* empire to devise a corporate growth strategy that doubled the stock value in under nine months. Although he insists that the messy real-world complications of applied math are, in the end, more satisfying than the abstract beauty of his old topological proofs, he hasn't turned his back on the ivory tower completely. His most recent article on cellular homology appeared in the June issue of the *Glasgow Mathematical Journal*, with no indication that he'd written the paper while lying on a raft in the Playboy Mansion's grotto, pretending to get mad when the Bunnies splashed him. Stephanie dumped him about two months after their first kiss, claiming—after he finally got up the nerve to quit their ballroom dance class—that he never let her get her way. She went back to her endless stream of prep school jocks.

Schwarz got over it.

Eric never managed to design a cheap computer for the third world, though he's still working on it, at least in his spare time. As far as I know, he hasn't made much progress on the Batman thing, either.

He became a legend at MIT, the birthplace of the hack, breaking down every system he could find until the day he was approached by Sphinx Systems, a secretive, well-endowed security company willing to pay big bucks for his expertise. They wanted someone who could think like a hacker—or, more precisely, *out*think the hackers and protect the status quo. The old Eric, naive, idealistic, high school Eric, would have turned them down flat. The new one was tired of never having enough money for a second slice of pizza. He bought his first suit and took the job.

He goes to Greenpeace rallies on the weekend and donates a chunk of every paycheck to Habitat for Humanity, the Red Cross, and the ACLU—but he's still convinced he sold out to the Man.

Bernard Salazar went first to Tufts, then to Wall Street, then to prison. He's currently serving a seven-year term for insider trading. It's a minimum-security prison—and, in case he gets lonely, his recently re-incarcerated father lives right down the hall in cell block D.

The Bongo Bums took their show on the road, abandoning Cambridge for sunny So-Cal, where they spent a couple years coasting through Cal Tech before ditching both hacking and higher education in order to pursue their screenwriting dreams. Ash now works the checkout counter at Click Clack Chicken; Gerald finally grew a mustache.

Samuel Atherton III, on the other hand, migrated slightly farther north, courtesy of his wife, who, upon discovering his affair, laid down the ultimatum: *Harvard or me.* Too busy groveling to conduct much of a job search, he took the first position he could find, guidance counselor at the fourth-largest vocational school in Juneau, Alaska.

Clay graduated from Harvard—just barely—without anyone ever finding out his secret. Midway through freshman year, he found his way to the Department of Visual and Environmental Studies—Harvard's code name for art. With his elaborate tattoos, black fingernails, ratty T-shirts, and monochromic canvases, he blended nicely, a poseur amongst poseurs. He and his fellow students made a wordless bargain: Clay wouldn't point out that their trust-funded punk posturing disappeared whenever they went home for the holidays, while they wouldn't ask him pesky questions about the trash he called art.

By senior year, the masks had hardened into reality. Several of the sculptors became regulars at the Yankee Doodle, and, with Clay's help, the painters learned how to pierce their own eyebrows and carve their own tattoos. In return, they taught him about post-post-modern analysis, abstract textuality, and how to survive on a diet of espresso and gallery-opening hors d'ouevres. He sold his first painting, a burned down joint pasted to the center of a white canvas, for ten thousand dollars.

It was called *Blunt*.

As for me?

I was right. I was convinced that *where* I went to college would determine everything that came later—and it pretty much did. Just not the way I thought.

If I hadn't gone to Brown, I wouldn't have met my roommate, a nationally ranked Scrabble player who's almost as smart as Schwarz and who became the first best friend I'd had since sixth grade. I wouldn't have developed a crush on my econ professor and ended up majoring in economics—first for him, then for me—and eventually landed on Wall Street, spearheading my firm's acquisition of Bernard's old company, once he'd driven it into the ground. They call me the Blondish Barracuda.

I wouldn't have rowed intramural crew or learned Swedish just for fun or gotten a concussion in the sumo wrestling booth at Spring Weekend. I might still have taken a class in Enlightenment philosophy, but at some other school, I wouldn't have befriended my study partner, a guy who dropped out of school the next year when he sold a pilot to Comedy Central and brought me as his date to the Emmys. If I'd gone to Harvard and stayed in Boston, I might not have broken up with Eric—or I might not have gotten back together with him a month later, then broken up, then gotten back together, etc., etc., until I'd maxed out my credit card on bus tickets, gone over my cell phone's minute allotment by at least nine hours a month, and eventually thrown up my hands and figured that, since I couldn't get him out of my system and he couldn't get me out of his, we might be stuck with each other for good.

Though the jury's still out on that one.

I'm not saying things would have been different if I'd gone to Harvard. I'm saying *everything* would have been different. Maybe worse—maybe better. I'll never know.

And I don't care.

This isn't meant to be a cautionary tale, or a manifesto, or a nostalgia trip. I'm not trying to show off or to redeem myself; I have nothing to brag about, and I think I've apologized enough.

This isn't for them, the guys, some kind of reminder of the rebellious youth they've left behind, even though it's all a little sad, the way Max cancelled his eBay account and Eric wears a tie to work every day. When Schwarz got his first pair of contact lenses, I almost cried.

It's not for Clay, who didn't deserve Harvard any more than he deserved everything that came before it, but who, after several years of hard work and almost no arrests, doesn't deserve exposure. Which is why "Clay Porter" is not his real name—because after everything, he deserves a break.

This isn't even for Bernard, who's only gotten slimier with age, but who has suffered enough.

This isn't for the gatekeepers, who mean well and already know their system is broken. And it isn't for you, because you could have figured that out without my help.

This is for me.

Because I still follow the rules; because my bookshelf is still stuffed with how-to manuals and the idiot's guide to everything. Because I'm still afraid, I'm still stressed, and I'm still determined to be number one at almost any cost—and because that *almost* is easy to forget. This is how I remember the one time things ran off the track—off the *cliff*—and left me stranded, without a guidebook, without a manual, without a clue.

I said I have no regrets. That was another lie, my last. Because I do have one regret: I regret that this story wasn't mine to tell.

You can be sure the next one will be.

DISCLAIMER
(Or, Don't Try This at Home)

1. Don't think this novel is suggesting you should try to hack Harvard—or any other college. In fact, you most definitely should *not*, as it would be both wrong and illegal. It would also be somewhat dumb.

2. If *you* are somewhat dumb, and thus decide to ignore #1, don't think you can use this novel as your guide. It is fiction, after all, and is in no way a primer on the actual admissions process.

3. Whatever the flaws of the admissions system, admissions officers are not to blame. They're good people with a tough job. And I'm not just saying that because some of my best friends are admissions officers. It's also true.

ACKNOWLEDGMENTS

Special thanks to Michelle Nagler, Bethany Buck, Michael del Rosario, Caroline Abbey, Sam Shah, Emily Grossi, David Roher, Natalie Roher, Brandon McGlynn, Barbara and Michael Wasserman, and, for all the inspiration and entertainment they've provided over the years, the former residents of Grays West 46, 36, 26, and Stoughton 19.

ABOUT THE AUTHOR

Robin Wasserman has always harbored a certain nostalgia for the college applications process. . . . That is, until she began writing this book and remembered what it was really like. She now realizes she would rather have her wisdom teeth removed—without anesthesia—than go through it all again. Which is to say: She feels your pain.

Having survived high school, college admissions, and college itself (which proved almost worth all the trouble), she now lives and writes in New York City. You can learn more about her own admissions tribulations and college capers at www.robinwasserman.com.

Lia Kahn was perfect: rich, beautiful, popular.

Until the accident that nearly killed her.

Now she has been downloaded into a new body that only looks human.

Lia will never feel pain again, she will never age, and she can't ever truly die.

But some miracles come at a price. . . .

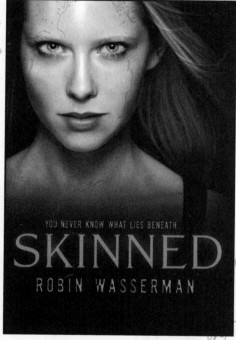

YOU NEVER KNOW WHAT LIES BENEATH.

SKINNED

ROBIN WASSERMAN

THE FIRST BOOK IN A GRIPPING TRILOGY

"A spellbinding story about loss, rebirth,
and finding out who we really are inside.
This intense and moving novel will wind up under your skin."

–SCOTT WESTERFELD

New York Times bestselling author of the Uglies series

From Simon Pulse | Published by Simon & Schuster

Seven Sins.

Seven Books.

Seven Teens . . .

. . . all determined to get what they want, when
they want it. No matter the cost, or the drama.

LUST   ENVY   PRIDE   WRATH
SLOTH   GLUTTONY   GREED

SEVEN DEADLY SINS
BY ROBIN WASSERMAN

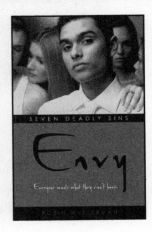

From Simon Pulse
Published by Simon & Schuster